Elven Borne

By
Scott Marcy

Elven Borne

Copyright © 2016 **Scott A. Marcy**

Second Printing, 2017

www.ScottMarcy.net

ISBN: 0692688994

ISBN 13: 978-0692688991

I dedicate this book to my mother, father, and God. Their love, patience, and guidance made this book possible.

Introduction:

Two elves sprinted through the forest, leaping over fallen trees and dodging debris. Black clouds, large as continents, spread across the sky, cutting off the sun, smothering the land; lightning stabbed the earth, and peals of thunder rolled over them. The earth shuddered and moaned beneath their feet. "Hurry!" shouted Vakhal. "It's almost shut."

Elora chased after him, branches raking her face, debris flying at her in the wind. "Don't leave me," she shouted. He paused and waited for her to catch up with him. He grabbed her hand and ran toward the Great Gate. Set atop a ziggurat, large as a water tower, and bright as the sun, the gate blinked, and the mountains staggered. Gale force winds blasted through the gate, and they fought for every step. "We have to make it to the gate," she screamed, but the storm's roar reduced her voice to a whisper.

He held her tight and struggled up the ziggurat's stairs. As they neared the great eye, they saw Eden, their home world, and Tobias, a human wizard. His hands raised and clutching his staff, he chanted in the ancient tongue, and his words split the skies.

"What is he doing?" Elora shouted. "He's closing the gate."

The rim of the Great Gate turned burnt red and began to fade. Vakhal sprinted across the top of the pyramid. "It's closing," he shouted. Holding Elora's hand, he whipped her forward and shoved her through the gate. The elva screamed and flew through the world portal, landing upon the shores of Eden. From the ground, she looked back and reached out for him. He took two steps, but the gate dissolved and then vanished.

Feet clamored up the stairs behind him. Burdened with sacks of gold, the dwarves Karamin and Azmor struggled to reach the top. When they arrived, Azmor asked, "Where's the gate? It can't just disappear." Vakhal dropped to his knees and looked upon the void in stunned silence, his heart filled with pain.

Karamin dropped his sacks and sat on a pedestal. "Tobias betrayed us." He removed his pipe from his inner coat pocket and lit it. As the smoke swirled, he added, "We're lost. We're stuck on this miserable rock."

"It cannot be," Azmor said. He groped the air and spun around. "The gate cannot disappear. It's eternal."

"The gate is eternal and so is the rhunite, but both are missing." He drew in a long breath and released the smoke through his nostrils. "He made the rhunite disappear; he put it to sleep." He nodded toward the surrounding hills. The rich, black veins of the mineral rhunite vanished, leaving behind quartz and granite. "I wouldn't have thought it possible."

"It's not. No one can do that," Azmor said. "I have to go home. My wife is waiting." Karamin shook his head and released another puff of smoke. "Don't just sit there. Do something!"

"There's nothing to be done. We're lost." The dwarves picked up the bags of gold and intercepted their brothers as they scrambled up the stairs. They trudged down the steps, their voices and steps growing faint.

Still on his knees, Vakhal raised his eyes to heaven. "Please, I cannot live without her. Hear my prayer." The weight of his isolation crushed him. "Please God, please," he whispered and lowered his eyes. He rose to his feet in numb disbelief — nowhere to go and a lifetime to do it.

A brilliant flash stung Vakhal's eyes. Elora leaped through the light and into his arms. A millisecond later, the gate vanished. He kissed her, then held her in his arms, and buried his face in her neck. "I thought I lost you."

"You almost did," she said and caressed his back. "Tobias made the Great Gate blink one last time for me."

He stroked her hair and looked deep into her eyes. "How could this happen? It's impossible."

"Tobias has gone insane. He divined a way to make the rhunite disappear into the void and cut off Earth from Eden," she said.

"Why?"

"He said, 'Mankind is oppressed by the ancient civilizations and monsters. They can never progress until they are free from Elven domination and daemia oppression.'"

Vakhal paced and combed his fingers through his hair. "Oppression? We are ever a friend to humanity, caring for them as parents. If we restrained them, it was for their own good."

She sat on a pedestal and clasped her hands in her laps. "He's delusional. He thinks that a golden age of humanity will dawn, and one day, when the gate reawakens, all of the worlds will witness a golden civilization." She chuckled, "He thinks men and women will rule the Earth as gods."

"I curse humanity," Vakhal said and glared at the homes and farms that dotted the fertile plains.

"It's not their fault. Tobias also cut them off from their families on Eden. Tobias betrayed us all. We must wait until the rhunite returns." She rose to her feet and held Vakhal's hands. "Is it such a terrible thing to wait with me?"

He caressed her cheek and a smile erased his anger. "I could wait ten thousand years with you, my love, and think it but a day. But we will be alone."

She caressed her belly and said, "Oh, but we are not alone." He threw back his head in laughter, took her in his arms, and swung her about. Their joy, however, annoyed the dwarves as they trekked back to their mountain stronghold.

Chapter 1

"The path diverges — the way is lost — but hope endures."
Poems of Elyazar Vol. 12

Where were you when the "Age of Man" ended? It was the single question on everyone's lips, a memory seared into our race consciousness. Sedated by our modern conveniences and apathetic to the warning signs, we lived with indifference, certain of our dominion and superiority. It was our Earth, our world; no one could challenge our authority or usurp our inheritance. However, our flawed thinking was an extension of incomplete history.

Before the dawn of recorded time, other races strode across worlds, titans of old. Giants of intellect and power, they ruled Earth with absolute sway, but when the Great Gate closed, they had no means to access our world. We relegated their deeds to fairy tales, clever stories told to children, dismissed as a fable. However, the Great Gate, the bridge between worlds, would reappear.

When our age ended, Jake Vakhal stood upon the precipice of his future, a mystery hidden by time. Like most college seniors, this vantage point offered him many expected paths. Well-worn roads diverging in some distant valley; they traveled apart and disappeared off in the distance. Would he apply to graduate school, work for a while, or return to family business? However, fate was cruel: it gave him no real choice in the matter. A hidden path awaited him, and once it began, he would long to return to this day, to this moment.

Unaware of his destiny, he prepared for one more year of college at Fort Defiant University, but this day would end far different than he imagined. Pompous professors piled assignments on him without mercy — research papers, essays, group projects, homework assignments, indecipherable textbooks, tiresome supplemental books, professorial appointments, and student activities — all demanded his attention. He hustled around the bedroom, throwing on clothes, stuffing supplies in his backpack, and hopping as he put on his shoes. Five smacks of the snooze button made him late, and the day would not wait.

From the second story, the suburbs of Fort Defiant, Colorado spread out before him. Filled travel mugs, wisps of steam appearing and then disappearing, briefcases in hand, keys clutched between their teeth, shiny new cars in the driveway, men and women hurried to work. A day of inflexible demands awaited them with expectant urgency. Children loitered at bus stops, hopeful for divine intervention to cancel school. Dogs peered out the living room windows and wondered when their loved ones would return. Cats, however, lounged and took a morning nap, certain that humans were an inferior species.

Senior college classes and a day at the library awaited Jake, yet he longed to throw off these obligations. He wanted to run through endless fields, to have a life of adventure, to embrace the possibility of the moment, and to live – unlike the life he anticipated. With a sigh, he accepted his destiny and started his day.

The aroma of cooked bacon wooed him to come and partake. Charlie Dahl, his cousin and best friend, was awake. He ran a brush through his platinum locks and then inspected his clothing. Neither his father nor the farming community accepted his New York fashion, and at graduation, his father expected him to don the traditional garb of Gleason, Kansas: blue jeans, a cotton shirt, and a baseball cap. Furthermore, his father expected him to move home and join the family business, an event he dreaded.

Pictures of summer vacations and fishing trips littered his dresser. In one of them, he held up a prize-winning trout, and his father stood behind him with a proud smile on his face. In another, he paddled a canoe with his mother.

Why couldn't life be like vacations, full of joy and expectancy?

He snatched up his car keys and grabbed his backpack. He hustled from the room and strode through the house. Charlie sat at the table, chin on her palm, elbow on the table top, and asleep. Her scrambled eggs and bacon sandwich grew cold. Jake dumped his rucksack onto a recliner and snuck over to the table. Quiet as a cat, he lifted her sandwich off the plate and ate in silence, savoring crispy bacon, egg, and cheese.

When he finished, he rose up from the chair and pretended to enter the room. "Come on girl, you need to get dressed." Charlie awoke and rubbed her eyes and yawned. "Breakfast is over; we need to get to class."

"Okay," she mumbled. She placed the plate in the sink and cocked her head. "I don't remember eating. I must be tired."

When a knock came from the front door, he hurried to answer it. Juliana Moore, his girlfriend, who lived down the street, waited for him on the front stoop. He kissed her and led her into the house, his arm around her shoulders. She trudged and said, "Professor Bates wants us to write a 10-page research paper on currency arbitrage."

"Charlie isn't dressed."

Having her boyfriend share a house with such a beauty dismayed Juliana, but then Jake informed her that Charlie was his first cousin, and the issue dissolved. After the death of her surviving parent, her father, Thor Dahl, Charlie lived with Jake's family, and the two were close as siblings. The idea of Jake sleeping with Charlie was absurd and repugnant. Even so, it disturbed Juliana that Charlie went about the house in her underwear, this day ivory silk panties and a matching chemise, a marginal covering that molded to her nubile body.

Cradling a cup of coffee in her hands, Charlie spotted Juliana and shuffled to her in furry slippers. "So how was your date?" Charlie brushed a fiery lock behind her right ear and blew the steam from the cup. "Jake never tells me anything."

"Well, it was —"

"Come on, I have to get dressed." Charlie grabbed Juliana's hand and led her toward the bedroom. Juliana shuffle stepped behind Charlie with a "help me" expression. Jake smirked and shook his head: Charlie lacked boundaries and a healthy sense of shame.

When his phone rang, he snatched it off the charger and saw his mother's photo. He listened for a moment, yawned, and then said, "Well, I'm talking to you, so I must be awake. How's everyone?" He tucked in his shirt and zipped up his jeans. "It's college, and it's always busy." His right hand on his hip, his face grew red and the arteries in his neck bulged. "I'm a senior. The professors gave them many books to study and work assignments. I'll come home to help with inventory during Spring Break ... That's not fair. It's a short drive, and then I'm home." He listened and rolled his eyes. His family also participated in a co-op farm and then sold their crops at a farmer's market — he was free labor. He rubbed his face and said, "Okay, it's five hour away, not the moon."

He glanced at his watch and snorted. It was the same guilt trip every year: come to youth camp and be with the family. He wanted to start his own traditions. He wanted to move to New York City and visit once a year. When his mom stopped talking, he said, "I will, after graduation. Listen, mom, I need to get going. I have to get to the library and work on an assignment. Call me when you get to camp."

Reggie Ortiz and Brian Krunk wandered from their bedrooms: Brian clad in pajama bottoms and an old T-shirt, Reggie clad in pink spandex athletic shorts and a matching black sports bra, shiny from an hour of dance aerobics. Lured by the aroma of brewed coffee, they hurried into the kitchen and savored their first cup of coffee; and in unison, they inhaled the aromatic vapors.

"Bye mom, I love you … I have to go, bye," he said and ended the call.

He joined his friends in the kitchen, rubbed the back of his neck, and growled. Jake, Charlie, Reggie, and Brian were best friends, but life tested their friendship. Jake grew tall and handsome: a Norse with flaxen hair, piercing blue eyes, a slender nose, and angular features worthy of a rock star. Brian, however, was short, chunky, and muscular, having a menacing countenance that made even his professors cower.

The girls also contrasted one another. Both were beauties. However, Charlie's diminutive body combined with flexibility won her a place on the gymnastics team. On the other hand, a pair of long legs, wavy black hair, Cupid's bow lips, creamy smooth complexion, a perfect nose, and coal dark eyes made Reggie more beautiful than a swimsuit model. She might have been the object of all men's desire, but her beauty came with thorns; and therein was the true contrast. A date with Reggie included Spanish lessons, a quiz, introductions to her extended family, a large meal, diatribes in Spanish, passionate debate, drama, endless questions, distrustful stares, veiled threats, and real dancing — not the vague gyrations of simulated dancing but authentic movements. On the other hand, Charlie laughed at everything, flirted with far too many boys, could out drink an Irish sailor, sang often — never with the right words — and broke into dance at random moments.

"Where is Juliana?" asked Reggie. She removed a hair white band and finger combed her thick, black locks. "Isn't she here yet?"

"They are in Charlie's bedroom," Jake replied and texted Juliana to hurry.

"Charlie bought seven new outfits yesterday," said Reggie.

"I'm glad I missed that," Jake said.

Brian rubbed his nose and yawned, "Missed what?"

Reggie rolled her eyes and shook her head. "Charlie is getting dressed. She has to try on every outfit, twice. It's a fashion marathon."

Brian nodded and said, "My first class isn't until noon."

"Come on," Jake shouted and pounded on Charlie's bedroom door. "We need to get going. I'm meeting Professor Brewer at the 'Coffee Bean' to discuss a research paper."

Chapter 2

Earlier that same day and in Gleason, Kansas, the shattering ring of the alarm drove Gunner from blessed slumber, and he grumbled as he wandered toward the bathroom. Linda, his wife, shuffled from the bedroom in worn pink slippers, clad in a frayed terry cloth robe and rubbed her eyes. She yawned, stretched, and wished for another hour of sleep. She paused in the living room, picked up her phone, and called Jake.

"Hi Jake, are you awake?" She ignored his disrespectful tone and asked, "We're fine. How is school?"

His indifference to home and family hinted at a deeper problem. If he started running from responsibility, he might do so the rest of his life, and when he reached the end, he might never know why he ran so fast or so far. Linda said, "I wish you were coming with us. You came to youth camp last year. Couldn't you take a break and join us?"

Jake was busy, again. It was always this way. During his military career, Gunner had the same attitude. She fought to keep him connected with the family. Now she bore the same burden with their son. "We appreciate that, but you have to make time for fun." With each excuse, the gulf between them widened. What had she done? Had life been so awful? He deflected her requests, said goodbye, and ended the call. "Okay," Linda sighed. "Bye."

She saw her reflection in the foyer mirror. The years created lines at the corners of her eyes and caused sags in her cheeks. Cosmetics concealed the truth of her age, but mornings were brutally honest. She descended the stairs and greeted the new day with a sigh.

"AUNT LINDA," Cindy shouted. "Bobby took my doll."

Linda was so tired, too tired to deal with it. She regretted having only one child and thought about having another. After Jake had grown into a man, she planned to travel or go back to college, but now that he was off at college, she longed to hold a baby and have it snuggle at her breast. Then her sister, Karen, had an unplanned pregnancy and gave birth to the fraternal twins. Karen was an unmarried executive with the USDA, and she viewed Linda as free daycare.

Linda snatched the doll from her nephew and handed it to her niece. The children paused from their bickering and watched her shuffle into the kitchen. After she was gone, Bobby grabbed the doll and raced away.

"AUNT LINDA," Cindy shouted and raced after her brother.

As the bacon sizzled and the scrambled eggs cooked, Linda looked up colleges on the internet. She pondered a master's degree, perhaps something in music. As a girl, she envisioned herself an actress upon the stage, starring in a musical. *It could still happen,* she mused and sucked in her stomach. A few seconds later, she inhaled and her tummy sagged.

Gunner, Linda's husband, charged down the stairs, still buttoning his shirt and tucking in the shirttail. "HONEY, have you seen my boots. I couldn't find them in the bedroom." He spotted them hiding with a potato chip next to the recliner. "NEVER MIND." After sitting, he stuffed his feet into his favorite hiking boots and pondered the spare tire of fat around his abdomen. *I need to hit the gym,* he thought, pinching the fatty ring. The smell of cooking bacon and brewing coffee drove the thought from his mind. He would begin his diet after breakfast.

The twins raced past Gunner, Cindy chasing Bobby. "Don't run in the house." His protests were ignored. When he opened the front door, he saw the newspaper sitting in a puddle of water. "Damn it," he sputtered. He crossed the faded blue porch, ignored the chipped paint and cracks.

Pinching the paper with two fingers, he picked it up and let the water drain. "Damn paperboy," he muttered.

He circled around the house and tossed the paper into the trashcan. He then wheeled the trash can to the curb. "I'm calling to complain." He was done being patient. "I'm going to have that kid's ass." It occurred to him how that sounded, and burst into laughter: medicine that took the bitter edge off life.

When he entered the house, Linda called, "Breakfast is ready." He hurried to the kitchen and took his place at the table. She placed a scoop of eggs, three slices of bacon, and two slices of toast onto a plate, and then she slapped it down before him. "You kids stop fighting and get in here." The children rushed into the kitchen and took their places at the table. Cindy made a face when she saw the eggs. "Just eat them," Linda growled.

"Gunner, if you were a CPA, we could move to the New York and live in Manhattan," Linda said.

His wife was in a mood. He checked the calendar on his phone. It was that time of the month, and he knew better than to argue with hormones. After he swallowed the last of his breakfast and gulped his coffee, burning his throat, he said, "We need to get down to the store. I want to get an early start." He eyed his niece and nephew. Their sleepovers occurred with such regularity that they lived with him more than at home with Karen. He loved the children, but he resented Karen. She deflected her responsibility with a wave of her hand and roll of her eyes. "Your sister is meeting us there. Right?"

Chapter 3

Through the frosted glass door, the security camera saw the movement of a lone shadow. The same figure it had seen for decades: a youth transformed into a man. Keys jangled, a lock clicked. When the door swung open, a security alarm greeted him with a lazy beep; why was he here so early? It was Saturday. Gunner hurried inside the store and stopped at the security pad. Old dust and mold made his nose itch. He fought the urge to sneeze and punched in the security code. The alarm yawned and greeted him. "Alarm disengaged."

"The gear is stowed at the rear loading dock. Pull your truck up to the loading dock," he texted Buford.

He paused at the checkout counter and stroked the rough wooden surface. He hated to lose the store, but there was no place for weathered hardware stores in the new economy. Homogonous big box stores usurped the creativity of hometown America and channeled profits to faraway urban centers. No matter where one went in the United States, one found the same set of stores selling the same products and the local citizens paid meager wages.

Gunner closed the door and locked it. He scribbled a note, "Will reopen October 20." His parents would never have approved, but they were dead: killed by a faulty heater. It shattered his world. He retired from the military and grieved their passing.

Out of the corner of his eye, looking through the plate glass window, he saw a luminescent pickup truck, bright and shiny, powerful like a stallion. As Toni circled the front of the truck, the drawn shade outlined her silhouette. Her curves and youthful form made Gunner come alive.

When a gentle tap came from the front door, his heart raced. He opened the door and saw a raven-haired beauty smiling at him. Only four years older than his son, she was forbidden fruit, but he wanted her; and desire is blind to the truth: an affair would ruin his life. She turned sideways and scooted past him. A low-cut neckline gave him a good look at the creamy swells of her breasts. When he closed and locked the door, she raised an eyebrow and smiled. "So you're really closing the store for two weeks?"

"I have to," Gunner said. "Jake is in college, and Lou just disappeared — again. He is on a drunken binge at his sister's place in Kansas City." As the Italian beauty strolled through the store, he turned the sign to "Closed", taped the note to the door, and drew the shade.

She strolled through the store. The narrow building had eight aisles and a custom assortment of merchandise – honed over decades – it still bore traces of his father's hand, a legacy given to him by two generations of Vakhal men. However, Gleason changed: big box stores sucked away customers like black holes. They also siphoned profit from the small town, and all suffered because of it; but who can resist a bargain? As a result, Gleason had high unemployment and low wages.

The wooden planks creaked as they passed through the store. He paused to straighten a "50% Off" sales sign on bolts, washers, and nuts. His stomach tightened. Every month the store sank a little more into the red. Both the building and the business were up for sale. He couldn't imagine life without them; they were home.

"I'm going to make a few entries in the books before we go." Toni climbed the side stairs to the office. The sway of her hips and the shortness of her denim skirt mesmerized him. He hesitated at the foot of the stairs. He loved Linda, but their marriage grew cold long ago. When Toni reached the top of the stairs, she glanced back at him and smiled.

———

Linda pulled up behind the store and parked near the concrete loading dock. Whenever Bobby poked Cindy, the girl kicked him. The constant bickering exasperated her; it had to stop. "You two stop it, or I'm telling your mom." It was an empty threat: Karen believed in permissive parenting: children sorted out their problems if ignored. Linda turned around and glared at the children. "You two stop it, or spankings will begin." The pair clasped their hands in their laps and cringed.

When Linda saw Karen's BMW, she sighed and sunk into the car seat. After exiting the car, she opened the trunk and hauled out the children's backpacks. Karen stepped out of the passenger's side of the car wearing a black skirt-suit. The pencil skirt was a bit too tight, and her steel-blue, satin blouse left little to the imagination. As she circled around the car, Linda observed the driver. The stranger leaned over and waved to her.

"Who's that?" asked Linda.

"That's Richard. He's a lawyer in my office. We've been seeing each other for the past couple of months." An introduction to her family meant the relationship was serious. "I got two weeks off from work and –"

Linda cut her off saying, "Oh no, Gunner and I are going to the youth retreat."

"I was going to say that we are taking the children with us. He owns a cabin in Ouray, Colorado." The children scampered to their mother and surveyed Richard with wary eyes. "You remember Richard, don't you?" asked Karen, her face tensed and lips tightened.

"No," they said in unison.

"Well, he's mommy's special friend. We're going to stay with him in the mountains. Doesn't that sound like fun?" Sour expressions answered her question, to which she said, "You two be good. Mommy likes him."

———

Toni inserted some receipts into a manila envelope and closed the metal filing cabinet. She then primped her hair and stole a furtive glance at Gunner. He sat at the desk and added up the bills. Tension displaced lust as he scanned the growing column of red ink. She sashayed to him and searched for the desire in his eyes. Finding none, angst arose within her. "What's the matter?"

"Bills," he muttered.

"Daddy will give you a loan if you asked him," she said with girlish sincerity.

"The bank would give me a loan, but I have no money to repay it." He sighed and leaned back in the leather chair. "A retail chain made an offer on the store. The amount stunned me."

"How much," she asked and sat on the corner of the desk. He handed her a legal document that detailed the offer amount. When she read it, her face lit up, and she squealed with delight. "This is incredible."

"I don't even have to see a lawyer or go to a closing. It's all computerized. With a keystroke, the system attaches my signature and takes my photo. Then it's done. What generations of my family built, I will sell. It seems so … sterile. No passion, no tears, just a computer entry, and my world changes."

"But that's a seven-figure offer. You would never have to work again," Tony said and sat on the edge of the desk. She kept rereading the offer price and slipped into a daydream. "You could do so much with it."

"I suppose," he said and drew in a cleansing breath. His index finger lingered above the "enter" key as memories drifted through his mind: his first job as a boy, the day he joined the army, the phone call informing everyone that he was a father, the sheriff reporting the death of his parents, and the party when Jake left for college. He stared at the acceptance contract and a great war waged within him.

The store was finished, and his marriage was empty. He brought down his finger and pressed the key. The screen thanked him and automatically sent him a confirmation email. When he switched to his email account, he saw the promised confirmation notice, which indicated court acceptance. In the blink of an eye, it was done. He had to admit, the millions Kansas spent on the court system upgrades worked great. When he checked his bank account, the money appeared as a credit entry. During his time in the military, he saw many economies fail and the devastation it wrought. He transferred it to his brokerage account with "The Denver Exchange" and converted his money to gold: markets fail but gold remains. He watched the transactions complete, and in less than a minute, a bin filled with precious metals, stored in a vault, bore his name. The company sent him a photo of his purchase and congratulated him.

He rose up from his chair and took one last look around at the dusty, weathered office that became home. A sharp bang at the garage door drove the melancholy from him. He brushed aside his cares: it was vacation time, time for fun.

He passed through the store and entered the rear storage area. The heavy aroma of motor oil reminded him of work. He navigated around a disassembled engine, its guts strewed around benches. He rebuilt engines at night for extra income. Between that and his retirement income from the Army, he made just enough to pay the bills. Of course, all that was at an end, but it seemed unreal, as though it was a wishful daydream instead of reality.

Releasing the lock, he pulled on the chain, and the garage door rattled opened. Through the increasing gap, he saw two yellow school buses. Refurbished and rebuilt for God's use, they bore the name "Gleason Community Church", leftovers from a failed Sunday school bus ministry: no one wanted to drive the old hulks, and unlike the days of his youth, no parent would send their child off to church with a complete stranger. The youth ministry inherited the buses, despite its objections.

Teenage faces peered at him through the glass windows. Buford waited at the loading dock. He rubbed his round belly and surveyed the pile of supplies. With a Georgia accent, he said, "We have to load all that? It's going to take half a day."

"Get the youth group to help you." He picked up a cardboard box and set it down on the edge. "We should be able to get everything loaded in a few minutes."

Buford waddled toward the buses. "Hey ya'll, we need some help." He waved his stumpy arms. The volunteer parents lingered inside the first bus, hopeful to avoid aching backs and sore muscles. "Come on now."

Logan stepped off the bus, stretched his back and looked at the sun with contempt. Although he was young, fit, and captain of the football team, he preferred to watch others work. He waved at the other teens and rallied the youth group. "Come on. I'm not going to be the only one." The young people poured out of the buses and congregated near the loading dock, eager to have their adventure underway.

Toni opened the back of the white trailer and supervised the loading process. Boxes of food, gear, and other supplies filled the long trailer. The supplies soon filled the trailer and the back of the pickup truck. "Okay," Toni shouted. "Get back on the buses. We need to get on the road. It's going to take us 6 hours to drive the 350 miles."

Buford rubbed the flat top of his crew cut and asked, "This camp is in the mountains?"

"Yup, it's halfway up a mountain and –" Gunner paused and watched a Cadillac Escalade cruise into the parking area behind the stores. Such an ostentatious display by a minister created controversy and alienated many within the congregation. The SUV cruised to a stop and the tinted window lowered. Pastor Jim Wilson removed his sunglasses.

Gunner said, "We're all set to go."

The pastor sniffed and played with the media control system. "I'll take the lead. The coordinates are programmed into my navigational map." Being tall enough to play professional sports and powerfully built enough to be a professional wrestler, Gunner had to lean over and twist to look through the open window. The high-tech instrument panel included a large computer screen, and unlike ordinary maps, it was three-dimensional and photo realistic, which included an interactive voice mode, the kind of tech that made men green with envy.

Sarah, Jim's wife, leaned over and waved. "Hi Gunner, we have everyone packed and ready to hit the road. Do you think we will be able to stop for laundry detergent? I ran out."

"We packed some." Gunner looked at the back. Their teenage children, Kevin and Grace, played video games as if in a trance. The electronic devices would keep the children sedated for the trip, but when they reached camp, he would confiscate all such items. It was best, however, to wait until they arrived to announce it. "Okay Pastor Jim, you take the lead. Buford is driving the first bus with the volunteers; I'll be on the second bus with the kids, and Toni will follow us in her pickup truck that is towing the white trailer."

"Okay, let's head out," Jim said and raised the window. The white SUV cruised away from him. Gunner rubbed his face and struggled to diffuse his anger. The new pastor irritated him: perhaps it was his brusque manner; perhaps it was his wealth, or perhaps it was condescending attitude – but Gunner wanted him gone.

"Everybody, get on board. We're going," Gunner shouted.

Linda gave her sister, Karen, a final hug and then the two children. "Okay, Bobby and Cindy, you be good and do what Karen ... your mommy says."

"Why can't we go with you?" asked Bobby.

"Youth camp is for teenagers. In three or four years, you will be able to come." She opened the rear door and gave them a pat. "Now hop in." Cindy scrambled across the seat and Bobby sat next to her. "Bobby, stop picking on your sister." She then said to Karen, "Cindy has a slight allergy to peanuts."

"I know," Karen chuckled. "I am their mother. You two have fun, and don't worry."

Linda waved to Richard and said, "Good to meet you. Bye, everyone. We'll see you in a week."

"BYE," they shouted as the car pulled away.

Linda watched the SUV disappear around the brick building. It takes more than being a woman to make a mother, and Karen lacked maternal instinct. Linda wanted to bring the children to camp, but no one would be their age. *No. It's for the best,* she assured herself. She climbed onto the bus and sat on the bench seat located behind the driver. She looked at the phone in her right hand and fought off the urge to speak with the children.

Buford waddled toward the lead bus, and Toni jogged toward the truck. Gunner scrambled up the stairs and hopped in the driver's seat. After closing the doors, he glanced up at the interior mirror. "Everyone take a seat. We need to get going." He then asked Linda, "How's your sister?"

"She's fine. She has a new man in her life. His name is Richard, and he is just her type, rich and handsome." Linda crossed her arms and legs. "They're taking the children on a vacation. I don't think he's the fatherly type." She leaned forward and whispered in his ear. "Pastor's SUV looks so expensive. How did they afford it?"

"The same way they bought their estate, their boat, and their vacation home in Belize: his daddy paid for it," he said. "Can you get those kids settled?"

She stood up and said, "Take a seat." The teens sat down and broke out their electronic devices. The girls hunched over their phones and texted, but the boys played games. Logan accessed his favorite pornographic site and admired the recent submissions.

Bain, Brian's identical twin brother, sat behind Linda. When Buford's bus pulled away, Gunner slipped the bus into gear and rolled forward. Pete passed between the brick buildings. It was Saturday morning: closed shops and empty streets made access to Main Street easy. The pastor cruised ahead of them and rushed through a green light.

"Looks like Pastor Jim is in a hurry," Buford said over the walkie-talkie. "I would pull him over and ticket him if I was 'on the job.'"

"I hear that," Toni replied. "How long do you think it will take him before he realizes we aren't behind him?"

"He'll probably make it to the highway," Buford replied.

Gunner twitched his nose and rubbed his neck. Interstate 24 was always busy these days, and they could easily become separated. "Linda, call Sarah. Tell her to turn on Jim's radio. That's why we bought them."

"Why aren't we just using the phone?" asked Linda.

"Because that's no fun," Gunner said.

"Oh, I understand," she said, but in reality, she had no idea.

When the light turned yellow, the convoy cruised over the Ruben Goddard Truss Bridge, and Gunner stomped the gas pedal. Through the steel girders, he saw the Jennings River amble on its lazy way south. Memories of warm summers and countless fishing expeditions drifted through his mind. Then the memory of his parent's unexpected death stabbed his soul.

When the phone rang, Christy, married to Gunner's cousin Rory, called. Gunner and Rory were close as brothers. "... Hey, Christy ... no, I understand. You just got home from a long trip. I'll put you on a conference call." She tapped Gunner's shoulder and said, "Christy wants to say something."

"Hi everyone," Christy Vakhal said. They shouted a reply. "Rory is still in bed asleep. I flew in early, and we had a late night."

"Did Bill drink himself under the table?" asked Gunner.

"Something like that," Christy said, "after he had an unexpected encounter with a transgender prostitute." Gunner threw back his head and roared with laughter. "Rory, Michael, and I will drive up later next week and join you. We have so much yard work to do."

"Don't work Rory too hard: he promised to go fly fishing," Gunner said. "Oh, and tell him to bring his bow. We might get to do some hunting."

"I will," Christy said. "I'm fixing breakfast, so I have to go."

"Bye," they all shouted in unison.

As soon as the call ended, Gunner said, "I don't see how Rory does it. Christy travels 9 months of the year. He's almost a single parent."

"She works for the State Department," Linda said. "She's doing important work."

Gunner grunted. "She should have thought about that before starting a family. Michael's going to grow up and not know his mother."

Linda stared through the window as if in a dream. The steel and glass structure of Nesbit K-12 transported her back in time. She recalled moving to Gleason and her first day in the fifth grade. Oh so nervous, she stood by Mrs. Jennings side, squeezed her hand, and chewed her index fingernail of the opposite hand. When the class looked up from their desks, she saw Gunner for the first time. His flaxen hair and sparkling blue eyes mesmerized her, and they had ever since.

Gunner tapped his phone and shook it. "Linda, did you bring the charger? My phone is dead."

"Damn it," Logan muttered.

"So is mine," Bain said. He sniffed his phone and screwed up his face. "Mine smells like burnt cat ... and it's hot." He tossed the phone onto the bench seat beside him.

"It's too late to turn back now. We will just have to wait until we can find a store and replace it." Bain's deceased father owned a civil engineering and construction company, which his uncle now managed; so, he could well afford to replace it. Gunner eased onto the northbound ramp of Interstate 24, and the bus groaned as it charged up the ramp.

The bus charged into traffic and matched the pell-mell highway speed. Perturbed at his son's indifference toward his family, he tried to distract himself. He watched the West Glenn Shopping District pass on their left. The sunlight gleamed off glass and steel buildings. They were near the mall.

The grid pattern of city traffic and rectangular buildings fell behind them. Off in the distance, the blue waters of Lake Hope sparkled in the morning sun. A pair of fishing boats raced through the glittery water, headed for a day of fishing. He wished to be on one of those boats instead of heading to a Christian camp. *I should never have let Pastor Jim talk me into this.*

"It is the only time we get to have a vacation," Linda said.

He hated it when Linda did that. It was as if she could read his mind. He was about to say something when all thoughts but one fled his mind. Strange ripples cascaded through the lake as if a million tiny pebbles suddenly hit the surface. "What's that?"

Chapter 4

Charlie stood before an old-fashioned dressing mirror, absorbed by every detail, a nuance of color, the cut of the garment, agonized by indecision. Juliana gave up trying to convince her that jeans and a blouse were acceptable. Before the current outfit joined the pile on the bed, she said, "I really like that outfit. It must have cost a fortune. You look like you could be in a movie."

"Do you really like it?" Charlie smoothed the knife pleats of her black leather miniskirt. They danced around her mid-thigh and threatened to flash everyone if she moved wrong. A matching bolero jacket – a garment that almost covered her sides – accompanied a waist cincher corset, which sculpted her torso into an hourglass ideal. This combination focused the eye on the gleam of her white satin blouse and the way it tented over her small breasts.

She inserted a thin black ribbon underneath a Peter Pan collar and tied it into a bow. When her scalp itched, she screwed up her face and scratched beneath a black semi-circular headband. It contrasted her vibrant red locks and held them behind her head. Charlie's stylist insisted that she have bangs, so she parted them in the middle and tapered them. Between her wine lipstick, blush, and green cat's eyes, she was stunning.

After tightening the laces on her knee high boots, she said, "I guess this outfit is okay." Juliana sighed with relief and stood to her feet. "But what do you think about my earrings?"

"Charlie, get moving! I am not going to be late," bellowed Jake. Several loud pounds rattled the door. He threw open the door and marched into the room. He scooped up Charlie, threw her over his shoulder, and carried her from the room. Draped over his shoulder, she brushed down her miniskirt, to keep from flashing everyone, and said, "Wait, I need my purse and backpack."

A smile appeared on Juliana's face. She pranced over and gathered the belongings. "I've got them. I'll meet you out in the car."

Jake marched through the living room with Charlie draped over his shoulder. "We're going." He carried the girl from the house and across the lawn. When they arrived at the old Chevy Suburban, he set her down on the driveway. Charlie studied her hands and twisted her face to one side. "What?" Jake snarled.

"I need my gloves," she said.

"I have them," Juliana said. She scurried across the lawn and handed the gloves to Charlie. A look of relief on her face, she stepped into the vehicle and slid across the bench style seat, the cool vinyl chilling her bottom. "Why is it so cold? It's only October."

"No idea. It was hot last night." Jake pounded the horn and honked for his friends. Reggie hurried out of the house, but Brian took his time; he stuffed a breakfast burrito into his mouth. After they had piled into the SUV, he backed the vehicle down the driveway and said, "You eat more than all of us combined."

Jake glanced at the dashboard clock and grew irritated at the thought of being late. Out of the corner of his eye, he saw Charlie's weather-beaten car. "You need to get the Beast fixed … and I mean by a real mechanic. That piece of junk is always leaving you stranded."

Charlie glanced up at him from her compact mirror. "The Beast has another 100,000 miles in it. All it needs is some loving care." She stretched her lips and applied a sealer coat over her wine lipstick, a color that complemented her red hair. "My dad was going to rebuild it."

"Loving? That car needs a faith healer. No. It's a zombie, and you should shoot it in the head. That car is the reason you lost your last three jobs, and no one wants to ride in it." Seeing her frown, he said, "I'm not trying to get on you, but you, at least, need to paint it." The car was half primer and half faded blue paint.

"It's all I have left of my father," she said. He knew this, of course, and he knew it was not up for discussion. Whenever she sat in the car, she smelled his black cherry pipe tobacco, saw his reading glasses, and wore his driving jacket.

It was an unexpected death. While driving home one night in a new car, a drunk driver crashed into the side of it, killing him. When the police stopped the driver, he tried to blame the accident on Charlie's father, Thor. The drunk said, "His car was dark blue. How was I supposed to see it?" The man posted bail and then fled town, never to return.

As the pair entered downtown Fort Defiant, red brick shops gave way to steel and glass office buildings. Merchants opened their doors and vagrants prepared to panhandle. Legions of shoppers parked their cars and rolled into town like a tidal wave. Bakeries, coffee shops, retail establishments, and private art studios welcomed them, eager to make a sale. A man glared at his phone in annoyance and shook it as his dog urinated on a light post.

The light turned green, and he raced to the next red light. A single car cruised through the intersection, passed over the Coronado Bridge that spanned the Misty River, and transitioned onto Trenton Boulevard. He glanced at the time display and irritation boiled within him. *It's wrong to hold up traffic for one car,* he brooded. *The old geezer could do his errands later in the day.*

When the light turned green, he punched the gas and nearly rear-ended the car ahead of him. "Hurry up," he said. The traffic cruised up to the next traffic light. He was too agitated to admire the beauty of downtown. It was a modern and attractive city. "Stay green," he said through gritted teeth.

It turned red.

"Why is this light so long?" He turned on the radio and tried to release the tension, but the country song did little to help him, and then his phone rang. When he picked up the phone, it was hot and the display was dead. "That figures," he grumbled. "I canceled the damage protection plan yesterday."

Brian nodded toward the "First National Bank of Gleason", and said, "Your phone isn't the only thing not working." The temperature and time display went blank; the sign stopped turning, and a puff of smoke rose from it. Several cars simply stopped, and smoke poured out from their hoods. The dumbfounded drivers stood next to their stricken automobiles, scratching their heads and cursing their broken phones.

Charlie said, "That's weird. I wonder what did that."

Chapter 5

Jake cruised on Rockland Drive, circling the campus. A towering wall of fieldstone, topped by black pikes, blocked their view of Fort Defiant State College. Many years ago, the campus belonged to a military school, but the school closed in 1957 and sold the campus. They made a right turn and cruised past the curved walls and an open gate, which no one remembered closed. A banner, above the main gate, proclaimed "Fall Harvest Festival."

Jake rubbed his face and grumbled. The whole world conspired to make him late. He joined the long queue of cars on the entry road to campus. Progress came in inches, if at all. "I can't wait. Charlie, take the wheel and meet me at the Coffee Bean. I'm walking." He threw open the car door and grabbed his backpack. She slid into the driver's seat, looking very much like a child driving the immense vehicle.

Jake strode past the long line of cars. In the great tradition of rural festivals, a crew of men in red vests signaled cars to park in semi-straight rows. Every so often, a driver would falter and park in the wrong spot. This caused frantic waving of yellow traffic flags and backed up traffic. In a baffling reversal, the cool morning transformed into a summer heat wave with the rising of the sun. It was October, not August and not December. He wished the weather would reflect it. However, despite the fervent heat, a sudden chill made Jake shiver — a weather inversion?

More birds — eagles, hawks, geese, ducks, crows, meadowlarks, blue jays, finches, and even humming birds —filled the sky. As if remote controlled, they flew in a single direction, west. He never knew there were so many birds. The sharp yap of dogs drew his attention back to earth. Packs of dogs fled west, weaving through traffic, on a heading for downtown and points beyond. The equestrian club's horses skittered about and neighed, eager to join the flight west.

"Red, come back!" a cowgirl shouted. A stallion raced through the parking lot, stirrups jostling and reins dancing. One of the red-vest attendants had his back to the horse. Jake cringed. At the last second, the attendant heard the pounding of hooves and leapt out of the horse's path. The crazed animal ran past the cars and then through main gates.

"That's weird," Jake said.

He trudged up the hill, his thoughts once again consumed by deadlines and obligations. The Coffee Bean lay within the student union and was a popular destination in the mornings. Jake jogged through the parking lot and past a car with an open hood. Several young men gawked at the engine, while the car's owner cursed at his dead phone. When a girl tried to start her car, she heard nothing, not even a click. She too checked her phone, only to find it dead. When he squeezed past the congregated crowd, terrible chemical smoke stung his eyes and burned his nostrils. "That thing smells like burnt hair," he said with a quiet voice.

The roar of an engine drew Jake's attention. Charlie drove the Suburban across a field. The four-wheel drive spit chunks of sod and left behind deep ruts. She jumped the curb and came to a stop. When Charlie exited the truck, she said, "The traffic was awful."

The grounds keeper threw down his cap and glared at the ruts with his hands on his hips. "Let's go inside before he calls security." Jake put his hand on Charlie's back and led her toward the shop.

"Damn it," Doug, the car's owner, said. "Does anyone have a working phone?" The others around him checked their phones and shook their heads. The grounds keeper kept hitting his walkie-talkie, hoping one more knock would repair it. The very air buzzed with electricity, and the smell ozone permeated the air.

Mr. Brewer stood out from rest of the patrons. The silver-haired professor wore the same sports coat with elbow patches and sweater vest every day. A steaming cup of coffee sat on the table next to his open laptop. When Jake approached the table, he noted that the elderly man appeared half in frustration and half in horror. Mr. Brewer looked up at Jake and said, "It just stopped working. All of my class notes, my tests are on it. My latest book project is also on it."

"Did you back them up?" Jake sat at the table opposite the professor. "If not, they are history. There's no getting them back."

"What? No. They can't be gone. I spent a year writing my latest book. A year – it's staggering. No, it's criminal. Has someone hacked me?" he asked and searched the café for the guilty party. When a teen wild, frizzy black hair and wearing all black clothes wandered past them, he glared at him.

"It's not just you," Jake said. "Everyone's phone and computer are dead."

The professor slammed down the laptop lid and tapped his lips with his index finger. "This is what we get for trusting technology. I have printouts from the last revision of my book. I'll have to work from them." He rose up from the table and said, "We'll have to reschedule our meeting." He stormed away mumbling and staring at the floor.

Jake rose up from his chair and looked about the cafe as if startled from a sound sleep. He searched for danger, but the mundane surrounded him. The coffee shop patrons, the wait staff, and his friends acted as if everything was fine. *What is wrong with them?* Then Jake wondered, *what is wrong with me?*

All of heaven became silent, and the Earth held its breath. When Jake exited the restaurant, he searched the skies and wanted to scream. Charlie hurried after him but saw no reason for Jake's distress. She rubbed his arm and said, "It's okay. You're just under too much stress. You need to relax." The festive atmosphere, the laughter of children, the cacophony of carnival rides, and the aroma of funnel cakes drove the apprehension from his mind. "Since your meeting was canceled, let's go to the fair. It'll be fun." Although reluctant, Jake agreed.

White tented booths spread across the athletic fields. A river of celebrants wandered through wide aisles between the tents, and circuit-traveling vendors shouted their wares. Charlie, Reggie, and Juliana paused at a jewelry table, and holding earrings up to their ears, they searched for a bargain. Although a dizzying array lay before them, they rejected most.

When Brain paused to examine a Buckmaster Survival Knife, Jake joined him and picked out a Swiss Army Knife. Various other bladed weapons, lying upon crushed black velvet, dazzled their eyes, and they examined many of the weapons. When Juliana joined Jake, she rolled her eyes and crossed her arms. A nearby clothing vendor caught her eye, so she rejoined the girl.

Jake purchased the knife, but Brian decided against it. The vendors had a reputation for selling imitations as authentic items. They caught up with the girls at a snack vendor, and despite the early hour, they each purchased a beverage and shared two funnel cakes. Live country music lured them deep in the heart of the fair. Men dressed in cowboy hats and western shirts performed on stage. The paused for a few minutes and then continued on their way. There was so much to see and do.

Dizziness made Jake's footsteps falter. He rubbed his temples and squeezed his eyes shut. When he opened his eyes, he whispered, "It's all coming to an end." God was about to turn the page and begin a new chapter. He turned to Juliana and said, "I'll be back."

"What's the matter?" asked Juliana, but the crowd engulfed Jake as he jogged from them.

The former military college believed in plain face buildings, somber and stark. They were red brick, rectangular – much like the minds of the men who built them – and three stories tall. Set up in a square, one could easily pass between buildings with a minimum of effort. The oversized windows often became stuck in the heavily painted tracks, but this did not stop the faculty and staff from forcing them open: the air conditioning and heaters never worked well.

Jake rushed up the concrete stairs. The stairs, like the buildings themselves, were worn smooth by countless student feet. He flung open the front door and ran past the bronze bust of George Washington without rubbing his bright shiny nose for luck. He scrambled up the stairs and burst into the dean's office. "Mr. Rogers, have you heard from anyone? Are there any alerts?"

Selwyn exchanged an unspoken but informative glance with Rose, his secretary. "Well, no. Our cell phone and computers are broken, but the hard-line phones still work. There haven't been any notices from the sheriff's office." He cocked his head and asked, "Why? What have you heard?"

"Nothing, it just feels like something bad is about to happen." Jake ran from the room with Charlie in hot pursuit. *White folks are crazy*, thought Selwyn. He returned to his office, intent on doing the impossible: doing his job without a computer. Then a strange feeling made his stomach quiver and toes tingle. He walked to the window and pushed aside the sun-faded white curtains.

The fair appeared a success despite the communication problems and the bizarre weather. Then he looked north to the central quad. A group of students played Frisbee; some lounged on blankets; others hurried to the fair, athletes ran on the track, and lovers kissed beneath the old apple trees. Life continued as it had been since time began, but a peculiar feeling settled upon him. It was as if he was leaving Fort Defiant, never to return, and these last images would have to last a lifetime.

He whisked the curtains closed, and mumbled, "He's just got me spooked." He sat behind his desk and tried to brush aside the feeling, yet it grew stronger with each passing minute. He slammed down his pen and marched from the office. He joined his secretary out in the hallway and spoke in a whisper. "Rose, contact the staff and have them —." A sudden clatter from outside the building caused him to pause. He furrowed his brow and narrowed his eyes. "What is going on?"

Chapter 6

Linda had a terrible premonition and rose to her feet. The highway turned north, exiting town before it went west. She swore she saw Fort Defiant off in the distance, although that was impossible. Fort Defiant was far away, but she looked toward it as if she could see it if she really tried.

She turned, looked out the back window, and studied the lake. "Something strange is going on at the lake." A boat exploded into a ball of flame. She gasped and pressed her hand to her chest. Bits of debris and a tiny figure of a man hurtled through the sky like a ragdoll. He tumbled, hit the waters, and sank below the murky water. "Oh my god, did you see that?"

"See what, babe?" asked Gunner.

"A boat just exploded," she said. "I think a man was killed." Logan and Bain scrambled across the bus and joined her staring out the window. Black smoke rose from the burning wreckage, but then it sank beneath the troubled waters. The second boat made a wide turn and sputtered to a stop. The driver and two passengers leaped into the water. The second boat exploded and a huge fireball rose into the sky.

"What happened to my phone?" Megan pouted and tapped her phone, trying to revive it. "I had the whole thing on video."

"It still might have posted to your 'YouTube' account," Tiffany said.

"Someone just died. Show a little respect." Linda looked for recognition in the girl's eyes but found a void. "That's somebody's brother or father." She turned to Gunner and asked, "Should we stop and notify the authorities?"

"No. Everyone on the dock saw it. I'm sure others have called the police by now." He picked up his walkie-talkie and pushed the send button. "Did you guys see that? Two boats exploded." He waited a few seconds and repeated the broadcast, but there was no reply. When he pushed the button again, he noted that the red LED never illuminated, and the battery pack was hot. Gazing up in the mirror, he said, "Everyone settle down and take a seat. The show's over." The highway curve carried them away from the lake.

"But what happened?" asked Logan.

"I don't know. Maybe their fuel lines ruptured," Bain said.

Gunner shook his head and said, "That would cause a fire, not an explosion, and it happened to both boats. We can look it up online when a story is posted."

He ruminated about the explosion. Short of a deliberate act, it mystified him. Then he heard the far-off wail of a siren. He searched the skies for a tornado, but they were clear. A car suddenly shot past on his left. Black smoke billowed from the hood. It swerved and launched down into the deep median between the raised highways. It tumbled end over end and came to rest.

"What happened?" asked Linda.

"I don't know. It just burst into flames." Gunner adjusted his grip on the steering wheel and glanced into the rearview mirror. His lips parted in a silent gasp and his eyes went wide. A swirling black vortex formed over Gleason. It gobbled up birds and an airplane, not even light escaped it. The sun smeared across the sky in a yellow streak. Out of instinct more than thought, he slammed down the gas pedal and dodged around Buford's bus. The engine roared as the bus hurtled ever faster. Pastor Jim did the same and floored his SUV. When the buses were parallel, he signaled Buford to floor it. Buford nodded and stomped on the gas. The bus shimmied and picked up speed.

Cars and trucks on the southbound highway slammed on their brakes. They slid sideways across the highway, leaving black skid marks behind, some crashing and some plummeted into the median. Those that remained spun around and smoke billowed from their tires. They raced the wrong way down the highway. A black SUV slammed head-on into a bread delivery truck and flipped in the air, crashing to the ground with a shower of shards.

"What's going on?" shouted Linda.

"Look behind us," he said. All necks swiveled and cries of terror arose from the teens. A black hole swallowed the sky, and the entire town warped as if viewed in a funhouse mirror. The image twisted and flowed like water. A helicopter rose from the airport and fought to gain altitude. Its engines failed and it plummeted into Jenning's Swamp.

"It's coming after us," Logan said.

The convoy reached 90 MPH, but cars still rocketed past them. The stampeding traffic raced from Gleason. Terrified faces looked back and screamed. An 18-wheel truck behind them launched off the road. It spun in a twirl and flew toward the event horizon. Cars joined it, and one by one, they flew off the road, flipping end over end as they disappeared into the void.

Reality folded like a sheet of paper and compressed. They traversed a hundred miles in a blur. When it decompressed, the pastor's SUV fishtailed and skidded. It shot through the guardrail and launched into the air. Smoke came from the tires of Buford's bus. It slid sideways and began to tumble. The yellow bus rolled down the highway, bodies flying out from the windows.

Reality began to snap back and forth: green fields and blue skies shifted to dense forest and sunrise – it kept switching ever faster until Gunner could no longer bare it. Gray mist settled over them, and everything, including time itself, slowed to a crawl. Mouths mid-scream, bodies flying, luggage in mid-air, the bus, and the world around them ground to a halt. Time stopped.

———

On its way toward Colorado, a passenger jet soared through the endless blue skies of Kansas. From the dawn of time, primitive men and women raised their eyes to watch birds in flight, and they dreamed of soaring through the skies, unfettered by the chains that bound them to the earth. Yet the passengers of Flight 819 yearned to walk the earth. After flying 12 hours from London and a two-hour layover at JFK in New York, they were once again airborne and bound for Los Angeles.

Jim Southern tried to sleep. The closed window shade, the travel pillow against the cabin wall, and two shot bottles of whiskey were supposed to make him sleep. However, the mind has no "off" switch. The crick in his neck, the small seats, the stomach upset from lunch, the window light in his eyes – the cacophony of annoyances ruined the flight. He looked to the next row of seats, hoping to persuade the occupants to close the window shade, but an enthralled teenager, Doug, stared out the window in a state of awe. Jim reached into his jacket, elbowing the plump woman next to him, and retrieved a pair of sunglasses. With the light dimmed, he closed his eyes and relaxed his mind. Rest. Sleep. He longed to fall into a deep slumber and awaken at the gate.

The earth was so small, a relief map spread out on a table. Tan squares that contained circular fields of green crops spread out across the horizon. It was so flat, so endless. The whole world could dine on the produce, or so it seemed. They flew through a wispy cloud, and he lost sight of the land. A moment later, they emerged. Doug furrowed his brow and cocked his head. "Mom, what's that?"

"Those are farms," Nancy said, reading a novel on her e-pad. "Your grandfather owns a farm in Kansas. If you look hard enough, maybe you'll see him waving."

"No mom," Doug said and pointed. "What's that swirling black spot. It looks like a tornado of darkness."

Nancy leaned to her right and looked past her son's head. "It's … um," she elbowed her husband, "Kent, what's that?"

"Those are farms," he said and sipped his rum and Coke. "A two drink maximum is unfair. They should allow four or five drinks. I can barely get a buzz going."

"Look," Nancy said and pointed.

He leaned over and saw a swirling black vortex, bolts of lightning stabbing from its dark heart. The sun smeared across the sky like a yellow streak. Electric red and orange light replaced blue skies. The "Fasten Seatbelts" sign illuminated and a bell dinged. The jet jumped and shimmied. Their seatbelts snapped tight and held them fast. The jet began to shudder, and the flight attendants raced up the aisle with the drink cart.

"Come on, damn it," Jim grumbled. He pressed the flight attendant button six times. "What's the problem?"

Doug went agape at the kaleidoscope of colors that enveloped the aircraft. Jagged rips raced across the earth, swallowing fields and entire towns. The crazed pattern of fractured earth pointed to a single location: Gleason,

Kansas, the epicenter. The airliner rushed toward a swirling black vortex.

"MOM!" Doug cried.

The aircraft disappeared, erased from the sky, swallowed by the vortex. A heartbeat later, The Black Mountains appeared. The flat lands rippled like waves upon the sea, short and high frequency, then long and devastating; vast crevices yawned; fractured rock burst from the ground like compound fractures, and the earth twisted beneath the load. The shockwaves changed the face of the planet and toppled the world of men.

————

The double doors flew open and Jake burst into the student union. He charged up to his friends, his face flushed and breathing hard. "We have to get out of here."

"Jake, what's going on? You're scaring me," said Charlie.

"I don't have time to explain, but we have to go. Something terrible is about to happen. His friends followed him from the building, fleeing from an unseen but felt terror." When they loaded into the old Suburban, he punched the accelerator and sped from the parking lot. They were so intent on leaving the campus that they failed to notice everyone faced east and stared at something.

They sped through town and illegally raced through several red traffic lights. After they had crossed town, a Cadillac ahead of them stopped at a yellow traffic light, much to Jake's annoyance. He recognized the owner; it belonged to City Councilman Doug Anders. Despite the rumor had it that he accepted bribes and was complicit in his wife's disappearance, he pretended to be a law abiding citizen.

"What is going on?" asked Reggie. "I feel like the world is about to collapse in on me."

"I thought it was just me," Brian said. "I want to bash something to bits."

Jake mumbled, "Something is wrong. We need to get back to the house." The sun smeared across the sky, a yellow streak forming a ribbon across a clear blue sky. The earth began to grumble as if awakened from a long slumber, and the river began to slosh, a wild dance of waves and white water. The Cadillac launched away from his car and raced through the red light. The scream of an air horn preceded the behemoth of a delivery truck. It slammed into the Cadillac, T-boning it. Tires screeched; metal bent; glass shattered; lethal shards flew; flames erupted; the delivery truck tipped over, crushing the Cadillac – Doug Ander's life ended.

The ground bucked like a bronco trying to throw them off it. He gunned the engine and whipped around the accident. "WATCH OUT!" screamed Charlie. Gasoline ignited and set the road ablaze. When he hit the brakes, an SUV slammed into his car's bumper, crushing the back-end. It propelled the SUV through the guardrail, and it glided in a smooth arc. It plunged into the frenzied waters with an enormous splash.

Jake blacked out for a second. When his mind cleared, he saw the deflated airbag and sensed the tightness of the seatbelt. The emergency lights blink and the horn blared synchronous to the beat. Blackness enveloped the car, and they slid down to the murky depths. Frigid water poured in through the window seams; the cold water shocked his system, and every breath became precious.

"Damn, that's cold," Charlie gasped.

Jake fought to release the seatbelt, yanking and pulling. The car plunged into the depths of the river. It hit the muddy bottom with jarring stop and the rear-end joined the front on the bottom. His thumb accidentally pressed the release mechanism, and the seatbelt retracted.

The water was already up to their knees. When Jake tried to open the door, it refused to budge. The water was up to their waists. Charlie pounded on the windows with her fists, an animal desperate to escape. The water was up to their chests. Juliana screamed, "Help us." Jake spun and kicked with his feet, but the glass refused to break. Brian and Reggie tried to force the other doors open, but the pressure held them tight. The water was up to their necks.

"God, help me," Charlie prayed and drew in one last breath.

Trapped in the murky waters, Jake slapped at the door handle and accidentally hit the window switch. It lowered a few inches. His trembling hands found the switch and lowered the window. His lungs burning, he swam from the car and rose to the surface.

He burst forth from the waters and sucked in a gasp. Explosions and fire erupted all around him. Bricks hit the water like rain. Juliana, Brian, and Reggie thrashed about in the water. They swam to shore and shielded their heads. "Where's Charlie?" The girl burst up from the water and wet coughs escaped her mouth.

"Over here!" Jake shouted. When she saw them, she too swam to the riverbank. They clung to the shore for dear life, terrified the earth would give way.

The river flowed the wrong way, piling up in heaps. Jake grabbed a scrub tree along the riverbank and climbed up to the road. He grabbed Charlie's hand and helped her climb. The earth shifted and again tried to throw them off it. When a tidal wave of water roared toward them, Jake's eyes went wide. He planted his right hand in Charlie's crotch, bunching up her denim miniskirt.

"Hands," she said, swatting at her bottom.

He planted his feet, grimaced, and heaved. The girl yelped as she hurtled up the embankment and landed on the street with a wet splat. A minute later, Juliana hurtled up and landed on the street beside her. Jake, Brian, and Reggie scrambled up through the weed-covered embankment, barely escaping the drowning wave.

Jake lay on his back, savoring the feel of solid pavement. However, the burning wreckage drove him to his feet. He staggered away from the wreck and tried to shield himself from the heat. The front end of the car that rear-ended his SUV lay before him. The windshield had a hole large enough for a cannon ball. Then he saw the mangled corpse of the driver. His body lay in an unnatural ball next to the guardrail.

"What should we do?" asked Charlie.

"We need to find the fallout shelter in the center of town." Jake staggered as the earth shifted underneath them and threw them to the ground with great violence. Charlie tripped onto the sidewalk. A moment later, a chunk of masonry plummeted and slammed to the ground next to her.

All of the five-story, red brick buildings staggered like drunks. Men and women released their death cry as debris collapsed upon them. Jake reeled like a drunk and fought his way to Charlie. He grabbed the girl and pulled her away from the building. They ran and then leaped into the river, plunging once again into the frigid water. The others copied them and leaped back into the river. The building next to them toppled: tons of brick, concrete, and steel plummeted. The debris hit the water and sank into the murky depths.

In the midst of this chaos, the heavens opened, and white tendrils reached out for them with a mother's love. These silvery fingers caressed, engulfed, and then transformed them. In a moment, "in the twinkling of an eye," they became beings of light, shining like the sun, creatures of lore.

Chapter 7

Jake rose into the sky, surrounded by translucent beings. They rose up from the deep water, but they were not alone: the dead rose up from their graves. They sparkled like glass and shimmered like sunshine upon the water. Some of the dead, however, became whiffs of black vapor – entities of darkness and malevolence – they also rose toward an ethereal path.

Jake soared, free as a bird, without the cares of life. He saw the land convulse, buildings toppled, and people die. Victims fell beneath the ruins, and entities of light and darkness rose up from the graves. The town grew small, and he rose ever higher, seeing all directions at the same time until the world's curve lay beneath his feet. The most wonderful peace, the greatest joy, filled and surrounded him – the kind a child experiences in a mother's arms – and it spoke to his soul, assuring him, comforting him.

He rocketed away from the Earth, joining the other entities, and rushed toward the stars. The universe wheeled around him: galaxies stretched around in a wondrous display, and then he saw a point of light. It called to him, wooing him into the light, but beyond the light, the darkness raged with murderous threats and hatred. Voices, beyond number, wailed and cursed. The dark vapors split from the light and fell into the void; and as they merged with the emptiness, new voices joined the chorus of the damned.

The light grew ever larger until it was the size of the sun. He raced toward it, but the temporal world beckoned him to return. Love and peace filled him with overwhelming joy, and a star like a beamed in the darkest night. He rushed toward the light and plunged into it, a drop of water into the ocean. All of his fears ebbed away, an eternal dance with entities of the light.

A powerful force ripped him from the light. He cried out, begging to return, but he plummeted to the Earth. Green forests and blue waters spun in a wild vortex. He rushed at the ground, a drop of rain falling from the sky. The world spun in wild, chaotic turns. His body floated face up in the river, and he rocketed toward it.

After he had entered his body, he drew in a sharp gasp, and for a few seconds, he hoped to return to the light; but like a newborn, his limbs thrashed and hands clawed at the water, seeking solid ground. When his right hand found green weeds, he clung to the riverbank, and wet coughs followed desperate gasps. He wiped the water from his face and rested. His strength returned, he climbed up the embankment again and collapsed onto the pavement.

He lay upon road, glad for the pavement's heat. He closed his eyes to dream, to sleep, but sleep fled as night from the day. Like the first humans who raised their eyes toward the heavens, Jake beheld a pillar of smoke rising into a vivid blue sky. Every type of bird imaginable circled in the sky above him.

He thought *I hope they don't crap on me,* and then passed out.

"Are you okay?" asked Charlie.

"No, clearly I'm dead," he said and tried to rest, but life demanded action; and he opened his eyes, squinted at the world and sighed. The worried girl brushed a wet red lock behind her right ear and gazed down at him. Using a bit of cloth, she wiped a trickle of blood from a cut on his forehead. When he arose, she held his arm to steady him. He said, "I'm fine. I got hit in the head when I was underwater. I have the worst headache."

He drew in a cleansing breath, and as the blessing of heaven receded, the pain of life began. His arm extended, he marveled at the new sensation that filled his body. Strength and vitality inspired him to leap for joy and shout. However, his voice was peculiar – the same but other. "Hello," he said, testing it. "Testing, testing, testing," he chanted. He was male; that much was certain, yet something was amiss. What, he could not quite say.

Someone burst forth from the water. Reggie splashed and screamed, "HELP!" Jake dove into the water and swam to her. He grabbed her as she went down for the second time. His arm wrapped around her, he swam to the shore and Charlie helped her onto the road. Raspy coughs spewed water from her mouth, and she sucked in wheezing gasps.

"Are you okay?" He cocked his head and touched her cheek. Reggie recoiled and brushed away his hand. She struggled to her feet and water pooled on the pavement. Although hints of his friend's face remained, a different woman stood before him, one with a timeless quality.

Jake looked past Reggie and saw his reflection in the water. A familiar face, strange nonetheless, gazed back at him from the rippling waters. Eyes, blue as sapphire, pointed ears, flaxen hair, and ethereal features caused him to have an Elven appearance. When he touched them, his ears sensed it. "What the —" his words faded into silence.

Charlie asked, "What's going on? What happened to us?"

"Why do you two have pointed ears?" asked Jake.

"Why do you have pointed ears?" echoed Charlie.

"What happened to the two of you?" asked Reggie. "You turned into elves."

"So did you," Jake said.

"No, I didn't. Only pasty, white people are elves." Then she felt her ears and studied her face in a fragment of broken glass. She whispered, "Madre de Dios."

A pile of bricks and debris toppled as Brian sat upright as if throwing off the covers from a winter's nap. He yawned. "Could you keep it down? I'm trying to sleep." With a twitch of his broad nose, he said, "I had the strangest dream. I could hear the heartbeat of the planet, and I could taste the goodness of the soil." He stood upright, letting the concrete and bricks fall off him. Thick as a tree stump, rippling with muscles, the broad-faced young man brushed off the dust. When he saw his friends, he grumbled, "That figures. All of you turn into Elves, and I turn into a dwarf, a really short dwarf." He scratched his new beard and frowned. "This thing is itchy," he said.

"The last thing I remembered is the earthquake," Jake said and searched his memories. "We almost died when that building fell. Maybe we did die. Is this heaven?"

"No," Charlie said and pointed at the piles rubble and the burnt out cars. "Heaven would look nicer than this."

"HELLO," a man shouted. "Is somebody there?"

Charlie cringed and grabbed a splintered board. She brandished the branch like a sword, ready to strike. Hiding behind Jake, she peered around his side. "Who is it?"

"There you are," said a stranger. "I thought I heard voices." A lanky man, a touch of gray on his temples, walked toward them. He wore blue overalls, and it had an Auxiliary Sherriff Volunteer patch on the front of the garment. "I'm Gary. Our club volunteers assist the sheriff with crowd control and rescue operations. I was just looking for survivors." He cocked his head and scratched his head. "Haven't I see you before?"

"I attend the University, and I'm always around town," Jake replied.

"That must be it," Gary said. "Were you up near the medical tents on campus earlier?"

"We were on campus earlier." Jake rubbed an ache from his left thigh and then the small of his back. "We were downtown when all hell broke loose."

Gary asked, "Are any of you injured?"

"No. We appear to be fine," Jake said, "just a bit sore."

Gary furrowed and narrowed his eyes as he studied; he mumbled, "That's a matter of opinion. Your ears look strange."

Jake rubbed his temples and winced. "I don't know what happened to them. Maybe they're swollen or something."

"I suppose. It's a day full of wonderment and mystery. What with those mountains suddenly appearing," Gary said.

"What mountains?"

"Look yonder," he said with a nod. "Damn things just appeared. I just can't stop staring at them." They turned, and for the first time, they saw a mountain range where there should be none. Black mountains capped with white snow rose into the sky and loomed over the town. They were enormous, taller than Mount Everest. "Those mountains just appeared out of thin air. How does that happen?" He shook his head and pinched the bridge of his nose. "I still can't believe what I'm seeing. I've been sober 31 years, but it's enough to make a man take a drink. Well, if any of you is injured, go up to the tent. There's a town meeting scheduled for tonight, but in the meantime, I need all of you to go home. We're keeping the streets clear for official use."

"Are there any transport trucks?" asked Jake, still staring in wonder.

"Not a one." Gary wiped the perspiration from his face with a handkerchief and took a swig of water. "All vehicles are broke down or burning. We got a pickup truck moving for about ten minutes, and then the damn thing caught fire. That reminds me: all of the gas mains and electricity are down. There's no telling when they will work again. Just go home and wait for further instructions. It's easy to get injured if you go traipsing around in this rubble."

Jake rubbed the back of his neck and twisted his head. "Most of us are here, but I haven't found my girlfriend, Juliana. Have you seen her? She's about so tall, blonde, and beautiful."

"Sorry, I haven't. You should look for her at her house. Most folks went home after the quake. If she's not there, if she's here under this debris ... well ... I'm afraid she's gone," Gary said. "I need to get going. You folks take care."

"Sure thing," Jake said with a wave.

He scanned the piles of rubble, the broken lumber, the twisted metal, and the many fires, a perfect visage of hell. He climbed on a pile of debris and moved several boards that had insulation attached. Then he began tossing red bricks from a pile. "Juliana," he called. "If you can hear me, make a sound. Tap on something." There were many sounds but none from her.

When a hand touched his shoulder, he turned and saw Charlie. "Let's look for her back at her house. I'm sure she's there."

"But why would she just take off and leave us?" He rubbed his face and surveyed the destruction once again. His gut twisted into a knot and panic welled up his throat. For the first time in a decade, he prayed, but the prayer seemed powerless, as though the heavens were made of brass as if God already decided the matter. The wall where he last saw her still stood and was clear of debris.

Splintered wood and bricks piled high upon crushed cars, and tattered insulation flapped in the breeze. Masonry building lay in heaps, and steel structures bent toward the ground. The products of a modern civilization became detritus, scattered about the chaos, and everywhere he looked, fires burned, thick columns of chemical-filled smoke formed pillars. Although far away, his eyes focused in like binoculars. A man's arm reached out from the debris, fingers twisted into a claw. There could be no doubt: he was dead.

Charlie caressed his arm and whispered, "It's time to go."

Hands on his hips and a sigh on his lips, he shook his head. "I hope that she's far from here and safe. If she is here, she's gone." A lump formed in his throat and agony tainted his soul. Juliana had to be home; she just had to be. "We need to go. I need to find her."

Chapter 8

No one thinks about a twelve-mile journey by car. The winding country roads make it a joy to travel, but by foot, it is a slow dirge. A red sun hung low on the horizon and cast crimson beams upon the new "Black Mountains"; a short time later, the sun vanished behind the Rocky Mountains to the west. They made it home as the last light failed. Brian collapsed onto the sofa; Charlie fell onto her bed, and Reggie lay on the floor; they ignored the hunger that clawed at their insides. However Jake had one objective: to find Juliana.

The power failed, so the refrigerator contents were warm. Yet a bottle of warm water never tasted so good. He chugged it, rivulets flowed down his neck and soaked into his shirt. After devouring two chicken legs and some cheese, he charged out of the house.

His neighbors wandered the streets as if in a daze. They hungered for any scrap of information. Drew Young hurried over to Jake with Herb and Henry Osgood close behind him. "Have you heard anything? Will they get the power back on soon?"

The question rung in Jake's ears, and he struggled to find the right words. "We were downtown when it hit. It's in ruins. The power is not coming back anytime soon. It will take months just to clear the debris."

"They have to get the power back," Drew said. "All of my food is thawed. We need to cook it, and the grill is out of propane."

Jake placed his hand on Drew's shoulder and said, "I'm sorry."

"What does that mean?" asked Herb. "We need power, lights, electricity."

"It's gone," Jake said. "Nothing is coming back." He turned and walked backward saying, "Go southwest toward Denver or northwest toward Fort Collins, but get the hell out of here – on foot if you have to."

"I have a bad hip," Henry said. "I can't walk that far."

Jake jogged past other congregated groups. Their eyes searched for his urgency. He charged up the lawn of a tiny, weathered house. The crabgrass, the ugly eggplant paint, the crumbling driveway, the sagging front porch, and the cupped shingles, Juliana's repairs vanished. Even her wind chime and wicker furniture were gone. He charged up the wooden steps and pounded on the front door. He was about to open the door when he heard heavy steps. The door whipped open and a black man growled, "Yeah, what do you want?"

"Where's Juliana?" He pushed past the man and entered the house. "Juliana, are you here?"

"Hey, get the hell out of my house." The man grabbed Jake's shoulder and spun him around. "What do you think you're doing?" Two children, one of them a boy and the other a girl, hurried from the kitchen. They held uncooked Pop-Tarts and gazed up at him with inquisitive brown eyes.

"Marvin, who is it? Oh Jake, how are you doing?" A woman exited the kitchen, drying her hands with a dishtowel. She cocked her head and asked, "You seem upset. Are you okay?"

"My girlfriend Juliana Moore lives here." He rubbed his face, his eyes glassy. "We were downtown when the earthquake hit. She disappeared." He sat down on the sofa and held his head in his hands. "This doesn't make any sense."

"Um ... Jake, we've known you for three years, since we bought the house from Ken Anderson. He moved back east to be near his sister. Where was that, Dan?" she asked.

"Pittsburg," Marvin said. "When his momma died in the nursing home, he had no reason to stay. At least, that's what he told me."

"What about Juliana? She lived here."

"We never met her," she said and examined him. "Are you feeling okay?"

"Yes — no, I don't understand any of this. It's like she never existed. Where is she?" He stood to his feet and dried his eyes. "I don't get it," he mumbled and shook his head. He took a deep breath and moved to leave. "I'm sorry to bother you."

Marvin took a step toward him and held out his hand; "We haven't heard the news. What's happening downtown?"

"The northern area and downtown are in shambles; the power lines are down; the transformers are destroyed, and the water mains are broken. It could be months or years before it is all fixed. If you have somewhere else to live, it would be best to leave." He exited the home and strolled toward his home, ignoring those around him.

"TOMMY," a woman called. She leaned over the porch railing, dread in her eyes. "Tommy, come home right now." Her husband tried to pull her back into the house, but she pulled away from him. "NO! I want my baby. He can't just disappear."

It was then that he noticed the Miller's home. The bright yellow home was white, and a stranger looked out the bay window. In fact, many of his neighbors were strangers. Then he saw someone dismount a horse on his front lawn. Towering above most men, rippling with muscles, flaxen hair tied into a ponytail, and a granite jaw, there was no mistaking the massive, Nordic man: it was Charlie's father, Uncle Thor — but he was dead.

"Uncle Thor," Jake shouted. "Is that you?"

Thor paused and looked about. His face brightened, and he walked toward Jake, his massive right hand extended. "It's good to see you, boy. When did you get into town?"

Jake shook his hand and said, "I live here. Charlie, Brian, Reggie, and I go to Fort Defiant University. We share a house."

Thor put his hands on his hips and narrowed his eyes. "Since when? Charlie lives here with a bunch of girls." The front door flew open, and Charlie burst from her home. She leaped off the porch and sprinted to her father, leaping into his arms. She clung to him and sobbed. "What's the matter, baby girl?"

She wiped away the tears and said, "A drunk driver T-boned your truck and you … you died. We buried you twelve years ago."

"What in the hell are you talking about? I'm not dead. Who could forget an accident like that? He sheared off the front end of my truck, but I lived." He stroked the girl's head and said, "Sweetheart, it's okay. I'm here." But Charlie clung to him and refused to let him go. After a while, he became self-conscious, and he scooped up the girl. She wrapped her legs around him and clung to him.

He carried her into the house and into the living room. She held him tight and pressed her face against his neck. Not knowing what else to do, he sat on the sofa, and she sat on his lap. She sniffled and said, "I missed you so much."

"I can tell, but I only live twenty-three miles from here on my horse ranch," Thor said.

She laughed and said, "I'm glad to hear that. You have horses?"

"Well … yes. Your horse, Cocoa, is waiting for you. We need to get you packed. I want to head out at first light. You're coming back to the ranch with me," Thor said.

The front door slammed and Jake entered. "I put your horse in the backyard; it's fenced in. I gave him water, but we don't have any feed. I guess he can eat the grass."

Brian yawned and stretched. "I needed that. What are we going to have for supper?" He squinted and scratched his head. "Mr. Dahl ... it can't be. You're dead."

"Why does everyone keep saying that? I would know if I was dead," Thor grumbled.

"Hmm, you're an elve, and a damn big elve. I can't believe this. Everyone got to be an elve but me. This sucks." Brian scooted onto a recliner, his legs too short to reach the floor. "Why did we change? I don't understand it."

"Because this is what we were always meant to be," Jake said. "My life never felt right. I tried to be like everyone else. You know, fit into the group. But I just knew I was meant to be something else, to do something else. I don't know how else to explain it. My life was wrong, and now it's right."

"Yeah, me too," Thor said. "When I was out on deployment with my unit, we saw lots of death and destruction. Everything was so temporary, like sandcastles on the beach, time and tide erased all, but I felt different. I sensed a call in my heart to rejoin my people as if I was a foreigner and not quite human. Now I understand it. I'm an elve, not a man."

"Me too, I mean, I was always meant to be a dwarf." Brian said and scratched his beard. "Whenever I used to discuss earth strata and how the continents formed in school, everyone would get so bored. I thought it was great. I've become what I was always meant to be."

"Juliana is gone; she just disappeared." Reggie wandered into the room with her arms crossed, in desperate need of a nap. "Why is Charlie sitting on that man's lap?" She rubbed her eyes and asked, "Don't I know you?"

"It's my daddy," Charlie said.

"You're daddy? What are you, 10?" She twitched her nose and looked up at the ceiling. "Wait. Your father is dead. Some drunk driver killed him." Thor growled and grew red-faced. Reggie sniffed and stretched, "Your father is back from the dead, and we are all elves. This has been one loco day."

Chapter 9

Knees bent, feet exposed, a spring poking his back, Thor lay upon the sofa and struggled to sleep. He beat the pillow, trying to fluff it, and settled upon it. He lay still for a minute, but then he growled and opened his eyes. He saw a figure silhouetted against the moonlight, and for a moment, his heart sang – he swore that he caught a glimpse of Mary.

"Daddy," said Charlie, breaking the trance, "can I sleep with you."

"Sure baby girl," Thor said. She scrambled over and snuggled up to him underneath the blanket. He held her and whispered, "I'm sorry you had to go through that," but she was fast asleep. He closed his eyes and drifted back in time to a warm summer day. In the middle of a field, under the shade of an elm tree, near a shimmering lake, He and Mary lay upon a blanket – the contents of the picnic basket reduced to crumbs – and as they watched clouds pass overhead, they imagined their future lives together. They watched clouds float across a vivid blue sky. His mind relaxed, and he drifted off to sleep.

A sharp knock jerked Thor from his sleep, and he sat up on the sofa. When several more followed, he rubbed his face and called out, "Hold on, I'm coming." When he opened the door, a young man pushed past him.

"Close the door. Hurry!" When Thor hesitated, he jerked the door from Thor's hand and slammed it shut. He locked it and set the dead bolt. "Do you have any weapons?"

"Who are you?" asked Thor. The young man turned and rushed for the kitchen. "Hey, hold on." He charged after this stranger, but he was fast and made it into the kitchen. When he threw open the door, he saw the crazed young man brandishing a steak knife. His eyes narrowed and assuming a fighting position, he said, "You definitely don't want to do that."

"You don't understand. They're coming. We have to get ready."

Light outlined the seam off another doorway into the kitchen. Charlie entered holding a candle. "What's going on?" She sucked in a gasp and jumped. Blood soaked into curly black hair covered his face and ran down his chest, soaking into his boxer shorts.

Jake entered after Charlie, and made a pair of fists, ready to fight. Then he studied the stranger. "Lane, is that you?" He took a step toward Lane, but Thor held out his hand.

"Put down the knife, man. You're freaking everyone out. This isn't funny."

"You don't understand. They're dead. They killed them, and they are coming this way." Lane turned around, leaned over the countertop, and looked out the window. He saw the horse, the fence, and the back yard. "We need to board up the windows."

"You're not making any sense." Jake held out his hands and moved toward Lane. "Take it easy. You're scaring everyone."

"YOU'RE NOT LISTENING!" Lane began to pace, waving the knife about in the air. "I—I didn't have a choice. I had to leave them." He covered his ears with his fists. "They kept screaming and screaming. All I did was run." Urine soaked into his underwear and trickled down his legs.

"What the hell is with all this noise?" Brian barged past Charlie. "I'm trying to sleep."

"Drop the knife," Thor said. "I don't want to hurt you."

Lane threw the knife on the countertop and sank to his knees. "I can't believe I left them. Someone make them stop screaming."

Jake picked up the knife and handed it back to Brian. "There's some whiskey under that cabinet. Charlie, pour him a drink." She nodded. After she had filled a glass, she held it out to him.

Lane reached out with trembling hands and took the drink. The fluid running down his neck and chest, he gulped it and then coughed. "More." When she refilled his glass, he curled up into the fetal position in the corner and slurped the whiskey. Jake eased over and sat down next to him. "I wanted to help, but they were all over us."

"Who was all over you?"

"Things … monsters," Lane replied. "When they crashed through the windows, the girls screamed. A bunch of people from the campus slept at our house. The campus is filled with people that fought back."

"Who attacked you? Were they looters?"

"What? No – not looters," he said and struggled to find the right words. "They were hideous. Their face sagged as if they were peeling off. Some had spider eyes, others had two, large black eyes. One that came at me with an ax had the face of an insect. I grabbed the ax before it split my head open, but I tripped and tumbled backward. When Bruce opened his bedroom door, the monster chopped Bruce right in the neck. His blood sprayed all over us. I ran – damn it – I just ran. How could I do that?" He beat his forehead with his fists.

"Alright," Jake said. "Take it easy." When he rose to his feet, Charlie sat down beside Lane on the floor. Jake, Thor, and Brian exited the kitchen. "It must have been looters in Halloween masks."

"Axe-wielding thieves in Halloween masks are raiding houses. That's all we need," Brian said.

"Do you have any lumber?" asked Thor.

"Yeah, we bought some plywood and two by fours to build a dog house, but then the dog ran off. What a disaster. We spent over two hundred dollars on that mutt, and he just ran off," Jake said.

"Get the wood, a hand saw, and some nails. We're going to board up the first-floor windows," Thor said.

"Now?" asked Brian.

"Are you getting back to sleep after that?"

"No," Brian said, shaking his head.

"We will wake up the neighbors," Jake said.

"I'll apologize in the morning."

"The batteries for the drill might still work. We could screw them up," Brian said.

"Yeah, we can screw up anything," Jake said. Brian grinned. "Let's get to work."

Chapter 10

The whine of the drill and hammer thumps jerked Reggie from a sound sleep. She pulled the pillow over her ears and tried to ignore it. However, such attempts are seldom effective. The day's events raced through her brain and denied her sleep. She shot up in bed, the covers piled on her lap. She yelled in Spanish and then said, "Cut it out. I need my rest."

She rubbed her eyes and searched the room. A flashlight beam penetrated her white curtains and illumined the room. She lit a candle and tried to make sense of her surroundings. Posters of handsome young men with six-pack abs adorned a fuchsia wall; panties and bras spilled out of an overfilled hamper; nursing books covered the top of a white desk, and athletic trophies filled white bookshelves.

She slid out of bed, and her feet touched satin. A satin crop top, black leather jacket, matching tights, bra, and panties lay in a pile on the floor. She hurried into the bathroom. There was no running water, so she used bottled water to take a sponge bath. After she had put on a blue terry cloth robe, yesterday's events barged into her thoughts. It all seemed like a dream, but it was too real.

Reggie picked up her dead phone from the countertop and cursed. Her family went to Houston for her cousin's Quinceañera. Just one phone call from them would relieve her, but all modern telecommunication was broken and not likely to return. She threw the phone into the trash, cursed under her breath, and shook head.

When she descended the stairs, she saw Thor. He wore a tool belt and puffed on a pipe. The pleasing aroma of cherry tobacco filled the room. "I'm sorry we woke you, but we had to prepare."

She brushed her long black locks behind her head and studied the windows. A crude covering of boards covered them. "What happened?"

"You missed the fun." Jake carried a bowl of cereal and sat on the recliner. "Lane broke in like a madman. Looters raided his home, so we boarded up the windows."

"They weren't looters," Lane said. "They were monsters. Why doesn't anyone believe me?"

"Relax," Brian said, "we're going to investigate."

"Do you have a gun?" asked Thor.

"I wish." He went to his bedroom and returned carrying a longbow. He slung the quiver over his shoulder and strapped a knife to his hip. Brian strapped on a long war-hammer, an expensive purchase at a "Comic Con". "Here," he handed Thor a machete. "This is the best I can do."

When they started to leave, Reggie and Charlie followed them. Thor stopped in the doorway. "Sweetie, it's the middle of the night. I need for you to stay here and lock the door after we leave." Charlie tightened her lips and crossed her arms. He said, "I'm serious."

"I just got you back. If you're going, so am I." When he gave her an angry glare, she responded, "I am coming. You can't stop me."

"Fine, but I want the two of you to remain in the street when we get to his house," he said.

When they exited the house, they saw chaos. Garbage and debris formed piles at the curb. Hood up, toolboxes open, bent over the fender, several men labored into the night and tried to repair their cars by flashlight. Any success was short-lived: either the fuel caught on fire or the electrical system shorted. The men threw down their baseball caps and cursed.

Lane's house was three and a half miles, which doesn't sound like much when driving, but it is very long when walking. The cool caress of the night was a welcome change from the heat of the day. It had been an unusually warm October. They turned left and then right onto a different street. The sounds of life faded behind them. After walking another mile, they studied their surroundings with apprehension. No bird sang; no insects buzzed, and no dogs barked. Front doors left ajar, cars abandoned in the street, clothes left drying with no one to collect them, the emptiness caused a dreadful silence.

Thor stopped walking when his flashlight fell upon an abandoned police car. He held up his fist for them to stop. Acrid smoke hung low upon the ground and the police car lay in the middle of the street, the driver's side door open, the dome light illumined the interior and a warning bell that signaled that the key was still in the ignition.

"Stay here," Thor said.

The absent police officer parked his car at an angle in the middle of the street. It sat behind a barricade, blocking the open door from Gunner's view. He placed his hands on the hood and rounded the bumper. The engine was still warm. Then he saw the bodies. Two officers lay dead in the street. Something blew their arms apart, chunks of flesh splattered about, and shrapnel shredded their faces into hamburger. His lip curled into a snarl, he drew his knife and examined the corpses. The twisted metal of a handgun frame jutted from one of the bodies, and an exploded revolver lay next to the other.

"What do you see?" yelled Charlie.

"Stay there." He stood upright and shone his light upon nearby homes. The front door of one home was open wide, and another home had its door ripped off the hinges. When he swept his light, he saw something lying on the foyer floor. When he focused the beam on it, a bloody mangled body filled him with dread. Someone hacked it into a blood pulp, taking the limbs and ripping open its belly.

He snapped his light to the other side of the street. Blood spray covered the bay window of one home, and the fresh corpse of a woman lay in the backyard of the house next to it. A hatchet wound severed her spine and stained her white dress with blood.

With a calm pace, he sat down in the police car and turned the key. The engine roared. He backed up the car and then cruised up to the others. "Get in the car. Now. Don't ask questions." When Charlie saw the officer's body, she scrambled into the car. Thor saw movement out of the corner of his eye. More movement came from the backyard. The woman's body was missing, only a bloody smear and pressed grass indicating the direction that someone dragged her. When the doors slammed shut, he fought the urge to stomp on the gas and pushed away the terror.

"What happened?" asked Charlie.

"Everyone is dead." When he glanced in the rearview mirror, he saw a monster moving about in a house. It raised a blood ax and roared. The word "Daemia" popped into his mind. A hundred others emerged from their hiding places. The nightmarish visage of the daemia were more gruesome with each one. He stomped on the gas and sped away from the carnage.

After too short a drive, they returned to the neighborhood. As he sped toward their house, the engine began to knock and smoke poured out from under the hood. He jumped from the car said, "Get to the house and block the second-floor windows." He cursed not having boarded them.

"Where'd you get the cop car?" asked Drew, pausing from his repair work.

"Everyone, come here," Thor shouted. Those who were awake at the early hour in the morning, which was most of the neighborhood, milled toward him. "It's an emergency." Curious men and women formed a semicircle around him. "Just one mile away, everyone is dead." While the truth was that the daemia killed them, they would never believe it; a believable lie would have to suffice. "Looters in Halloween masks killed everyone, including the cops."

"They killed the police?" asked Henry. "Are they maniacs or something?"

"Listen, we have to get ready. They are coming. Grab whatever weapon you can and come to our house. There is safety in numbers. Come on. Get moving. We haven't got much time. Hurry," he shouted. "If you stand around talking, you will die. Now move."

Henry and Herb broke from the group. At first, they walked, and then they ran. The others then ran back to the homes. Parents woke their children; men charged into their homes and sought out weapons. They emerged bearing baseball bats, golf clubs, axes, and machetes. When old man Simpson emerged bearing a shotgun, it exploded in his hands and ripped him apart. Women screamed and children hid behind their parents.

"NO GUNS. The ammunition explodes," he shouted. When Drew tossed away his revolver, it exploded. "Get a handheld weapon and come to my house. We need to fight together. Don't stay in your home alone." Some of the terrified people hurried from their homes, but others rushed toward his house. Thor scrambled into his backyard and grabbed his horse's rope. He led the horse to the front yard and then into the house.

"You're bringing the horse inside too?" asked Drew.

"He's more valuable than a car right about now," Thor replied. Hammering came from the second floor. He charged up the stairs and into Reggie's bedroom. Jake nailed boards over the window. "Remove the doors. Nail them over the windows; but lower the window first, so you have good firing position."

By the light of a full moon, he saw a mother, holding her 4-year-old boy, running toward the house. Three daemia sped between backyards. Thor sprinted from the room and scrambled down the stairs. "HURRY," he shouted. A daemia Archer stepped out from the corner of a home and slotted an arrow. When he drew back, a different arrow sailed over Thor's head and hit the daemia in the right shoulder. A shrill squeal came from its mouth, and it stole back to the shadows. The mother charged up the stairs and into the home. Thor jogged backward and then ran into the house. The moment the door slammed shut, three arrows hit it with a thump.

"They're here," he shouted. "Grab a weapon." Those still unarmed rushed into the kitchen and raided the cutlery. Something pounded the wall, a mother screamed and clutched her baby, and pictures crashed to the floor. Claws scratched at the door and roars made their skin crawl.

"They're climbing up the walls," Jake shouted. Thor sprinted up the stairs and rushed into the room. Savage hands ripped away the boards. Thor chopped with his machete and cut off an arm. Black blood sprayed out from the severed limb, and the creature roared in agony.

"They're coming in this way," Reggie shouted. Thor charged down the hallway as one of daemia broke through the window. It came at Reggie with an ax, but Thor blocked the blow. The two wrestled, their bodies straining. An arrow flew past Thor and hit the daemia in the neck. The stricken creature continued fighting even as its life's blood sprayed onto the wall. Another daemia pushed through the window, and Jake struck it with an arrow.

"HELP ME," Charlie screamed. Brian sprinted into her room and swung his war hammers. The daemia blocked it, and then he swung at him with a baseball bat. The blow knocked Brian into the wall. The daemia screeched and arched its body; Charlie stabbed it in the back.

Men and woman rushed into the rooms. Bats, knives, and axes rained down up the invading hordes. Blow after blow pushed them backward, but more daemia broke through the windows. Herb wrestled with one in the hallway, the pair broke through the railing and plummeted to the floor. Henry stabbed a daemia as it stabbed him, the pair falling together in death. Brian hit a daemia in the neck, shattering its spine.

His eyes wide, his heart pounding, Drew swung wildly at three daemia in an animal frenzy. He battled for his life as they pressed toward him. "HELP," he shouted. Three men pressed into the room. Thomas slammed into one and knocked it into a wall, knocking over a dresser, sending mementos crashing to the floor. The daemia slashed at his throat, severing an artery, and he clutched his neck, red blood flowing through his fingers; a moment later, Drew stabbed the daemia in the belly and kept stabbing.

The mothers hid their children behind them and fought a desperate battle. Thor jumped from the second floor and rushed at the daemia. He chopped off an arm and cleaved a neck. When the remaining daemia turned to attack him, the women stabbed it in the back. It screamed in agony and tried to run, but Thor hacked its leg and then took off its head.

Two daemia wrestled Charlie onto the bed. The girl kicked and screamed as they tore at her clothes. Brian bounded into the room. He hit one in the kneecap and hit the other in the side. He swung back and hit the first one in the face, his spiked hammer sinking deep into its head. Charlie scrambled off the bed and grabbed her knife. Clad only in tattered rags, she lunged at the daemia and stabbed it in the side. The pair fought in a wild frenzy: stabbing, crushing, swinging and slashing. When the daemia sunk down in the corner, she stabbed it repeatedly in the neck and covered herself in black blood.

Thor rushed to the den window where two daemia ripped away the boards. He hacked and chopped at them. When the horse screamed, it made his blood run cold. The animal kicked its back hoofs at Daemia coming through the bay window in the living room. "JAKE, I need help."

Jake stood upon the stairs and released an arrow. It sank deep into a daemia's chest, and the other turned to run. He loosed another arrow and it hit the daemia in the spine. He leaped through the broken window and sprinted to the daemia. As it tried to crawl away, he grabbed a fistful of its greasy hair and cut its neck.

Thor piled up furniture in front of the window. Through the last gap in the window, he said, "Get back in here." Jake returned to the house and grabbed the dining room table. Two of the women helped him drag it into the living room, and they tilted it on end, blocking off the window. The horse skittered about, looking for a daemia to kick.

His chest heaving, Thor inhaled gulps of air. Everything became silent. He hurried from the room, and he joined Jake as he scrambled up the stairs. When Thor looked into Charlie's bedroom, he saw the girl in tatted clothes and covered in black blood. She kept stabbing the daemia corpse. He leaped over the top of her bed and stood before the window. Fires burned in several of the homes, and its occupants lay upon the ground: dead and dismembered. The daemia carried away the severed limbs and other prized objects. They weaved between houses and scrambled over fences. Then he saw the fire climb up the side of the house.

"We need to put out those fires." He dragged his daughter from the corpse. She kicked and wrestled as he dragged her from the room. "Baby, calm down. It's okay," he said and held her tight. She dropped the knife, buried her face in his chest, and sobbed. "We don't have time. We have to get out of the house. Grab some clothes and get out."

"Okay." She wiped away her tears and thought for a moment. Flames, the dead, and ruins about them, she asked, "What outfit do you think I should wear?" Thor threw back his head and roared with laughter.

Chapter 11

The gray zone melted, like snow in the spring, and time started. The yellow bus hurtled through a dense forest. It bounced, tossed Gunner about, and made the screaming youth group. They crashed through vines over roots that broke the pavement into rubble. Gunner steered around a massive root, a wall of wood. The tires screamed and so did the people. When they swept around the root, the bus bounced over debris and fishtailed. Gunner stomped the brakes and the bus twirled to a stop.

"Damn." Gunner pushed so hard on the steering wheel that he bent it. He forced himself to remove his hands. A scream ripped from Julie. The girl scrambled backward down the aisle and fell onto the floor. Gunner leaped to his feet, turned, and drew in a sharp gasp.

Seated in the back of the bus, Megan and Tiffany withered into old women: ancient, balding heads, skin sagging on their frail bones. Tiffany tried to rise up from the seat, but she collapsed onto the aisle. Gunner took two steps toward them but stopped. The bodies desiccated and turned to dust. Rotted clothes filled with dry bones collapsed to the floor. Rust tendrils spread forward from the back of the bus and ate through the ceiling, exposing dense foliage and sparse skies. The vinyl seats cracked; rips exposed stuffing; brown leaves and rusty pine needles accumulated; the thick mat rotted; the tires exploded; the bus sank, and settled on the ground; grime covered the window, and a few shattered.

Logan and Kevin scrambled over seats, but the decay — spreading from back to front — caught Kevin. His skin turned mottled black and gray as if covered by mold and slime; his eyes shriveled and then eight black, marble-like eyes, replaced them. He gurgled and arched his back, releasing a bloodcurdling moan. Claws grew from each fingertip, engorging muscles ripped his clothes, and jagged, dagger-like teeth sliced out from his gums. Part roar, part scream ripped from his tormented mouth. He crashed through a window, rolled, and then sprinted into the forest.

"Get out. NOW!" Gunner snarled and moved away from the corpses. Stale air, rotting flesh, dead leaves, damp earth, animal dander, and vegetation stunk; and he became nauseous. He covered his mouth with his handkerchief and fought to breathe.

"Everything is getting old, including the trees," Linda said. They looked out the windows and saw a primordial forest.

"This isn't possible. People do not grow old like that. What's happening?"

Tom, the youth group president, stared at the bodies in numb disbelief; Gunner scrambled around him. He grabbed the door release mechanism, but rust fused the hinge. His powerful muscles strained, and he leaned into it. The hinge groaned and released. The ancient door opened a bit. It was all Gunner needed. He pushed open the accordion doors and jumped out.

Bain, Logan, and the other teens scrambled, shoved, and fought their way out of the bus. Tom was the last to exit. He leaped from the bus, but the decay raced toward them. It overtook Tom, and he exploded into dust. The yellow paint faded; grimace covered the exterior, leaves piled atop the roof, and roots grew into the engine compartment like tendrils.

"Look!" Julie shouted and pointed.

Through a gray haze, they saw Toni's pickup truck. In the air, tires off the pavement, tilted to one side, the trailer askew, Toni gripped the steering wheel and grimaced, as if an action movie stuck on pause. When Gunner stepped toward the gray mist, Linda grabbed his shoulder. "Stay away from it."

"Mountains," Julie said and pointed at an opening in the forest canopy. White capped mountain peaks loomed over the land. They sliced through clouds, rending them asunder, and stabbed at the sky. They were monolithic, titans of old, taller than Mount Everest.

Gunner picked up a rock and threw it at the mist. As soon as it entered the gray mist, the rock froze in mid-flight, like a fly stuck in amber. He threw another, and it had the same effect. Gunner picked up a long branch, broken from a recent storm, and stabbed the mist. It became stuck, and when he tried to pull it away, the embedded tip snapped off – the wood fragments hovering in mid air.

"Back away from it," Gunner said.

"I don't understand any of this." Bain attempted to pick up an old plastic bag, but it turned to dust. Likewise, a fragment of pavement crumbled in his hand. "It takes a thousand years for plastic to decompose, and the pavement turned to dust, but the highway in the gray mist is still new." They could only see a short way, as though the land was locked in a deep fog, but the highway was intact; and as the mist receded, they saw into the past: mangled cars on fire, pileup crashes, and men running in terror.

Gunner's thoughts turned toward Pastor Jim and Buford. He jogged off the remains of the highway and scrambled down an embankment. The other bus lay on its side with the front end raised upon a boulder. Dark red rust and clods of grass covered the undercarriage, but the bus' body was gone: a jagged edge of rusted metal skirted the frame and marked its former location. The contents of the bus were detritus, fragments soon to be buried underneath the forest floor. Bain dug through the loam and found a crushed aluminum can; it crumbled into tiny fragments.

"Over here," Reese shouted. They scrambled around the bus and joined the petite girl in the forest. The front end of a rusted hulk emerged from the forest floor, like some dinosaur skeleton rising from the ground. The SUV was a mass of rusted metal and rot. Bain dropped to his knees and dug with his hands. A window collapsed and soil poured into the rotted interior. A skull with empty eyes gazed back at him in astonishment. Gunner jerked Reese away from the macabre scene, fearful they might become contaminated.

"How can they all be dead?" asked Reese. "They were alive a few minutes ago." Her face contorted, and she dropped to her knees. Bent forward, she cried out in agony. A bulge grew between her shoulder blades, and it soon ripped through her
blouse. She sat upright, threw her head back and screamed. A pair of orange and black butterfly wings

unfurled. Gazing up at the sky, fists grabbing loam, her mouth agape, she sensed something grow out of her skull: a pair of green antennae emerged from her short, boy-cut black locks and moved about independently. Likewise, her ears grew long and pointed. She closed her eyes and contorted her face. When her eyes opened, her irises sparkled like slivers of sapphire.

Reese rose to her feet and looked about the forest as if seeing for the first time. She kicked off her tennis shoes, stripped off her blue jeans, and ripped off her blouse. Clad only in emerald satin panties and a white silk camisole, she sprang into the air and fluttered into the sky with her new fae body.

"REESE," cried Linda. The girl giggled and flew over the treetops, disappearing from view. "What's happening?"

Gunner rubbed his face, his mind overwhelmed by what he witnessed. It could not accept what his eyes beheld. When he climbed the hill, his boots slipped on dead leaves. He grabbed an oak tree for support. Crawling up on all fours, he struggled up the hill and stood upright on the flat ground. All that remained of the highway were two parallel, flat strips, covered with grass and sparse foliage. Linda hurried to his side with the others in hot pursuit.

When a rock hit the ground, he glanced back at the gray mist. The stick and rock lay on the ground. His eyes went wide when he saw the mist approaching the front end of Toni's truck. "Get out of the way!" He pushed the others off the road, and they all tumbled into a pile. The truck exploded from the mist and bounced. With only inches to spare, it rocketed past them. The truck slammed on its brakes and the trailer jackknifed; the hitch snapped, and the trailer rolled down the road.

"We need those supplies." Gunner scrambled to his feet and sprinted to the trailer. "Bain, get Toni out of that truck."

The trailer lay on its side with the back door ripped open. The contents spilled all over the ground. Gunner charged up to the trailer and wildly threw out boxes, bags, and supplies. The other survivors joined him, throwing the vital supplies onto the ground.

"Let me go!" Toni yelled and thrashed. Bain dragged her out of the truck and away from it. She struggled to her feet and jerked her arm free. "What are you doing?" A look of astonishment on Bain's face perplexed her.

Toni turned, and her lips parted in a silent gasp. The tires rotted and popped; the paint faded; the body rusted; the interior rotted, and fire consumed it, only to extinguish a moment later. Her new truck, the one paid for with her hard-earned wages, decayed into a charred hulk. "Awe, come on," she groaned and crossed her arms. "That's not fair. I just made my last payment." When pointed ears poked through her black locks, she touched them and asked, "What's going on with my ears?"

"Back away," Gunner ordered. The trailer aged and collapsed right before their eyes. He ripped open a box filled with groceries. They seemed fine. "I think it worked: we got to them in time."

"What are you saying?"

"Look around," he said, gesturing at the trees. "This highway hasn't been used for thousands of years. We must have been stuck in that gray mist for a long, long, long time. When we came out, time must have contaminated the vehicles like radiation."

Linda cocked her head and touched Gunner's ears. Her face contorted, she caressed his face. The spark of youth returned to his eyes, and the green of his youth returned to his flesh. The young man she loved as a girl returned to her.

Gunner caressed his wife's cheek and marveled. He said, "You look like a teenage girl. I-I can't believe it." They embraced and kissed.

"Great, everyone is an elve, and I'm a dwarf," Bain grumbled. When they began to laugh, Bain tried to fight it, but seconds later, laughter exploded from him. They laughed until they cried.

When the moment passed, Linda asked, "What do we do now?"

"There's nothing else to do. We have to gather our supplies, and hike out of here. We need to move out while we still have daylight. I want to get away from that gray mist. There has to be civilization somewhere around here."

Chapter 12

A restless sleep ended with the crack of thunder. Gunner shot upright and alert; his Elven eyes searched the darkness for threats, and his Elven ears listened for an attack. The soft fall of the sound of rain soothed him, yet something lingered in the darkness: a presence beckoned him to follow. He slipped from the sleeping bag. Linda stirred but fell back asleep. He gathered his belongings and exited the tent. The last few drops of rain fell upon his face and the clouds parted.

The stars, luminescent diamonds, shimmered, and the black silhouette of trees contrasted the midnight blue sky. As if a switch flipped, his eyes beheld the world in monochrome clarity. He raised his right hand and turned to it. It was clear and crisp, as if on some old black and white television program. Likewise, the camp, the forest, and the sky were visible, as if he shifted to some other reality. For the first time, he saw the nighttime landscape as any predator might.

When he finished dressing, he strapped a knife to his right hip and a quiver of arrows on his back. Bow in hand, he followed the mysterious siren song, a melody that hung in the air, familiar, beautiful, yet so strange. As he wandered through the camp, he heard the sounds of sleep: soft breaths and restless turning.

From the moment he entered the forest, it reminded him of home: safe, familiar, a place he desired to remain. When he touched the rough bark of an oak tree, he sensed the flow of energy through the tree, and as he lingered, that life force flowed through him. He knew trees were living things, but it was as though he experienced them for the first time.

He wandered through the forest, a stranger in paradise, and the song grew louder with each step. At first, the leaves crunched and twigs snapped beneath his feet, but when he took care, he made no more sound than a cat, movement with a quiet stealth. He shifted to a run, and the ground flew beneath his feet. Despite his great size, he ran like a deer, leaping over logs, shifting around trees, and moving with speed.

After an hour of running, he thought, *I should go back,* yet the siren song compelled him to follow. He broke through some dense undergrowth and stopped. Broken pillars, pathways of white, footbridges over still waters, a circular temple, having an oculus dome that looked toward the heavens, the ruins lay before him in all their glory.

He followed the curved path toward the reflecting pool. The water appeared transparent as glass, and fish seemed to swim through the air beneath him. When he crossed the bridge, timelessness settled upon him and drove troubled thoughts from his weary mind. The song led him through the ruins of the oculus temple.

When he scaled the stairs, destiny took control: a moment he was fated to live, destiny unfolded and guided his steps. He passed between the pillars in a state of awe. The purest light from a new moon beamed through the oculus and fell upon the "Dragon's Eye Amulet". The golden amulet was the size of a pocket watch, and set in the center, a red dragon's eye stone stared back at him. He took two steps toward it but stopped.

"Come to me, my love," a voice whispered. As if in a dream, he entered the shaft of moonlight and an ethereal glow made him appear timeless, radiant. When he extended his right arm, the pendant floated into his hand. "I've waited for so long for you to find me. We shall never more be parted. I will be with you and your descendants forever."

All dreams must end with the red glow of dawn. Reality snapped like the flash of a camera, and he found himself alone in the forest. The amulet filled his right hand, the gold chain draped over the side. *What have I done?* thought Gunner.

Chapter 13

Bain sat upright, causing the sleeping bag to pile up on his lap. He rubbed the small of his back and groaned. The hard ground made him ache. His sleep was restless and troubled, filled with fitful dreams.

The aroma of cooking bacon made his stomach rumble. Bain unzipped the blue nylon tent and beheld the wild forest. This strange wilderness – with all its night terrors and emptiness – consumed the safe, familiar vistas of his youth. The twisted trees and the naked skies offended some new instinct: a deep longing that craved the comfort of soil and stone.

He crawled out on all fours and stepped on the wet grass. A passing cloud pissed all over the ground, and he stepped in it. "Crap," he grumbled and put on his boots. The expansive skies still held menacing clouds that threatened those upon the surface. As he trudged through camp, the vague field and the dark forest beyond filled him with anxiety; how he craved a cave or even a hole to crawl in for relief. However, the smell of cooking eggs, bacon, and toast distracted him, and a stomach grumble urged him onward.

After he had passed around a blue tent, he saw the others gathered around a campfire. Toni stared into the flames with empty eyes, and Julie sniffled. He dismissed female emotions as a nuisance and grabbed a blue plastic plate. After he had filled his cup with orange Gatorade, he took a big slurp and sat down on a log, hopeful that he would be the next to eat.

When Toni looked up from the fire, she squinted and cocked her head. Bain glanced to his right and left, trying to discern what she saw. Toni rose to her feet and circled around the fire, her eyes fixed on him. "What?" asked Bain. "Do I have a bug on me?"

"Your ears, they're pointed but floppy." Toni reached out but withdrew her hand. "Do they hurt?"

"No. My ears don't hurt." When he touched them, his fingers felt two wide ears with floppy points at the top. "Do your ears hurt?"

A scream ripped through the camp. Bain dropped his cup, letting it splash around his feet, and drew his knife. He charged around the fire, leaped over a log, and raced between the tents. The girls barely had time to rise to their feet before he was gone.

Bain held his knife before him, ready for action. He saw some strange redheaded girl. When she saw him out of the corner of her eye, she spun around to face him. She cupped her breast through her shirt and asked, "Why the hell do I have tits?" Bain furrowed his brow, perplex by such a strange question. She grabbed her crotch and said, "They're gone. What the hell happened to my junk?"

The girls lingered behind Bain. Toni saw a girl with blonde hair and blue eyes – a stranger – yet there was something familiar about her. "Who are you?"

Linda asked, "Do you live around here?"

"It's me … Dylan." Tight blue jeans and a Lycra top made it clear that her nubile form belonged to a girl and not Dylan. She combed her fingers through her long hair and exposed a pair of elegantly pointed ears. "What the hell is going on?"

Gunner burst from the woods and dumped a pair of dead rabbits on the ground. He gripped his bow with his left hand and drew an arrow with his right. He slotted and drew the arrow in a heartbeat. "What's the matter? I heard a scream."

Everyone stared at him. Flaxen locks grew long during the night, flowed over his shoulders, and his pointed ears poked through them. He had the same muscular frame, but he had a leading man's good looks. "What's going on? Somebody speak. Who is this girl?"

"I'm Dylan, and I'm not a girl."

Toni studied Dylan's crotch. The denim fabric stretched over the smooth contour at the junction of Dylan's thighs. "Well, you're no boy." When Dylan glared at her, she replied, "I may not be a doctor, but I know a girl when I see one."

"Shut up!" Dylan replied.

"What happened to your ears?" Linda asked Gunner.

"I have no idea." He released the tension on the bow and returned the arrow to his quiver. "When I woke up in the middle of the night, my ears were pointed, and the moon was so bright. The whole world was black and white but clear."

"Bain's ears are pointed and floppy," Toni said.

"I can see that. He seems a bit wider too," Gunner said.

Bain frowned and scratched the thick stubble on his chin. "I'm just big boned."

"And thick as a tree stump," Toni said.

When Bain flexed his short arms, he sensed the bulge of powerful biceps. His entire body rippled with unearned muscles. He held out his hand and saw five meaty fingers, and when he made a fist, he was sure he could crush stone. "What is happening to us?"

"I feel fine," Toni said.

"Well I don't," Dylan said. "You just don't go to bed a boy and wake up a girl. I want my junk back." It was strange to hear such language come from a teenage girl.

Gunner picked up the rabbits. "Let's have some breakfast and try and figure all this out." They followed him back to camp and sat around the fire. Linda prepared the eggs while Gunner dressed the meat. He threw it into a stewpot with some potatoes and carrots. He then placed it near the fire for a slow simmer.

Nibbling on bacon, eating toast, devouring the eggs, they ate in silence. The events of the past day pressed in on them. Logan yawned and wandered into the circle. "What was all the noise about earlier?" They all looked at each other and shook their heads.

"What are we going to do?" asked Linda.

"We're going to base camp here for a few days." He began to clean the rabbit pelts. "Bain and I will set out on mini expeditions. We need to find civilization."

"What about going home?" asked Toni.

"Too far, and those mountains are in our way. We need to find civilization and return with help." He stabbed at the fire, and embers rose into the air. "If we don't find anyone, then we can pack up and head toward Interstate 70. There should be several towns between here and there. Besides, if any rescuers come after us, we don't want to stray too far into the wilderness."

"There aren't going to be any rescuers," Bain said as he chewed. "You saw what happened. The town vanished; mountains appeared; the highway aged 500 years, perhaps more; the bus turned to rust, and Dylan got an instant sex change – so I think we're in deep sh–" seeing Linda's disapproving glare, he corrected himself and said, "trouble."

"Hold on. You're saying that's Dylan." Logan narrowed his eyes and studied the girl. "Are you sure it's Dylan?"

"Yes it's me," Dylan said, crossed her arms, and pouted.

Logan screwed up his face and rubbed the back of his neck. One could see his mind struggle to comprehend the situation. Then a quizzical expression appeared on his face. His fingers detected sharp lumps. He felt the back of his neck and then the small of his back and detected many more; all appeared connected to his spine. Sore spots on his head demanded an investigation. His fingers moved through his thick, brown locks and detected a lump, perhaps a knob. There were more, six that ringed his head, and when he drew back his hand, a clump of hair filled it.

Heart racing and nerves tingling, he jumped up from the log and ran back to his tent. He scrambled into his tent and ripped open his backpack. Spilling his belongings onto his sleeping bag, he found a small mirror. Holding it away and behind, out of the corner of his eyes, he saw the bony spines. He stripped off his shirt and snarled in horror. Large blotches of gray, leathery skin covered his torso. When he touched them, they seemed hard and yielded little sensation.

His mind groped for answers, and his trembling hands searched the rest of his body. When he heard voices and footfalls, he scrambled to button his shirt and yanked a stocking cap over his head. After he had exited his tent, he tucked in his shirt and wrapped a scarf around his neck. Pain, like the cut of a knife, sliced through his stomach. Hunger, beyond any he had ever known, drove him toward food.

When he rejoined the others, he heard Linda say, "I don't like the idea of splitting up. We should stay together. You have no idea what could be out in the woods. If you're going, so am I."

Gunner pulled her aside and whispered, "I've spent the night searching the nearby woods around the camp. We're safe here, but I have no idea what might wait for us out there. I need to get my bearings, and I don't want to put the children at risk while I do it. I need to know that all of you are safe."

"But what about you? What will we do if you're injured or killed?" Linda crossed her arms and turned away from him. "I don't know what I would do without you."

He caressed her shoulders and savored the perfume that still lingered upon her. "I'm not going alone. I will take Bain and Logan with me. If we see anything that looks like danger, I … we will turn around and get out of there. I'm not looking for trouble. The three of us can get out of danger a lot faster than the group."

"I suppose," she said and turned toward him. "I'm worried about Jake."

"Jake is smart and an excellent woodsman. He can take care of himself. We will find him." He rubbed his chin and detected no stubble; in fact, his face was still baby smooth. "Leave the tents up, but keep the rest of the gear ready to go. We may have to leave fast."

"You're not making me feel good," Linda said with a frown.

He scratched an itch and contemplated his next words. "I don't want to scare you, but back on the bus, we changed into elves; but Kevin also turned into something … well … terrifying. He is still out there, and I worry more him. A word entered my mind, daemia. It's their name, but I don't know how. All I know is that they are dangerous."

"And you want us to just sit in camp and wait for them? What if these daemia attack?" asked Linda with a shiver. "You could be gone an hour when some of those things stumble upon us. Carnivores move all the time. They need fresh hunting grounds."

"I think this whole area used to be in a gray zone. They probably don't know about it." He rubbed the back of his neck and gazed off into the distance. "But you have a point. We stay together." When they returned to the group, Gunner shouted, "Break camp, we are moving out."

 Linda asked, "But what about the stew? I just put it in the fire. It will take half a day to cook."

"By the time we get this group up and moving, it will be noon. Logan and Bain, I want you two to scout ahead. The rest of us will follow behind you." The rest of the teens mumbled their agreement.

Hours later, they collected their backpacks, put out the fire, and were on the move. Dead foliage formed a thick mat, and trees blocked their path like a besieging army. Their feet slipping on the damp loam, they struggled up a steep hill. A bare rock penetrated the ground at the top and jutted like a broken bone. Gunner scrambled onto the rock and surveyed the wilderness.

A lone white cloud floated through a vivid blue sky and trees spread as far as the eye could see. The shimmering waters of a river lay to the northwest, and the biggest mountains he had ever seen lay to the west: white capped Titans, their sharp peaks scraping the sky. In a slot that used to be Colorado, they traveled south in the gap between the Black Mountains and the Rocky Mountains.

Chapter 14

"Take a look at this," Bain shouted.

Gunner jumped off the rock and strode to Bain. A concrete slab snapped like a cracker, both the broken ends thrust into the air. Julie saw a bit of orange and dug an old plastic cup from the ground. "The Waffle House," appeared in black letters. "My dad stopped here to eat every time we left town. He was crazy about this place. But it didn't look like this. It was just off the highway and on the prairie. A whole shopping plaza was next to it." Her eyes became glassy, and she put her right hand on her hip. "I hate this. The whole world has gone insane." The other girls gathered around her and offered empty comfort.

"My family ate here too. That means that something transported us 100 miles to Interstate 76, and Sterling, Colorado is about 2 miles west. There are a bunch of hotels and restaurants at the off ramp. We could stay the night." Then he twitched his nose and surveyed the terrain. Jagged hills with ambling streams between and sharp rocks stood between them and rescue. "It used to be flat. I mean pancake flat here." He pointed to the southwest. "We need to head toward that hill, the one that looks like the front ramp of an open rifle sight."

"I don't see a shopping mall," Toni said.

"I don't see I76," whined Dylan. "That's a long hike. It will take us most of the day to get down there. Are you sure that we want to go that way? I mean, there is nothing there."

When Logan moved to the bushes to relieve himself, he removed his baseball cap to scratch his head, a clump of hair came with it and fell to the ground. The top of his head stung, and when he felt it, his fingers detected small horns growing out of his skull. His heart hammered, and he slapped his cap back on his head. He jerked up his shirt from his jeans and saw that the leathery, gray flesh merged into a solid band. It grew up and down his torso.

As he cursed, he sensed salty fluid in his mouth, so he spat. Red blood mixed with black spattered on a plate size rock. When his index finger explored his mouth, it knocked a tooth loose, and it tumbled out of his mouth. "What's happening to me," he whined and spit out more teeth and blood. His gums felt sore, and when he touched them, he felt the tips sharp spike teeth. They grew out at irregular angles, and tips appeared to be hollow, like the snake fangs. Fluid flowed out from the holes, and when he removed his finger, a drop of green venom sat upon the tip.

Back at the hilltop, Bain lounged upon a rock and crossed his stubby arms over his barrel chest. "Then where would we go? There is a huge mountain range between Kansas and us, and we are only miles from Sterling."

Dylan sniffled, which caused the other girls to become glassy eyed. "I ... I'm sorry." She wiped a tear from her cheek and tried to repress her pain. "I didn't mean to –" It was too late; tears rolled down their cheeks. "Damn it, I don't want to cry. I want my life back. I want my family back." The other girls also joined her and everyone wept.

"What's going on?" Linda emerged from the bushes. She rubbed Dylan's back and held her. "Why is everyone crying?"

"D-dead, our families, are dead," Julie sobbed.

"Oh sweetheart, you don't know that. We survived. They might be waiting for you in some survivor's camp." Linda hugged Dylan, and they had a group hug. "Let's keep a positive attitude."

Gunner wanted to join his wife and encourage them. However, he hated group hugs, and the situation was dire. He tried to reason a scenario where they might have survived, but it was impossible. Whether fate buried it underneath a mountain or time turned it to dust, the city of Gleason was gone, and reason insisted that it would never return; but hopelessness was cancer to moral, so he remained silent. Overwhelmed. Grieved. When he and Bain locked eyes, they shared the truth without words.

"We need to keep moving." Gunner rose up off a rock and brushed off the dirt. "If there is a survivor's camp, I want to find it soon, preferably before nightfall. I could use some hot food and a shower. Where is Logan?"

"LOGAN, where are you?" called Linda. "We need to stay together."

Cutting pain radiated from Logan's fingertips, and as he watched in horror, his fingernails reshaped into claws. He whimpered and tried to cry, but his eyes were so dry. For a moment, he went blind. He dropped to his knees and grabbed his face, feeling the place that had once been his eye sockets. A sudden flash of red stabbed his brain and then a panoramic explosion of vibrant light tormented him. His hands trembling before his face, he saw the world through eight eyes that never blinked.

A gasp came from his left. He turned and saw the thermal image of two figures. The faces were brilliant yellow, the breasts burned orange, and the bodies a molten mixture of orange and red. A scream ripped from the larger female. "Stay away from me," said Linda. When he tried to speak to her, gurgling grunts and growls came from his lips. He coughed out the last of his human teeth and roared in agony. His body twisted and muscles grew thick.

A white-hot male rushed through the bushes, and Logan backed away from him. The man squatted down and held out his hand. "Logan, it's okay. I'm not going to hurt you." He recognized Gunner's voice, but it sounded warped and brassy. Sounds, no matter how small, pierced his brain. Desperate for darkness and silence, he fled, screaming in agony and rage.

Chapter 15

How do you abandon a teen you that you were to protect? Because of his military training, Gunner tracked Logan for a mile, but it took him too far from the others; so he gave up and returned to them. When Linda saw him alone, she wrung her hands and took a step toward him. "Did you find him?"

"No. He moved too fast. I gave up when the trail led me to a sheer rock wall. He scrambled up it as though he was on level ground. He's gone." He caressed the handle of his knife and rubbed his neck. "I'm not sure what I would do if I caught him. The Logan we knew is gone."

"We need to go," Bain said. "I don't want him coming back after dark. We need to get to Sterling."

"We can't just leave him," Toni said. "We have to go after him." A din arose as quiet dissent turned into open rebellion.

Gunner held up his hands and waited for silence. "Whatever Kevin and Logan became, they are dangerous to themselves and others. We have no way to help them.

Bain is right. We have to keep moving and find help. Now I'm sorry about this, but we have to go."

With no choice, they began their descent. Loose gravel and thirsty soil covered a steep incline. They had to sit and climb down on all fours. Every so often, someone would lose their footing and slide. When they reached the bottom, they found a shallow creek that meandered through a field of tumbled rocks, jagged rocks lining the shore. The creek weaved between the hills on a crooked path southwest.

Unwilling to risk another climb, they followed the creek. However, it held many dangers: loose stones, sharp rocks, frigid water, and gravel that spilled from the heights. When three teens fell into the creek, they gasped and sprang out of the frigid water. Bain scrambled on a large, angular rock and helped them out of the water. Soaked and shivering, they stripped off their wet clothes and changed into dry clothes in their backpacks. Bain surveyed the way ahead of them and whispered, "I wish this place was still flat."

"Me too," Toni said, and the others agreed.

It took Bain by surprise, and he scratched his head. Someone next to him would have had to strain to hear his voice, but they heard him from afar. Then he remembered that they were elves, and elves have superb hearing. For some reason, it angered him. He wanted to tell them to "go to hell", but he wasn't sure why.

After four hours, they traveled only a few miles. Cuts, scrapes, bruises, and icy wet feet resulted. There was plenty of light left in the day but little enthusiasm to keep going. After a short rest, they once again moved west, each one cursing the rugged terrain.

Eager to be rid of the frigid water, they climbed a steep embankment and found themselves on level ground. They found themselves on I70, but the road lapsed into disorder. Brown grass broke up the pavement, and the guard rails rusted to dust long ago; and the road buckled at points, causing crevices over which they could leap, but it offered them a fast mean of travel.

They walked for several more hours and stopped only for a quick bite to eat. After offering a prayer, the large group consumed what remained of the supplies. All had a mouthful of food, but most remained hungry. Gunner surveyed the desolation ahead of them and pondered his next decision. The night would be upon them soon and they required shelter from the elements.

"My father built a new outlet mall not far from here. Well, it was new. I'm not sure about now, but there might be people. It should only a few miles down the road," Bain said.

Gunner rubbed his face and nodded. "Come on, let's keep moving." The youth group groaned as they rose to their feet. "Bain said that there is an outlet mall just ahead. I want to make it there by nightfall." The idea of food and shelter revived them.

After two more hours of hiking, they arrived at what used to be an off-ramp. The corpse of the outlet mall lay in the middle of the unkempt field. What had once been a five story hotel lay near it. The interior, however, collapsed in the middle, leaving a hollowed out hulk with brittle walls. The group stared at the eyeless windows and the gloomy black exterior in disbelief.

Gunner rubbed his aching lower back and shook his head. "We camp here for the night. We'll put up our tents in that field." They were so fixed upon the ruin that they failed to notice the field. Golden wheat spread out as far as the eye could see. After they had crossed the road, Gunner stripped kernels from the wheat. They were the size of marbles, thick and soft. After he had ground them up between his hands, he blew away the chaff. He popped them into his mouth and chewed. They reminded him of a nut flavored chewing gum. He washed them down with plenty of water and ate more.

It was not what they expected to eat, but it filled their bellies. After they set up the tents, Gunner said to Linda,

"Bain and I are going to check out the ruins. There may be something we can use."

"I'm coming too," shouted Toni.

The trio crossed the fields in search of adventure. In its glory, the glass walls and ceiling of the hotel filled the atrium with light. Now, the shattered glass let in the rain and black mold covered the walls. Wild, green weeds rose up through the rectangular window frames, a jungle where once men abode. The doors lay on the ground, bent and corroded. After they entered, birds launched into the air and flew to open sky.

"It looked better when my dad built it," Bain said.

They pushed through the vegetation and stood before the railing that overlooked the common area. Brilliant sunlight beamed through the windowless dome and illuminated the lobby. Rainwater filled a central fountain and a circle of trees drank from it. As if stumbling upon some lost paradise, they descended the stairs in a state of awe.

Broken and burnt out shops lined the walls, and looters carried off anything of value. Yet a quiet reverence permeated the structure as if they wandered into some ancient cathedral, and it revived their souls. Gunner picked up the tattered and rotted remains of a ragdoll. He laid it aside and grieved the fallen.

"Apples," Toni said and bit one with a crunch. "It's good," she said with a full mouth. Brain and Gunner removed their shirts, buttoned them, and tied off the sleeves. They filled them with apples, and Toni found blackberry bushes and filled her cap. When Gunner returned, Linda showed them how to turn raw wheat and a few other ingredients into flat bread. A few of the boys caught fish in a nearby creek. That night everyone lounged around a fire, enjoyed the bounty of food, and shared stories; and their burden seemed a little lighter.

Chapter 16

The boys fished, and the girls picked berries. Nature provided abundant strawberries, blueberries, and blackberries. Pots, pans, and coolers overflowed with produce. Dylan and Toni even spotted a wild vine heavy laden with grapes. As the girl's picked them, Toni brushed a raven tress behind her pointed ear and gave Dylan a furtive glance. "So, how are you doing?"

"My back is a little sore from picking strawberries." Dylan squatted beside a cooler, and a tan cotton skirt, decorated with a floral print, draped over her bare thighs. She placed each cluster of grapes with care into the cooler. "These things are huge." The cluster filled her petite hand to overflowing.

"No … um … I meant, how are you doing … after switching teams?" asked Toni.

"Oh, I'm fine. I wish I had something other than a skirt to wear, but my hiking clothes are still drying. Not to mention wearing panties," she whispered as if it was some dark secret. She pulled open her peasant blouse and gazed at her chest. A pair of creamy swells filled out a white nylon bra. "Not to mention other things."

She picked a heavy cluster and popped a grape into her mouth. However, a disturbing memory negated the sweetness of the fruit. "When I bent over this morning, I caught Billy Jensen staring at my butt." She turned toward Toni and put her right hand on her hip. "I don't like boys staring at my butt. He kept staring, as though he just seen big foot. It made me feel weird." She looked around and whispered, "Knowing what he wanted to do."

Toni shrugged and brushed a lock from her face. "That's what boys do. It's even weirder when older men do it." Dylan grimaced and crossed her arms. "You're a girl now. You have a different role in sex. Someday you'll be a mother with a baby on your hip."

Dylan's arms hung limp and blushed. "What if I don't want to have a baby?" She placed the grapes into the cooler. "I just became a girl; I don't want to be a mother."

"Nature is conspiring against you. It will do everything to get you pregnant. My dad always said, 'Your body is a baby factory. Just keep it closed for business a while longer,'" said Toni.

Dylan sniffled and said, "But I don't want to have a baby or have sex with a guy."

"I'm sorry," Toni said and gave her a hug. "You don't have to do anything you're not ready for."

The clip-clop of hooves and the grind of wheels interrupted them. A solitary horse, blinders on its head, drew a wagon filled with ears of corn. Straw hat upon his head, soiled trousers, worn shoes, and a sun-faded shirt, the farmer rode atop a wagon. "Ladies," he said and nodded at them.

"Excuse me," said Toni. "Where are you going?"

Chadwick pulled back on the reins and stopped the wagon. "I'm going to the market." He studied their quizzical expression and added, "The market in downtown Sterling. It's just over yonder, past the old overpass."

"How many miles away is it?"

He screwed up his nose and looked up at the sky. "Hmm, I'd say it's about three miles or so. Are you girls lost?"

"Kind of," Toni said. "We're new to the area."

"Just go through the overpass and follow the road. It curves to the left toward town. You can't miss it."

"Thank you," Toni said. The girls picked up the produce and rushed back to the camp. "We have to tell the others."

Chadwick raised his hand and parted his lips to speak. However, the girls disappeared into some bushes. He rubbed the stubble on his chin and wondered if he should warn them. Then he saw Gunner off in the distance. If they had such a formidable elve to guard them, they would be safe. He slapped the reins and rode toward town.

Chapter 17

Their feet moved with joy and laughter filled the air. Civilization awaited them in a few miles. Despite the weight of their packs, a few jogged ahead, but Gunner called them back. He wanted them to stay together.

The rolling hills grew larger as though waves of a wild sea. When they crested a tall hill, Sterling lay before them. However, it bore little resemblance to the town of their memories. A vast array of gray slate roofs spread out before them. Horse-drawn wagons carried heavy loads on a relentless trek to the central market. Smoke from countless chimneys rose into the air and carried the aroma of cooking food: eggs, bread, bacon, and sausage.

The teens scampered down the road toward town. Gunner raised his hand to stop them, but there was no restraining them. They rushed down the hill and raced toward town. He strode after them and pondered their situation. The town appeared medieval: no cars, electric poles, or telephones. What sort of life awaited them in this future world?

Narrow cobblestone streets funneled them toward the city's center. A woman dressed in a long brown skirt and gray blouse paused from sweeping to watch them pass. Her weathered face and tired eyes testified to her hard life, yet kindness lay behind her eyes, and that was encouraging. Likewise, a group of men cradling mugs of steaming coffee paused to watch them. Their brown and gray, cotton and wool garb suggested a pre-industrialized society. The teen's yellow, red, and white clothing seemed out of place, perhaps even garish in such a setting.

The crowds grew dense and flowed in a circular current around the central fountain. Heavy canopies spread over wooden wagons. Each wagon bore different treasures — spices, clothes, jewelry, tableware, produce, meats, and other items — and the merchants bellowed their chants, each one trying to top the others. Likewise, other merchants fought to lure patrons into their shops. When a woman stopped to shop, the merchant performed for her, reciting a wondrous spiel about marvels of their product. While amused, the woman searched the product for defects and argued price.

"Stay together," Linda called. But what young person listens to such advice? They diffused through the swell of the crowd and gawked at the goods for sale. Julie returned a few minutes later, a pout on her face. "What's the matter?" asked Linda.

"They won't take my money." Julie clutched a twenty-dollar bill in her hand. "He said, 'It's worthless paper, girl; get some coins from your mother.' What are we supposed to do?"

Out of the corner of her eye, she saw Gunner enter a jewelry store. "Come with me." They struggled to pass through the crowd and were quite frustrated by the time they traversed the plaza. When they entered the shop, they saw Gunner standing before a glass counter. His right eye peering through an eye loupe, the merchant, Edgar Hallsby, held a diamond necklace above an examination lamp.

"Flawless, absolutely flawless," Edgar said and rubbed his bulbous belly. "I've heard tales of your people, but I never imagined. This is the most magnificent specimen I have ever seen."

"And I have the matching earrings." He opened a black velvet case and slid it across the counter. A pair of 5-karat diamond earrings twinkled like stars in a midnight sky. Edgar once again donned his diamond loupe and examined the stones.

"Perfection," he whispered. "I take it you have a mind to sell them?"

"I do," Gunner replied.

Edgar twitched his nose and rubbed the back of his neck. "If you will pardon me," he said and approached a silver-bearded man that appeared old as time. He ushered Juan through a set of curtains. The pair spoke in hushed voices, but Gunner's Elven ears allowed him to hear their conversation.

"Where did you get those?" asked Linda.

"An early anniversary gift," Gunner said. "I was going to take you on an early morning hike and give them to you on a mountain top. But we need the money."

Edgar returned and stroked his double chin. "I can pay you 15-gold for them, and I tell you, I am generous."

Gunner said to Linda, "I saw another jeweler across the plaza. Perhaps we should try there."

"Now, now, there's no need for that." Edgar rubbed his belly and stared at the countertop. With a twitch of his nose, he said, "I'll give you twenty, but not a coin more." His face tensed and hands clenched. Gunner eyed a hulking man in the far corner of the store. The guard caressed the handle of his sword.

"Done," Gunner said, and everyone breathed a sigh of relief.

"You've made a fine choice and struck a fair price." Edgar slapped his partner on the back, nearly toppling the old man. He brought out a bottle of his finest whiskey and gave them a drink. Gunner took a sip and pondered his next words.

"Say … um … what do you know about those mountains appearing? Any idea how that would happen?" Gunner tried to hide his embarrassment with a smile. Edgar paused from filling out a receipt and furrowed his brow.

"Well, every school child knows that tale." Edgar glanced at Gunner's pointed ears and nodded. "But perhaps it's different with the elves." He rolled his eyes toward the ceiling and twitched his nose. "Let me see, my papa told me the story. 'In the previous age, the earth was flat, not a ripple or a bump. All of the farms produced so much food that the people grew fat and indolent. God looked down from heaven and grew angry. He broke the foundations of the earth and mountains shot up.'" He chuckled and then said, "Supposedly, the Black Mountains just appeared out of thin air over a thousand years ago. Scientists say that's impossible, though."

"It's blasphemy," Juan said and slid onto a stool with a groan. "My old bones are sore this morning. God made the Black Mountains in heaven and dropped them onto the earth, chock filled with elves, the dwarves, trolls, gnomes, daemia, drathva, and other such things. It's how your people came to be."

"Uh huh," Gunner mumbled. "What happened to the people before?" Their blank expressions prompted him to say, "You know ... the humans before the mountains arrived."

"Oh them, they died out with the 'Golden Age,'" said Edgar.

"Not all of them," Juan said, "or we wouldn't be here."

"We're descended from the righteous," Edgar said and handed a receipt and a bank draw to Gunner. "They were the ones who stayed faithful to the God of gods and his demigods. Bernadette is my goddess. She brings wealth." Juan nodded in agreement.

"Thanks for the information." Gunner took the documents and exited with Linda by his side. They found a group of pouting teens congregated near the fountain. Most clutched worthless money and scowled at the merchants. "Come on," Gunner said, "I have to go to the bank, and then we are checking into a hotel."

As they traversed the plaza, Linda asked, "How did we afford those earrings and necklace."

Gunner smirked and said, "Well, you remember my buddy, Jim, who worked for Homeland Tool Manufacturing?" She nodded. "He got them for me. They are … um … manufactured diamonds. I was going to tell you … at some point. They are the same as natural diamond, better in fact. They're flawless."

Linda rolled her eyes and then clung to his arm. "You are so bad. But, we can use the money." He nodded and put his arm around her waist. "We need to go shopping."

———

Despite a brass bed, a soft duvet, and the soft glow of a fire in the hearth, Gunner woke after three hours as if it was eight. He threw aside the duvet, snatched his clothes off the chair, and stabbed his legs into his jeans. "Can't sleep?" asked Linda, still underneath the covers.

"No. It's like I'm trying to nap at noon. Why am I so wide awake?" Gunner washed his face in a basin of water, and his right hand glided over baby smooth skin. Ever since he transformed from a boy to a man rough stubbed that covered his chin. Now, however, his beard vanished, and his platinum locks grew long, not the look a retired military officer desires. He threw on a leather jacket and a baseball cap.

He opened the French doors to the balcony, and the cool night wind refreshed him. The sound of laughter drew his eyes down to the glow of a tavern window. He sat at upon a metal chair and gazed past the roofs and up at the full moon. It appeared larger and hypnotic. Linda bundled up in a blanket and joined him on the balcony. "Do you think Jake is okay?" she asked and sat next to him on the bench.

He shook his head and said, "I wish I had a clue. We're 1,000 years in the future." He lapsed into silence and drew in a deep breath. "I have to go looking for him. He might have been thrown in the future." It seemed a feeble hope, but he had no other. He put his arm around his wife and hugged her. "He's okay. I can feel it."

"How can we be a thousand years into the future?" Linda snuggled into him and joined him staring at the moon. "It makes no sense."

"Mountains appearing, turning into elves, the world reshaped ... Dylan becoming a female elve," Gunner said, "it's enough to drive you crazy. All I can say is that it did happen, and we have to adapt."

The hours dragged, but the first rays of dawn broke over the horizon. When a knock came from the door, Linda rose from the bench and scurried across the cold wooden floor. When she heard voices, Linda moved closer to hear.

"The girls are missing," she said. The moonlight glowed upon the silken gown that adorned her hourglass figure, and the breezed lifted a golden lock. She crossed her arms and shivered. "When Bain went to check on them, he found their rooms empty and bed untouched."

"They are probably out exploring. It's what I would do." He rose up from the chair with a groan. "I'll go look for them. I can't sleep."

When he exited his room, he saw Bain across and down the hallway. He stood in the doorway and had a worried look upon his face. "Dylan is gone, but her bags are still here." Gunner furrowed his brow and walked to the threshold.

Toni searched for clues. "The last time I saw her was in the middle of the night. Neither of us could sleep, so she went for a walk. I told her not to go far."

Gunner scowled and said to Linda, "I want you to get yourself and the rest of the teens dressed. Stay in our room with the door bolted, and be ready to go. If we don't return by dawn, leave without us."

He marched down the hotel stairs with heavy steps. The clerk looked up from the registration desk, a thousand excuses and denials in his eyes. When Gunner strode over to the desk, the weasel-faced man, Sid, took a step backward, but Gunner grabbed his shirt. He dragged the man over the counter, spilling the registration book and other items onto the floor. His muscular arm hauled back, and a massive fist smashed into the clerk's jaw. The slender man spun and spattered blood onto the painting on the wall. Gunner jerked the man back and gave him a powerful blow to the gut, lifting the man's feet off the floor. The devastated clerk's legs wobbled and held up his right hand. "Stop. I don't know any —" Another blow flung him across the room, and he crashed into a writing desk. "Stop hitting me. I'll tell you everything."

"I'm listening," Gunner growled.

"The Black Brotherhood has them," Sid said.

"Who?"

"Everyone knows them. They deal in slaves and black market goods. Normally all Elven females wear choker necklaces, in addition to wedding rings. They were so beautiful. You can't blame us; they wanted us to take them," Sid said.

While Gunner was curious about the necklaces, he focused on his immediate concerns. "How many of them are there, and where are they keeping them?" When Sid hesitated, he hauled back to punch him again.

"Wait, they don't tell me where they take the girls," Sid said. "I swear. Would you tell me the location of your secret hideout? Rumor has it that it is in the ancient sewer system, but the dwarves constructed 100 kilometers of tunnels. You'll never find them."

"How many of these 'slavers' are in Sterling?"

"Three or four as I recall," Sid said with a shrug. When Gunner hauled back, Sid cringed and raised his arms for protection. "Two dozen, perhaps more," Sid shouted. Linda scrambled down the stairs, clad in her new cappuccino brown leather boots, tights, vest, and waist jacket. She had a slender rapier strapped to her waist, and she clutched a sheathed Elven saber and matching knife in her right hand.

Bain stood on the threshold of a closet and held Toni's backpack for all to see. His eyes turned to Sid and burned with raw hate. "If anything has happened to them," Bain said.

"They've kidnapped the girls, and they are going to sell them as slaves," Gunner said. "We're going after them." After he had strapped on his weapons, he met her eyes and touched her hand. "If we are not back by noon, lead the youth group out of town and don't look back."

Chapter 18

A jet of crystal water rose up from a nozzle and then plunged into the fountain with a splash. Gunner and Bain approached every merchant, but everyone denied knowing of such things. The morning was running out; if he couldn't locate Dylan by noon, they would have to abandon the search. He and Bain shared an uneasy, silent exchange.

A fastidious man wearing a hat with a red plume, crimson cape, and black boots approached them. He stroked his goatee and sniffed. "I am Sheriff Merrimack. Concerned citizens informed me that you search for the Black Brotherhood. They are a criminal organization." He swept back his cape with his right elbow, put his hand on his hip, and exposed his sword basket grip. "You would do well to avoid them."

"They've kidnapped a child under my care. I have to find them," Gunner said. Bain looked past the sheriff and saw four men skulking about, pretending to shop at nearby carts. "Do you know where we might find them?"

The sheriff twirled his handlebar mustache and narrowed his eyes. "I know of a few taverns where such people congregate. They might, for a price, release the girl." He examined his gloved right hand. "Um, another man was reported missing last night. Do you know anything about his disappearance?"

"Me? No. I don't see how people live this way, people being kidnapped off the street. It's outrageous." Gunner shook his head and crossed his arm. "The missing man, he was kidnapped too?"

"Who can say? People just disappear. We dutifully investigate these cases, but few of the victims are ever located." He sniffed and said, "I was informed that you made a large sale yesterday."

"I made a few coins," Gunner replied.

"If you like, I could act as an intermediary, negotiate on your behalf." When Gunner nodded, he said, "Very well. I will make some inquiries. Stay in the plaza where I can find you." After he had departed, two of the men remained and lingered near the fountain.

"Hello there," said Chadwick. "How fair you are this fine morrow?"

"Not well," Bain replied. "One of the girls under our care was kidnapped. The sheriff is going to negotiate with the kidnappers."

"Hmm," Chadwick said and looked out of the corner of his eyes to his right and left. He leaned close and whispered. "Rumor has it that Sheriff Merrimack is a member of the Brotherhood. He's more likely going to lure you into a trap and rob you."

"Do you know where the hideout is?" asked Gunner.

"I'm sorry. I know it is in the sewers somewhere, but I wouldn't know where," Chadwick said. "My granddaughter disappeared two years ago. What could we do? He has dozens of the worst sort of people. There was nothing we could do." He cleared his throat and rubbed his forehead. "We miss her."

"I guess we will have to buy her back," Bain said.

"Hmm, I wouldn't do that. They will take your gold, kill you, and sell her anyway. I've seen it happen. Take it from me; there is nothing you can do." Chadwick removed his hat, stared at the cobblestones, and wandered into the crowd.

The bright sunshine reflected off the turbulent water in the fountain. Shoppers milled about enjoying the day, and the aroma of cooking food wafted out of restaurants. It was a perfect, except for the rage in his heart. Gunner rubbed his face and could think of no plan to save Dylan. He could search for years and not find their hideout; Linda and the other children would be at risk. There was only one reasonable plan, and he hated himself for thinking it. "Go back to the hotel and tell Linda what's happening. We're going to leave."

"Without Dylan?" asked Bain.

"We don't have a choice. We could lose five more girls while trying to save one. The sheriff and the Brotherhood will come after us, and this is their home ground. We'll lose. We don't have a choice." Bain lingered a few seconds and then strode away. Gunner never felt so impotent.

"Use me," whispered a tiny voice in his mind. He looked about but saw no one. "I can save her." The pendant beneath his clothes burned as if on fire. He almost forgot about it and the peculiar way he found it. "You didn't find me. I found you."

"How can we save her?" he asked, feeling a bit foolish.

"Watch and learn." A golden ember glowed on the ground before him. It rose into the sky and exploded. Gunner jumped back, nearly toppling into the fountain. A curtain of gold light spread out to his right and left, extending across the horizon. It passed through the Earth and extended into the heavens. "Pass through it." When he hesitated, the pendant said, "Don't be afraid. You'll be safe."

"But —" he began to say.

"Trust me," the pendant whispered.

Driven by need, he stepped toward the curtain.

As though stepping through a waterfall, liquid light poured over Gunner's head and flowed over his body. His mouth closed in reflex, and he held his breath. For a moment, he floated weightless beneath an ocean that spanned the universe, yet with his next step, he emerged from the curtain of light and stepped foot onto solid ground. Sucking in desperate gasps, he struggled to regain his senses. A grimace on his face, he stood upright and could scarcely believe his eyes.

Darkness enveloped the fountain plaza. Awnings retracted, doors closed, merchandise covered, locks secured, the vending wagons were closed. When he gazed at the sky, he saw a passing cloud float between the moon and the stars. "What happened?" he whispered.

"It is the previous night. If you hurry, you can save her," whispered the pendant.

Gunner jogged and then sprinted through the city streets. He made a right and then a left on the main road. The moonlight illuminated both the grid pattern of the paver stones and the balconies and roofs of the residences. Wisps of smoke swirled in the air, and meager light escaped beneath tavern doors.

Two men exited the hotel. A bound, gagged, and hooded girl writhed in their arms. "Hold on to her," said one of the men, as he struggled to hold onto her legs. "They're will be hell to pay if she gets loose."

"I'm trying, but she's a wildcat," the other man replied.

Gunner drew his sword and rushed at them. The startled men dropped Dylan and drew their swords. Gunner lunged and drove his sword through the first man's heart. He grimaced and released his death cry. The other man ran for his life and disappeared into the shadows of a narrow alley. Gunner cut the girl's ropes and removed the gag. "Are you okay, Dylan?"

"I'm fine," she said and rose to her feet. "They grabbed me when I went past an alley. They were too fast for me."

"Help me," Gunner said and dragged the dead man by his feet.

"Is he dead?"

"I hope so," Gunner replied. She grabbed the corpse's arms and they dragged him to a storm drain. Gunner pushed the body through the narrow opening, and a splash came from the drain a second later. "We need to go back to tomorrow."

Dylan cocked her head and parted his lips to speak. A golden curtain shot up before them and extended to the horizon. Through the translucent curtain, they saw the opposite side of the street, well lit at noontime. He grabbed Dylan's hand and dragged her through the curtain.

When they emerged on the other side, Dylan sucked in a gasp of air. "What was that? What happened?" She spun around in a circle, dumbfounded by what she saw. An elderly woman waddled past her and viewed the girl with curiosity.

"Come on," he grabbed Dylan's hand and led her into the hotel. They rushed up the stairs and circled around the railing. The door opened and Linda emerged.

"Dylan, you found her. Bain said we would never find her." The other youths joined them in the hallway. Linda embraced Dylan, and Gunner gave her a brief account of their tale.

"Grab your gear," Gunner said. "We have to get out of town before they come after us."

Chapter 19

The proverb, "Better a friend that is near than a brother who is far away," was never truer than with Chadwick. He showed up on the outskirts of town with two wagons. After they had loaded onto the wagons, he and his wife carried the teens far from danger. When they traveled 30 miles, they approached the outskirts of Fort Defiant. Chadwick made his final farewells and returned home.

The sun leaned west on an endless sky, and the shadows of the Rocky Mountains reached out for the Black Mountains. Carved through the hills on a gentle slope, a dirt road greeted their eyes like an old friend. Wherever it led, they would follow. Pine trees on their left, a gradual slope on their right, clouds of dust risen from their feet, hills that rolled like waves on the sea, aching backs, sore feet, they trudged toward an uncertain destination.

Every step came a little harder than the one before it. The dirt road took a hairpin turn and traveled away from Fort Defiant, an eerie omen. They continued east and everyone's spirits soared. How long would it be until they encountered civilization? Perhaps a car or truck might give them a lift. Some technology had to survive the collapse. Rescue might be around the next bend.

After they passed the hairpin turn, they stumbled across some fallow ground, and Gunner agonized over Jake's fate. A dingy sign — faded by a thousand winters and summer, blistered and battered — read "Welcome to Fort Defiant." It stood high in the air next to the ruin that was Highway 24. Parallel lines of grassy mounds marked what had once provided four lanes of traffic; the rusted hulks of abandoned vehicles appeared like fossils from a bygone age, and only the concrete pillars of an overpass remained, vestiges of a civilization lost.

Across the river, they saw windowless office towers; towers that reminded one of the eyeless corpses, burnt, dingy, mottled gray, and rotted – a long dead forest of concrete and steel. Most of the residential buildings collapsed in upon themselves, now a home for birds and foxes. Rust turned the railroad bridge to an artist palate of orange and red hues, much of it now collapsed into the Misty River. Dead leaves and muck covered abandoned vehicles, and piles of debris stretched off to the horizon. Filth covered the windows; their rotted tires lay flat, and weeds grew upon them. They jammed the city streets as if abandoned during a calamity. Gunner traveled the world during his military career, and although he saw the ruins in Greece and Rome, he felt nothing but a vague sense of nihilism. Now it was his home, his world, and his hometown that lay in ruins.

Pain filled Gunner's heart, and his eyes became glassy. He brought a trembling hand to his face and wiped away a tear. Some of the youths dropped to their knees and wept. Linda refused to believe her eyes and demanded they see something different. Gunner parted his lips to speak, but no words departed.

Use me, the pendant whispered. His thoughts shifted to the Dragon's Eye Pendant hidden beneath his clothes. Its presence vanished from his mind like a dream upon waking. He touched it with his right hand and wished, "I want to save my son."

A golden translucent curtain rose up before them and shot up to the sky. The teens scrambled away from it, terrified. Mouths agape and eyes wide, they surveyed it in awe, their minds baffled. A translucent, curtain of light hung before them. It rippled with waves of energy and moved as if caught in some ethereal breeze.

When Gunner stepped toward the curtain, Linda said, "Be careful."

"We have to do something. I'm not losing Jake," Gunner said, his visage set like granite to the wind.

"Wait," Linda said. Her right hand thrust out to grab him, but it was too late. Golden light swept around him like a cloud, and he vanished. "Gunner," she said and took two steps toward the curtain.

The city was new and alive. The "Welcome Fort Defiant" letters were brilliant white and set on a field of blue. Stricken automobiles covered Highway 24; some burned; some were upon their side; some lay in piles, and everywhere the mutilated dead lay like scattered leaves upon the ground. Cows escaped an overturned trailer and grazed along the side of the road, glad for the midday meal. Someone made crude repairs the Coronado Bridge with lumber placed upon the concrete piers.

Fort Defiant burned. Pillars of black smoke rose up to the heavens, and explosions echoed in the dying city. A lone police cruiser sat in the center of an intersection. The mutilated corpse of a deputy lay on the ground next to an open car door, a rivulet of blood flowing from terrible wounds. A creature – more terrifying than any he had ever seen – lay upon the ground near him, a war club near its open hand. The two fought to the death, and they were not alone.

A terrified businessman staggered down the middle of the street, blood flowing from a wound on his head. He tripped over a dead body and fell to his knees. Mangled corpses littered the streets, and red blood splashed every stone. The man rose to his feet and called out, "Deborah, where are you?" No one replied.

Gunner recoiled and looked away from the carnage. He was a veteran and fought in many wars. The dead became as common as stones lying on the ground, but never, in all his years, had he seen such savagery.

Linda and the youth passed through the curtain. The look of wonder on their faces turned to grief. She covered her mouth and gasped at the slaughter. "What would do that?"

He turned to her and said, "We need to keep going."

It took her a few seconds to shake off the shock. "What ... what about those things? We should go back."

"Back to what, back to the Brotherhood in Sterling? There's nothing behind us but a strange world that wants to murder and enslave us." He caressed her cheek. "We need to find Jake, we need to save him."

Chapter 20

The sun blazed with merciless cruelty, which contradicted the month of October. The reek of death hung in the air and dead bodies abounded. Most lay where they fell, unwept and unburied. Gunner, Linda, and the teens trudged south on Lakeview Road.

"This is the youth group trip from hell," Dylan whined. "I'm tired and hungry. I want to go home."

"Let's take a break." Gunner nodded toward an old oak set upon a knoll. The lush, green grass bid them rest like a soft mattress. The teens collapsed onto the ground and fell fast asleep. He took Linda's hand and helped her up the hill. They sat next to the tree and leaned against the trunk. He put his arm around her and pulled her close. She laid her head on his shoulder and slipped into a deep slumber.

The deep blue waters of the Misty River skirted the road and followed a sharp bend. Sunlight reflected from a thousand watery mirrors, shimmering just for him. Weariness made his eyelids heavy, and he drifted off to sleep.

"LOOK!"

He snapped awake and scrambled to his feet. Michelle stood at the water's edge with an expression of horror on her face. Blood red water floated past her, and bodies floated in the creek. They spun around in circles as if performing some watery ballet, and they became hung up on the curve. Bodies — some human and some monsters — were entangled at the bend. They floated around the bend in the river and continued their journey south.

Gunner jogged down to the river and waded into it. He grabbed a man's body and turned him over. Gauged bloody flesh and vacant sockets made him scrambled backward. The dead body rolled onto face down again and floated away on its journey south. When he wiped his hands on his shirt, it left behind bloody smears.

"Who are they," asked Linda, standing on the shore, "and what at those things with them?" Then she remembered Kevin and Logan. She covered her mouth and grief filled her soul.

"People turned into daemia," he mumbled. When he turned around, he saw the youth group; they gaped in horror at the macabre scene and clung to one another. *I need to say something,* he thought. "It know it looks bad – " he paused; he was about to offer an empty platitude and trite advice, but he thought better of it. "I know

Page 163

you're afraid. So am I. If we stay together, we have a better chance of survival. After we find my son, we're going southwest to Denver. Rescue services are probably there and ready for us. If any of our families and friends survived, that is where we will find them."

Julie crossed her arms and began to tremble. She stared as if hypnotized. When he turned, he saw limbless bodies spinning in the swift current. Many were gutted, their organs eaten. He climbed out of the water and said, "We need to keep moving. I want to get away from here as soon as possible." When the youths failed to respond, he said, "Come on … move!"

They left the river behind and headed toward the suburbs. The trees in a small forest rustled; he swore he could see them grow. Several burnt out homes — shattered windows, smashed doors, and bloody smears upon white paint — filled him with dread. Bloody trails marked the drag paths where the attackers dragged the dead. They merged into a glistening red trail in the center of the road and traveled out of sight.

"That's Jake's street," Linda said. She released Gunner's hand and ran toward it. When she neared the corner, she stopped. He hurried to her side and joined her.

A crude patch of boards covered broken windows; burnt patches and soot stained the exterior; shingles and plywood littered the ground and exposed the house's wooden bones. The yard had a very large hole in it, dirt flung aside as if an animal dug it.

"Come on guys. We need to get going. We wasted half a day." Jake jogged out of the house and scrambled down the stairs. He was dressed in hiking gear and wore a backpack. Brian and Charlie followed him. Jake furrowed his brow and took two steps toward them. "DAD," he shouted.

He sprinted to his parents and threw his arms around them. "We thought you were dead." He wiped the tears from his eyes. "What happened? How did you get here?"

Gunner recounted a brief version of their trip, the Dragon's Eye Pendant, Sterling, and the nightmarish scene at the river. When Thor rounded the corner, Gunner's face went ashen. Now it was Gunner's turn to run. He ran to Thor, threw his arms around him, and the two huge men embraced. "You're dead. I was a pallbearer at your funeral." He grabbed Thor's upper arms and shook him. "Damn it, you're ALIVE!"

"I wish everyone would stop saying that. It's damaging my calm." He rubbed the tip of his nose and glanced at the assembled teens. "Jake told me all about it. I don't know what to say."

"I know what to say. The 'Sons of Thunder' are back together again," Gunner shouted.

"Alright, alright, keep it down. We're behind enemy lines. We haven't slept. I'm told that some people are holding up in old Fort Defiant. We have to get out of here before nightfall. This house won't take another night of combat." Thor glanced at the graves. "We lost three more people in last night's attack. It was relentless; they kept coming."

"Was it anyone I know?" asked Linda.

"We buried my friend Lane and four of my neighbors in a mass grave." Jake squatted down at the foot of a grave and picked up a handful of dirt. "The daemia dug up the bodies and stole them. I didn't know him very well. When I saw him on campus, I waved … I don't even know his last name. He was from back east, but I don't have a clue if he has a family."

Thor spoke in a low voice, "They always carry off the bodies." Thor told Gunner of the daemia and the attacks. When he looked up at the sky, he said. "We managed to get a diesel pickup truck working. I had to shield the hell out of the electrical system." He picked up a black rock from the dirt and threw it at a stop sign. When the rock hit the sign, it exploded and disintegrated the sign. The old fort is 36 miles from here, and most of the streets are blocked. We have to make it by sunset."

Chapter 21

Sunset plunged the world into shadow, and the Fort Defiant rose like a lone warrior, its bulwarks set against the growing darkness. The engine roared as they rushed toward the eastern gate. A guard on sentry duty atop the wall called out, "survivors approaching the western gate."

Gunner rubbed the sweat and fatigue from his face. Deep thumps and scrapes came from two massive wooden doors. When the right door swung open, the defenders, men and women clad in crude plate armor and brandishing even cruder weapons, stood in the gap. They poised their weapons, ready to strike. An elderly man pushed through them. He wore old army fatigues, a faded memory of youth and service to his country.

"We are exhausted," Gunner said. "We need to get these children inside before the daemia attack."

"Tom Collins, like the drink," the man said and extended his hand. Thor reached through the window and shook his hand. "You're a big pair, aren't you? We could use your help. The fortress is large, and there are too few of us to defend her."

"We will do what we can," Thor said. The old man nodded and signaled the guards to move aside. The truck cruised into the fortress and cruised to a stop near a grassy patch of earth. The spent teens piled out of the truck and collapsed. Most fell asleep in seconds, backpacks used as pillows.

Gunner and Thor walked with Tom through the camp. Grimy faces looked upon them with weary eyes and then returned to staring at a campfire. A ragtag assembly of tents and tarps replaced home and hearth, and a society of plenty now knew hunger. A few of the defenders watched them pass, hope for news of rescue. "We've done our best, but events overtook us like a storm." He glanced at the truck. "Twice we got trucks working, but they were no more outside the gate when the electrical system shorted. How'd you manage it?"

"We pulled the electrical system and rebuilt it inside a Faraday cage," Thor said and opened the hood. "A copper cage is tied to the truck body." He pointed at a crude box made of copper wires. "It protects the electrical components from the electron wave produced by radio frequency. That is what keeps shorting them out. It also keeps the radio from working; all we get is static." He patted the fender. "Those damn black rocks don't bother her a bit now."

"Rhunite," Gunner said, as if it was common knowledge, "those rocks are called rhunite." Thor nodded his head in agreement.

George raised his trouble light, illuminating his grease-smeared face and scraggly red beard. He cocked his head and studied Gunner's ears. "What the hell are you?"

"I'm bone weary and angry. Button this thing up. We're going to make a run to town," Gunner said.

"It's getting darker by the second," Tom said.

Gunner studied the people around him. "These people are on the verge of defeat. They need food, blankets, and weapons. We can't wait until morning. I'll lead a raiding party."

Tom rubbed his chin and nodded. "Okay, you take some troops with you and make a run. We need to mount the walls. The night is nearly on us."

"Thor, you stay here and keep our families safe," Gunner said. Thor nodded and drew his machete, resting it on his shoulder. "Okay, I need six volunteers for a raiding party."

"I'll hook up the trailer." George, Tom's assistant, said. He and two other men rolled a rectangular trailer behind the truck. "I used this for my lawn mowing business."

Gunner climbed into the driver's seat and started the engine. The diesel motor roared with a noisy clatter. Linda approached the truck, and he lowered the window. "Couldn't someone else go?"

"We need supplies," Gunner said. "It can't wait."

She caressed the back of his neck and kissed him. "Come back to me." She stepped away from the truck and crossed her arms. Five men climbed into the back and a sixth sat in the passenger's seat.

"Bradley Cooper," a teenage young man said. Gunner shook his hand. "Where are we off too?"

"We need supplies."

Bradley rubbed his chin and twitched his nose. "There's a strip mall not too far from here. It's got a grocery store and a hardware store." Guards opened the gate as they cruised toward it. Weary eyes watched them pass, and prayers bid them success.

Gunner pressed on the accelerator. Burnt out automobile hulks were scattered about visitor parking. The charred ruins of the ranger station lay in the center. He cruised through the lot and made a right turn on Simms Road. The wind rushed through the open windows and cooled them. Just driving in a real truck again filled Bradley with hope and made his spirit soar.

When they reached a gun shop and shooting range, Bradley said, "Man, I sure would like to hold a shotgun or rifle again. We'd show those … what did you call them?"

"Daemia."

"Right, we'd show that daemia what killing really means." Bradley sighed. "But I suppose that's a thing of the past."

Mere minutes later, they completed the 12-mile journey. The shopping mall appeared like a dark specter, a symbol of their former life. He made a right turn and weaved around abandoned cars. Mutilated corpses littered the ground. A crow stood atop a man's corpse and pecked at his eyes.

They cruised to the grocery store and up to the front doors. He pressed the front bumper against the sliding glass doors and pushed through them. When he backed away, he put the truck in "park" but left it running.

"Three of you gather supplies. Skip the meat and produce. We need canned goods and bottled water. Move fast, I want to get in and out before we're discovered." They jumped off the truck and ran into the store. "You come with me."

When they neared the hardware store, they saw smashed doors, and a dead man lay face down on broken glass, three arrows jutting from his back. "We need weapons."

They ran to the garden section and dumped machetes, axes, meat handling claws, and knives into carts. "Dump these in the truck and then meet me in the sporting goods sections."

"Got it," Bradley said. He and Virginia scrambled away with their supplies. They raced through the open door and back to the truck.

Gunner jogged toward the back of the store. His Elven eyes adjusted to the dark and the monochrome world illumined before him. A daemia stepped out from the plumbing aisle. A crown of ten horns ringed his knobby head, and his face was a nightmare of spider eyes and jagged teeth. The brawny creature raised a wooden baseball bat. Bits of hair, blood and brains coated the spikes at the tip. A serpent's tongue shot out of its mouth and tasted the air. It spat a glob of poison at Gunner, but he dodged it at the last second. The poison splattered a tile display and oozed toward the floor.

Gunner crouched in a combat position. He clutched his machete in his right hand and a hunting knife in his left. "Come on, you ugly bastard. I want some payback."

The daemia roared and rushed at him. It brought down its bat in a crushing blow, but Gunner deflected it. He spun to the left and chopped his blade at the daemia's neck. The daemia jumped and rolled. It recovered and readied itself for another attack. Its forked tongue flicked in the air. It swung the bat at Gunner's head, but Gunner ducked out of the way. The spikes struck a metal shelf and sent sparks flying. Gunner slashed and drew black blood from the daemia's chest. This sent the daemia into a frenzy. When it grappled with Gunner, its putrid breath stung his nostrils; its beady eyes and bared teeth were inches from Gunner's face. Gunner kicked the daemia in the groin and swung his right elbow, striking the daemia's head.

The daemia staggered, and Gunner pressed the attack. Blow after blow rained down upon the daemia's back. The savage force brought the daemia to its knees. The machete cut the bat in half and chopped into the daemia's skull, but it still lived. Gunner stabbed his knife through one of the daemia's eyes and twisted. The daemia fell to the ground, and as it died, it whispered, "Thank you."

Bradley and Virginia sprinted up to him. "We heard the noise." They looked on the daemia with revulsion. Gunner stared at the dead creature, stricken by the revelation. This creature, this monster had once been a man. "We need to go," Bradley said. He patted Gunner on the back and said, "That was a good kill."

Gunner retrieved his weapons and trudged after the other two. He stood in the middle of the sporting goods department and surveyed the items. The others filled several carts with bows, arrows, baseball bats, and golf clubs. However, he spotted swords in a display case. He smashed the locked display case and broke into the cabinet. He emptied all of the weapons into a cart and selected a broad sword. He drew the weapon from the sheath and extended the gleaming silver weapon. Its razor sharp edge seemed to split the light, and it felt like an extension of his arm. He strapped it and its twin to his back. Then he strapped on a pair of curved hunting knives with Elkhorn handles.

They were about to leave when he saw something out of the corner of his eye: a pair of long-necked warhammers, having a metal shaft, solid steel heads, a square face, and reverse spikes. It was a mean looking weapon, beyond the ability of most men to wield. They would struggle to lift it and if swung, it would jerk the man about. However, he knew just the right person to wield them. He placed them into the cart, and they fled the store. It was imperative that they return before it was too late.

Chapter 22

Flaming arrows streaked through the pitch black, starless sky. They rained down upon the old fort, but they bounced off the granite structure. Bonfires lit up the night and teams of daemia rushed the walls with ladders. The largest daemia Gunner had ever seen stood upon a small hill and roared orders to his warriors.

Gunner stomped the accelerator, and the engine roared. The truck surged forward and moved faster by the second. "The gates will be barred. We have to turn back before it's too late," Bradley said. "We won't get through."

"Everyone I love is inside there. We aren't turning back. Jump out if you want." The truck, however, was already up at 90 mph. Daemia turned as the truck slammed into them, hurtling them through the air, tumbling in wild cartwheels. Body after body bounced off the truck and flew away. "OPEN THE GATE," Gunner shouted and clenched the steering wheel.

Bradley raised his arms and screamed. The gates swung open wide, and the truck flew through. The gates slammed shut behind them, and the bolt snapped shut. The truck slid to a stop, spraying rocks, and the trailer jackknifed. When Gunner opened the door, he saw Thor striding up to him, and he wore steel armor with a bronze hue. "It's about time you got here. There's killing to do."

"Where'd you get the armor? You raid a museum?" asked Gunner.

"Actually, yes." Thor patted the interlaced bands of the breastplate and tugged on the gauntlets and chainmail sleeves. "They had an old arms and armaments museum in the fortress. It was supposed to attract tourists. I found this in the fantasy section. I figured: I'm an elve now, so what the hell. I saved you a seat." He tossed Gunner a blue duffel bag. "Here's yours."

As the others tossed weapons to defenders, Gunner said, "That set is for Thor." He handed Thor the warhammers. "I thought you would enjoy these." When Thor raised his hammers, a lightning bolt split the night and thunder rolled over the black skies. Gunner shook his head and laughed. "I bet you can't do that again."

Thor grinned. "Not everyone can come back from the dead and face a horde of angry daemia." He swung the hammers and said, "These are great." In his hands, they appeared light as fishing poles. "They have a good feel."

When Gunner jerked the armor from the bag, he saw a set similar to Thor's and started stripping off his clothes. Charlie and Jake rushed over to them. Both Jake and Charlie wore knee high boots, brown leather tights, brown scale-chainmail tunics, and green leather jackets. Charlie said, "Don't we look great?"

"You look amazing sweetheart, but who is defending the fort?" asked Gunner.

"We are, but the daemia come in waves," she said. "It's like the tide coming in and going out."

"They keep trying to breach our walls. They used wooden ladders last time, but we set them on fire." Thor wiped the sheen of sweat from his face and leaned close. "They're not stupid. I can see them reasoning out a way to break into the fort, and time is on their side."

Gunner strapped his armor over his thick leather clothing. Families huddled in fear around their tents, hoping someone else would fight on the walls. He sniffed and scratched his nose. "We would never make it out here with all these people in tow, and we don't know what is waiting for us. It might be like this all over."

"Charlie and I were talking," Jake said. "We could go for help. We move really fast, and we could let the military know what's happening."

"You two go back to the wall," Thor said. "Gunner and I need to talk." After they had departed, he said, "More of the daemia show up all the time. It's like someone or something is driving them south. Food is running short, and they only eat meat. If we don't get help, they are going to take the fort." A trumpet blast summoned them to the wall: they were under attack.

Chapter 23

Thor and Gunner sprinted up the stairs and stood at the wall. The deep thrum of drums shattered the silence, and the yellow blaze of bonfires lit up the field and tree line. The drums grew louder by the second. "There," shouted Jake. Siege ramps — crude sheltered towers constructed on flattened cars — passed through the forest on the dirt access road. "I count six."

Gunner turned. Bathed in shadow and firelight, he saw the look of terror on everyone's face. He searched for some solution. Then he spotted the truck. He asked Tom Collins, "You said that you made a few Molotov cocktails. Do you have any left?" Tom stared at the ramps in horror, unable to answer. He shook Tom and asked, "Do you have any?"

"Yes, lots," Tom said.

"Jake, you're with me. Thor, Brian, and Bain, you organize the defenders." Charlie, Bain, and Reggie followed Gunner and Jake down the wall. "I need all of those incendiaries in the back of the truck. We're going to take the fight to them."

"What," asked Charlie. "That's insane."

"It's called an active defense, and I don't have time to explain." He put his right hand on his son's shoulder and said, "I need you to drive." Jake nodded and climbed into the truck. "Bain, open the gate for us, but wait until the last possible second; then slam it shut behind us." Bradley, Louis, and Gunner climbed into the back. When Charlie and Virginia started to climb in, Gunner held up his hand and said, "We got this. Help them defend the wall."

The girls looked at one another, and Charlie said, "We're coming." They climbed past him and readied their bows. Charlie pounded the roof. "Get going." Jake gunned the engine and sprayed dirt from the back tires. They sped toward the gate and at the last second, the guards opened it. They raced through the gap, and crashed into four daemia, sending them hurtling, breaking their bodies.

Jake made a sharp right turn, and the rear end of the truck whipped around, and slapped a daemia clutching a spear. The jolt threw them against the truck bed. When Charlie climbed out of the pile, she locked eyes with Louis and then saw a spear jutting from his chest. Blood coated the spear tip and dripped from the sharp point. When he tried to speak, blood flowed from his lips and bubbles formed. He slumped forward and died in her arms.

The truck tires slammed into potholes and then launched into the air. A daemia pointed a spear at them and shrieked in some strange tongue. They flew toward the siege ramp. Charlie and Virginia used lighters and ignited the Molotov cocktails. As Jake swept by the first ramp, Gunner and Bradley hurtled four incendiaries at it. The glass bottle shattered; gasoline sprayed and ignited; Daemia leaped off the burning ramp.

They raced down the side of the dirt access road. Gas bombs flew from their hands. Daemia raced about on fire, slapping at the flames, and the first three ramps burned, lighting the forest on ablaze, blocking the road. The last two ramps were intact. Jake spun the truck around and stomped on the gas. The enraged daemia notched arrows and let them fly.

Charlie screamed and ducked. The arrows pelted the truck and made tiny thumps as they bounced off it. When she looked up, Virginia had three arrows embedded in her chest. She gazed up at the stars and whispered something. A second later, Virginia slumped over onto Louis' body; her head tilted back, eyes open, and still gazing at stars. Tears flowed down Charlie's cheeks.

"HOLD ON," Jake shouted. It was too late. Bradley's eyes went wide. They ran down three daemia and launched over a ridge. The truck and its passengers flew into the air.

Bradley did a somersault and hit the ground. Charlie grabbed the rear tailgate and screamed. When Bradley struggled to his feet, six daemia tackled him like a defensive lineman. They slammed him to the ground, stabbed, and ripped him apart.

Gunner shook Charlie by the shoulders and shouted, "Find the lighter!" Blood sloshed back and forth in the truck bed as she searched. When she found it and lit it, the light exposed the truth: blood covered her. Her hands trembled and the flame flickered. Gunner lit gas bombs and hurled them at the two remaining ramps. They too burned.

Jake raced up the opposite side of the road. Flames burned the left side the truck, and daemia ran into the headlights. Too late to avoid them, he ran them over or sent them flying. A second after Gunner threw the last two bombs, the truck glanced off a tree and the fender slashed the tire. Jake kept the pedal pressed to the floor, launching fragments of the tire. Soon they were down to the rim, but they charged up the hill toward the fortress.

The daemia by the Fort blocked the road with felled trees. Jake smashed through the leaves and branches; fragmented branches stabbed the engine, mortally wounding it. The truck bounced and slid sideways.

Gunner grabbed Charlie and scrambled out of the back. Drawn by the scent of blood and flesh, daemia piled into the back and feasted on the bodies. The others chased after Jake, Gunner, and Charlie, but the feasting roars caused them to turn around; and they joined in the revelry.

Drawing their blades, Jake and Gunner fought their way to the gate. When they killed a daemia, the others would rip it apart, devouring their comrade. Their blades flew in wild, chaotic chops and slashes. The gate opened with a loud bang. Brian and Bain led the charge. They drove back the attackers, and Gunner, Jake, and Charlie sped past them. They returned to the fort, secured the door, and slammed the bolt shut.

When they were inside the fortress, a volley of flaming arrows lit up the night sky, killing or igniting several defenders. Numb, Charlie saw something peculiar. The firelight illumined a sign screwed to the inside archway of the gate. It read, "Weapons play is strictly prohibited. Report any violations to a park ranger. Enjoy a safe visit." Amid the screams and shouts of battle, she covered her mouth and laughed herself to tears.

Hours later, war drums pounded like distant thunder from the western road. A flaming arrow shot past Gunner's head. His Elven eyes cut through the night and beheld an army. These daemia were different. The humans that transformed into daemia still wore the tattered rags of human clothes, but leather and plate armor covered these new daemia. They brandished fearsome weapons, and their roars filled the darkness with hate.

"What is it?" asked Bain.

"More siege ramps," he shouted, "everyone to the western wall." When he grabbed Tom Collin's shoulder, the man fell over backward. An arrow jutted from the front of his forehead and a trickle of blood flowed from the wound. The bodies of the dead and dying lay all about him: young and old, men and women, human and daemia lay entangled, as if asleep.

Defenders scrambled up the stairs and searched the darkness for their enemy. When the siege ramps entered the light of the many bonfires, their faces turned ashen. Three stories tall, car hoods for protective plate, siege towers rode atop abandoned trucks. Telephone poles served as poles to push the ramps forward.

"What's that?" shouted Reggie. The others without Elven eyes squinted to see. Real trolls – their bodies made of stone and limbs more powerful than ten men – pushed the poles, and their master's whips cracked on their backs. Four of these ramps emerged from the night.

A few of the girls wept, and several of the boys stared with empty eyes. The dead lay entangled at Gunner's feet, and when he met Thor's eyes, they shared a moment of unspoken truth: they would never survive the night. The look of defeat was in their eyes

Five more pickup trucks lay in the center of the compound. Teams of mechanics labored to shield their electronics, but it would take then another 8 hours to complete. From somewhere in the darkness, a man played "Nearer my God to Thee" on his violin, and people clung to each other and whispered a final goodbye. Gunner lifted his eyes toward the heavens and whispered a prayer, "Lord, save us."

Lightning rent the heavens and God's thunder rolled over the land. A curtain of water dumped from black skies. The deluge extinguished the bonfires and washed over the ground like a river. Pools formed outside the fort and soaked into the bare earth. The drums defied the torrent, and the rock trolls pushed their heavy load. The tires, however, began sinking into the mud and soon the crushed cars sank up to the frame. Whips cracked, and the drivers shouted obscenities. The trolls heaved, but the towers were too heavy. The commanding daemia stood upon a boulder and roared in rage.

Gunner and Linda held each other, and Jake joined them. The violinist played a jig, and they danced and splashed in the puddles. Shouts of victory echoed across the camp. Afterward, Gunner closed his eyes, leaned upon the wall, and offered a simple prayer of thanks.

Chapter 24

The morning sun broke over the horizon like an avenging angel. Its golden beams chased the daemia into hiding, and even the few selected for sentry duty fled the light. The siege ramps sank deep in the mud far from the walls. After a night of the combat, they were exhausted, but everyone welcomed the sun and let it beam upon their faces. In the midst of their revelry, another sun appeared in the sky. It hovered above the new "Black Mountains" and burned with white-hot light. The earth shook; the ground ripped; the fortress toppled; massive stone blocks spilled, and screams ripped from their lips.

Jake found himself lying face down upon the open ground. He struggled to his feet and wiped the dirt from his face. The fortress lay in a heap behind him. Its defensive walls reduced to chaotic piles of rectangular stone. Whimpers and cries of distress urged him to action. He scrambled over the debris and pulled Charlie from a pile of rubble. Gray dust covered her, and a trickle of red blood rolled down her cheek from a cut on her head.

Bain and Brian bounded over the stones and rescued people from the rubble, but there were few survivors.

Gunner and Thor lifted a massive block off of a man, and he cried out in agony. They tossed aside the block, and it hit with a thump, raising a cloud of dust. Linda rushed to aid the stricken man, a stranger, but the rock crushed his chest. He struggled to breathe, but bloody froth came from his lips. Despite Linda's best efforts, the man passed out and died in her arms. Tears cut a track down her cheeks.

Thor surveyed the catastrophe. "Damn kids, can't leave them alone for a minute. You can't leave them alone for a minute." A laugh burst from Linda's lips, and she gave him a hug.

"It's good to have you back," Gunner said with a grin. He brushed off the dust and grabbed his backpack. "Everybody get up. We have to get going. I want as many miles as possible between us and this place by nightfall." Others already had the idea, they trudged out of the fortress and scattered in every direction. "Gather what is left of our group."

Later, they assembled in the courtyard. Toni and most of the youth were missing — killed, captured, or dispersed. Only Linda, Gunner, and Bain remained from the group that set out from Gleason. Gunner's soul ached as he remembered the faces of those who set out that morning.

How would he ever face their parents? He whispered to her, "Is there no one?"

She lowered her gaze and shook her head. "We lost six last night in the battle and two in the earthquake. When I was on the wall, I saw Tommy, Brooke, and Bruce off in the distance. They were heading north to Fort Defiant. When I called out to them, they looked at me but kept going."

Gunner rubbed his face. With his hands on his hips, he pondered what to do. It was a torturous decision: to save his family or go looking for the youths. Thor put his hand on Gunner's shoulder. "They have a right to look for their families. It is what we would do in their situation. If they come with us, they are certain to never see them again."

"They're just children," Gunner said.

"There are no more children. Everyone has to grow up fast." He picked up his pack. "Are there any working vehicles?"

"Nope," Gunner said.

"Then we walk," Thor said. He rubbed Gunner's back. "I'm here now. You don't have to bear the burden alone." Gunner nodded and gathered his belongings. They decided to wear their armor since it was the easiest way to carry it and one never knew when an attack might happen. "LET'S GO!" Thor shouted with a wave of his hand.

They climbed over the rubble that used to be the wall. Gunner scanned the tree line to the north, hoping to see the youths return. However, only the corpses of the dead remained. Bodies beyond count lay upon the field: dismembered, burnt, lethal wounds gouged into their flesh. They weaved around the dead daemia; their ugliness caused grimaces and nausea.

"Look, it's Virginia," said Reggie. The girl's body lay next to the burnt out hulk of the truck. "We should bury her."

"No time," Thor said and tugged on his daughter's hand. "We need every scrap of daylight to get away from here. Her soul has returned to God: the body is just a shell."

After they had passed through the field, they neared the burnt out hulks of the siege ramps. They still smoldered, and the heat kept them on the edge of the road. They looked for Bradley's body, but all that remained was a bloody stain upon the dried field. As they walked, Charlie asked, "So where are we going?"

"Denver," Thor said, "and from there on to a new life, perhaps in the Rockies."

"We have to build a new home," Gunner said. "And this time, we will be living in the same place. The days are over when families lived apart." This revelation disturbed Jake. The many years of his education prepared him for a life that was gone, vanished when the Black Mountains appeared.

Chapter 25

Midday found them at the edge of the unknown, far south of Fort Defiant. Baked by the sun, sweat and dust caked upon them, and eyes cast up to the heavens, they stood before the curtain of light. It danced across the sky like the Aurora Borealis and rippled like a golden curtain of light. "… So you say we just walk through it?" asked Thor.

Gunner removed his hand from the amulet. "That's what we did last time. I asked it to transport into the future. I figure all this upheaval and war business will be over and life will be back to normal. Once you cross through it, you will be in the new time-period, and then the curtain vanishes." He looked to his left and right. The curtain extended beyond his sight and seemed to form a giant circle around Fort Defiant.

Hood up, engine exposed, doors wide open, Jake and the others rested inside a broken sedan. The electrical system stunk of chemical char, but the bucket seats were comfortable. He adjusted the rearview mirror and saw Charlie in the back seat. "How much do you think the owner paid for this?"

"$45,000 or $50,000," Charlie replied.

"You think he'll come back for it?"

"I would," Reggie said. "I had to work 40 hours a week as a waitress just to pay my living expenses." Brian grunted his agreement and threw pebbles at a concrete barrier; it kept motorists from colliding with a road repair project. "This is a really nice car. Maybe we could spend the night."

"Break time is over," Gunner said and leaned into the car. "Did you search the trunk to see if there was anything useful?"

"Just a collapsible shovel and two suitcases," Bain replied. "There was girls' stuff in the suitcases."

"Bring them; there might be something your mother and the girls can use." After they had exited the car, he said, "Weapons," he said drawing his sword, and the others joined him in the middle of the road. "It's pitch black on the other side. I hope that means it's nighttime. I'll go first, and if it's safe, the rest of you join me. I won't be able to see you once I pass through the curtain."

Gunner held his breath and stepped through the veil. He floated in a sea of golden light and burst forth from the other side as if stepping from a golden waterfall. He drew in a deep gasp, and his eyes soon adjusted to the darkness. A swath of stars twinkled in the black of night, and off in the distance to his left, he saw a light beam through rectangular windows. A sleepy town lay in the valley amid the rolling hills. A cool breeze carried a faint hint of smoke and a hint of cooking food, which made his stomach grumble.

After he had signaled, the others emerged. He pointed and said, "There's a town. We need to stop there and get supplies."

"How can it just go from day to night," Charlie yawned. "It doesn't make any sense."

"The pavement is gone," Jake said, squatting and feeling the ground. The stars provided plenty of light, and he scooped up a handful of soil and weeds. The asphalt was nothing but microscopic black specs in the cool brown soil. He stood upright and brushed off the dust. Looking up the hill, he noticed something peculiar and walked through waist-high weeds. A rectangle of rust marked the spot once occupied by a car, and the concrete barriers disintegrated to dust. "How long does it take for a car and concrete to decompose?"

"Two thousand years, perhaps more," Gunner said. "Many of the Roman structures were made of concrete, and they still stand over 2000 years later. Maybe it's 3000 years." He scanned up and down the road. "It appears that wagons have worn ruts into the road."

"I want to follow the road into town, and see if we can get some sort of lodging." They followed Gunner down the sloped road. It curved along the side of the hill. Gunner kept a watchful eye on the grassy slope of the hill and the tree line of the forest. It would be easy for an enemy to assume the higher ground and attack from the cover of the forest.

The road became level and passed through a small patch of evergreens. It carried them toward the town at the bottom of the valley. The sound of music and voices soothed their fears. The road approached two homes and passed between them. Designed with ancient and reliable materials – fieldstone for the foundation, wood to frame it, mud and daub walls, thatched roofs, and primitive glass for the windows – the homes appeared warm and inviting. When they passed between them, firelight silhouetted them in black. A well lay in the center of town, and braziers filled with orange flame made the center circle glow with soft light. The town's people wandered around tables that were laden with food. The women wore dresses down to their ankles, peasant blouses, and kerchiefs in their hair; the men wore brown trousers, tan cotton shirts, and dark vests. Red, blue, and orange decorations hung from twine strung between buildings.

Gunner and Thor reached entered the town's center first. Being very tall, muscular, and clad in armor, they caused an immediate gasp from the townsfolk. The music ceased, and mothers grabbed their children. Brian and Bain circled around them, bearing warhammers and axes. Jake and Charlie appeared next, arrows slotted on ready bows.

"Want to get out of the way," Toni shouted. When Thor and Gunner moved aside, Linda and Toni entered the center of town. "So, we're having a party. What's the occasion?"

A gray-bearded man emerged from the crowd and approached them. "I am Mayor Karl Simms. You honor us with your presence. Your two great peoples are welcome to our harvest celebration. Please, feel free to partake in our bounty."

"Um ... thank you," Linda said. "This is a festival?"

"Yes. We celebrate the end of harvest every fall." He waved to his wife, Marta and his daughter, Clara. A slender woman, long past the flower of youth but with kind eyes, moved to his side. A young woman, the image of her mother, lingered behind them. Marta held out a tray filled with cheeses, meats, and bread. "Please, sample our wares."

Linda picked up a wedge of stinky cheese, and despite the offensive smell, she ate it. It tasted better than it smelled, and she picked out another. "Come on," she said between bites. Gunner sheathed his sword and moved to her side. The rest followed behind him. The young women gathered around Jake and looked upon him with doe-eyed desire. However, the serving girls passed by Brian and Bain as though they were potted plants. At the mayor's signal, the music resumed, and the din of conversations resumed.

"Your entry took us by surprise. We sent invitations, but we did not think you would attend," Karl said. "It is an honor."

"Our people?" asked Linda.

"The elves," Karl said and noting Brain and Bain, "and your people also." Two serving girls handed Gunner and Thor a pair of goblets filled with ale. "It's been fifty years since elves visited Crow Valley. Are you here on a social visit, or do you have some commerce in mind. I do not wish to pry, but as mayor, it is my task to know such things."

"We're travelers from Fort Defiant," Gunner said.

"Fort Defiant?" echoed Karl. "That name is not familiar to me."

"You remember," Marta said, "the ancient ruins to the north."

"Oh yes, the ancient fortress," he said. "I visited it once as a boy. I loved climbing upon the toppled blocks and pretended I was in a fierce battle. Now that I am old, I wish to avoid such dire circumstance. I prefer peace and a warm embrace. You say that you came from there?"

"What happened to the town ... the one near the fort?" asked Linda.

"Town? No. There is no town, just the ancient ruins. Every year a team of archeologists from Denver travel northeast to our village and rent cottages. They travel to the ruins by day, conduct surveys, and dig for artifacts. The King of Colorado, Edward Mountbatten III, has a great interest in such places. It brings welcome coins into the town's coffers. You have some interest digging in the ancient ruins?"

"No," Jake said and then swallowed a bit of cheese. "I used to live there."

"Live ... in the ruins?" asked Karl. "You jest with me."

"Nope, I really lived there ... um, before ... before the town was destroyed," he said. "But it looks like that was a long time ago."

"That was in the last age, 'The Age of Man,' over 3000 years ago. It cannot be." He stroked his beard and searched for some hint of Jake's age in his youthful features. "You lived in the Gold Age? I heard elves were long lived, but I had no idea." He shook his head and said, "I cannot conceive of living for so long."

A young woman, Naomi, stepped out of the crowd. "What was it like? I've heard our ancestors had endless parties and traveled in magical carriages. It must have been wonderful before the daemia and haugr arrived. They spoil everything."

"You smell like you've been fighting them," Carson, a young man, said and cast a sideways glance at Jake. "Your clothes are ripped, and you're covered in their blood. It's a strange way to dress for a party."

"Don't be rude," Marta said. "They are our guests."

"Perhaps our guest would like a celebratory bath." Carson refilled his mug from a keg. All the young men gathered around him, and Jake perceived that Carson was the alpha male, used to being the center of attention.

"A bath and change of clothes would be nice," Linda said. "We are so tired."

The great hall lay at the center of town, across from the fountain. It sat upon a small hill, two stories tall, proud, dominant, ruling over the village; its timbers were the size of trees with carved magical symbols, and it upheld a thatched roof. The mayor led his guests to it in a grand procession. The men occupied a bunkhouse in the southern dormitory, and the women occupied two small rooms attached to it.

"Here we go," Marta said. She and the other women carried in armfuls of clothes. "A while ago, a group of elves stopped in our village. They were moving west to the Elven homeland in the Rockies. Anyway, when several of their horses went lame, they had to abandon some of their belongings. It seems only right you should inherit them. We also have some donated dwarven clothes. We could not wear such small, odd clothes." Both Brian and Bain grimaced at the last comment.

The men's clothes were simple and elegant: elastic brown trousers, ecru linen tunics, wide leather belts, green jackets that reached to the knees, and leather gauntlets. "We've provided basins of water, towels, and soap in the bathroom. Let me know if there is anything else you need," Marta said. After she had visited with the ladies, she exited the room.

Jake stripped off his soiled clothes and wrapped a towel around his waist. He soaked a cloth and lathered it with soap. As he washed, he said, "I was hoping for a hot shower. I'd settle for a bath, but I guess that's a thing of the past."

"I was hoping to see over the countertop." Brian set the white basin of water on the floor and washed. Bain tried to shave off his beard, but it was too dense. Jake gave them a glance and smirked. He hardly recognized his friends: they were true dwarves, barrel chested and brawny.

Jake picked up a pair of leather tights and sat on a wooden bench. He inspected the bathroom. Wood defined the room, the building, and the people. They made art from it, sat on it, and ate it. Despite the many centuries, the facility appeared well maintained and attractive. "I really just want to sleep," he said to his father. "I am exhausted."

"So am I, but we need to socialize. They are our hosts, and we need their help." Gunner stomped his foot and slid it into a boot. "Just socialize for a while and then we will get some rest. "Besides, you might meet someone nice."

"I had someone nice, and she vanished," Jake said.

Gunner patted his son's shoulder. "I'm sorry. I know how much you cared for her, but she's gone. I'm sure she lived a good life."

Jake stiffened and furrowed his brow. It never occurred to him that she was dead. Their travel through time was so abrupt. It was as though she was somewhere far away waiting for him. "Are we really never going to age?"

"That's what everyone keeps saying," Thor said. He tucked in his tunic. "I wish this thing had buttons."

"Not in your size," Jake replied. When a knock came from the door, he said, "Come in." The door opened and the festival din spilled into the room.

"You all look so wonderful," Linda said.

"Thank you for the clothes," Charlie scurried into the bathroom and twirled. "What do you think? I feel like a princess." The long blue gown, made of chiffon and satin, combined with her red locks, and pointed ears made her appear mythical. She looked to her right, cocked her head, and searched the other room. Charlie reached in and grabbed Reggie's wrist.

"No, no, I can't." Reggie struggled a little and then shuffle stepped into view. A pair of stretch, black leather tights cleaved to her like a second skin and a pair of knee-high boots delighted the eyes of men. Likewise, a black vest-corset with a sweetheart neckline and stone boning that emphasized her curves, and a white satin blouse, gleaned from the suitcase, focused the eye on her considerable breasts. "What do you think?"

"You look amazing," Brian said.

"Wow," Bain added.

Reggie primped her long, black locks. Her beauty mesmerized Jake. "You're an amazing elva (a female elve – a term Jake used without thinking)." He put his hand around her waist and escorted her to the great hall. "Smile, you're going on stage for your first performance." Reggie smiled and drew in a deep breath. Jake opened the door. Applause thundered as she entered the great hall. She gave her best parade wave and entered the main floor. All of the men swarmed her and asked her to dance.

"Um ... well ... I'm not sure –" Reggie started to say, but Carson pulled her into his arms and began to dance. Charlie watched with amusement. As the pair swept across the room, Reggie learned the steps and moved with an easy grace. Another man asked Charlie to dance, and Jake asked one of the girls. Even Brian and Bain found dance partners. The music played; the ale flowed; the young people danced, and Gunner and Thor devoured the refreshments. Only Linda paused to marvel at the turn of events and wonder what a new day might hold.

Chapter 26

Elves are a special breed, sleeping little, if at all, able to go months without rest. Like a shark, they shut down parts of the brain and sleep in stages. After a mere three hours, Jake awoke, refreshed and ready for the day. Brian and Bain, however, snored like grizzly bears, so loud they shook the walls. He climbed down from his bunk bed and carried his clothes into the bathroom. After dressing, he slipped out into the main hall. Gunner, Thor, and Linda were already awake and sipping coffee.

An obese man moved like a parade balloon, clad in a brown wool robe, much like a Franciscan Friar. A ring of red hair trimmed the top of his bald head, and a pair of black, horn-rimmed glass hung from the tip of his button nose. The cherubic man filled his plate with breakfast items. When he felt the weight of Jake's stare, he gave him a quick look, twitched his nose, and returned to the scrambled eggs.

When Jake approached the broad oak table, Karl said, "Master Jake, I would like to introduce you to Brother Henry."

"He's a priest?" asked a Jake.

"Oh … um, no. He's a wizard," Karl said and cocked his head.

"A common mistake," Henry said, "wizards lack the piety of a priest, but we have a monastic devotion to our craft."

A gaunt old man, with a pinched face, seated at the other end of the table, glared at Henry and brooded over his empty plate. He cleared his throat and tapped his plate with a fork. If Henry understood the man's objection, he ignored it and piled his plate high. Henry said, "Fill your belly, young elvan. We have a long trip ahead of us."

"We do?" asked Jake.

"Your father asked Brother Henry if he would guide us. He and Thor want to try and find work in one of the Elven cities," Linda said.

"Yes, work is always easier to find in the city of your people," Henry said. Charlie shuffled out, still wearing her bedclothes. She yawned and poured a cup of coffee. Cradling it between her hands, she let the wisps of steam curl about her cheeks. When Henry eyed the sleepy elva, he furrowed his brow and pouted with his chubby cheeks. "I'd like to get an early start. The weather is turning, and I want to beat the early snow."

Brother Henry gulped down his food and returned for more. When Brian and Bain woke, they carried off most of the breakfast items, devouring everything within reach. The old man returned from the restroom and grimaced at the empty serving table. When Reggie emerged, she sat beside Jake and picked food off his plate.

A young man named Kendal sat next to Reggie and stared at her. "Forgive me for staring but you are so beautiful. I've never seen a woman so lovely …." She accepted his compliments with grace but took none of it seriously. He was an infatuated boy, many years her junior. A burst of laughter from the other side of the room gained her attention. The celebrating families reminded her of her missing loved ones, and she wondered if they survived the cataclysm.

Brother Henry cleared his throat. "Yes, she's lovely." He gazed at Reggie and Charlie's throats. "I've never seen an elva without a choker necklace."

"A necklace?" asked Jake.

"Hmm … what?"

"What type of necklace?"

"Elves have many types of choker necklaces, depending upon rank or clan, and humans have picked up on the tradition," Henry said, rubbing his chin. "Brides wear magic rings when engaged. Slaves wear magic necklaces one when branded; warrior women wear a choker necklace bearing their master or mistresses seal, and elvas wear one when reaching the age of Ascension. It protects them from the many evils in this world. They mark social status and rank within the royal court. It all depends."

"We don't wear those necklaces," Clara, Karl's daughter, interjected. She paused and her face grew red. Anger welled to the surface, and she said, "You men force it upon girls, too young to know better. It perpetuates a patriarchal system that prevents women from taking their true place in society. And you elves are the creators of this injustice. It would be bad enough if you controlled your women and let us be, but then you export it to our society. Our nobles use it to subjugate their wives and daughters, and they use it to enslave women who challenge them. You're afraid of what women might become. If the world was run by women, there would be no wars, no magical necklaces —"

Karl slammed his hand, ratting the table setting and roared "Enough! They are our guest. Be still or be gone." The girl stormed away from the table and slammed the door as she exited the hall.

Henry cleared his throat. "Yes, the tradition is not universal among humans of this world. On other worlds, all women wear them. As I said, 'It depends.'"

Jake changed the topic and asked, "What's an elva?"

Henry rubbed his flabby neck and looked down the bridge of his nose at Jake. "You're like a newborn; aren't you? An elva is a female elve, and an elvan is a male elve. That's what you are." The words sparked recognition in Jake as though he already knew it and was foolish to ask. Many other things lingered in the twilight of his consciousness, just out of reach.

Marta emerged from the kitchen carrying a tray. She said, "Here we go. I hope you all are hungry." When she set it down in the middle of the table, the gaunt old man rushed to the table, his cane clicking, determined to reach it ahead of Henry. The wizard inhaled the tantalizing aroma of cooked ham, hash browns, bacon, scrambled eggs with cheese, and such the like; and his stomach rumbled in approval.

"You are a marvelous chef," said Brother Henry. Brother Henry ate … and ate … and ate. After Henry had consumed all his food, he returned with a stack of pancakes, three blueberry muffins, and a sweet role. Even the old man got his fill, and Jake understood the reason for Henry's girth. Even after the meal concluded, Henry munched on crisp bacon. Charlie ate only a few obligatory mouthfuls, and Reggie drank only coffee.

"So Brother Henry, do you have to leave so soon?" asked Karl. "You only just arrived.

"Hmm … oh, yes. Lord Gent commissioned me to go on an urgent mission. I am to meet with the king in Lentel, the Elven city in the Black Mountains. My mission is most urgent. I must be on my way." He rubbed his knees and said, "My legs aren't quite what they used to be." He pondered a moment and added, "Perhaps, I should hire a travel-pony."

Gunner set down his coffee cup and put his arm around Linda. "We've been through a real odyssey. The Black Mountains appeared; our hometown disappeared; everything electronic burnt up; gasoline exploded, and daemia slaughtered everyone in Fort Defiant. We are exhausted. Do you have any ideas why all this happened?"

Brother Henry gaped in silence, and his eyes narrowed as he stared Gunner's chest. He appeared deep in thought as if pondering a crossword puzzle or contemplating some deep mystery. He rubbed an itch from his nose and broke the trance. "The events you speak of came with the return of the Great Gate. It is a portal — an energy field that forms an unseen conduit — a link between Earth and

Page 210

Eden. Those within my order agree that the gate brought this destruction upon Earth when rhunite awakened. It carried a portion of the "Wolf's Maw Mountains", which is what we call the Black Mountains, to Earth, and it transferred a portion of Earth to Eden — one swapping places with the other. Also, the rhunite emitted an electromagnetic pulse across the planet and caused ion storms. The technology of men employed became useless. Without their great machines to carry them about and to harvest food, many starved to death. The thought of it brings great sorrow to my soul."

"And rhunite is?" asked Gunner.

"Rhunite is an enigma that drives scientists mad," Henry said. "It's a mineral: inert yet energetic, harmless to the living but pernicious to technology, used in weapons and armor manufacturing, also used for growing crops. To quote the poet, 'It's a madman's fantasy concealed in a fitful dream.' Some have spent a lifetime studying it and still do not understand it."

Gunner sipped his coffee and pondered Henry's words. Linda said, "We keep traveling in time. Yesterday, we were 3,000 years ago in Fort Defiant fighting for our lives, and the day before that, it was 2,000 years ago; and slavers almost captured us in Sterling. It's very confusing."

The entire discussion confused Marta. She collected the dishes and wiped the table. "You could always travel by carriage. It's lovely this time of year." Charlie and Linda rose to help her, but Reggie remained seated. Charlie scurried back, grabbed Reggie's hand, and dragged her to the kitchen.

"But I want to hear." When she was in the kitchen threshold, she said, "Wait until I get back to discuss the good stuff." Charlie yanked Reggie into the kitchen and the clatter of pans made the men chuckle. The men remained seated: cleaning was a woman's work. They chatted about current affairs, many small kingdoms, unstable republics, Parliament alliances, and endless political intrigues.

After breakfast had concluded, Henry said, "If you are coming with me, we must leave this morning."

Chapter 27

Grass
by Carl Sandburg

Pile the bodies high at Austerlitz and Waterloo.
Shovel them under and let me work-
> *I am the grass; I cover all.*

And pile them high at Gettysburg
And pile them high at Ypres and Verdun.
Shovel them under and let me work.
Two years, ten years, and passengers ask the
conductor:
> *What place is this?*
> *Where are we now?*

> *I am the grass.*
> *Let me work.*

Three thousand years erased the footprints of man, and like sandcastles on the beach, even the fortress was a mere shadow: a few blocks above the sod, a wall fragment here, a tower there, and ghostly scorch marked on stone. Jake searched for his house, but rolling fields and sporadic trees now occupied the land.

Jake remembered the Misty River as little more than a canal, enhanced by the Army Corps of Engineers, suitable only for crop irrigation. This Misty River was broad, deep, and swift as the Mississippi, but the frigid water appeared almost black, a byproduct of runoff from the Black Mountains. The turbulent waters rushed on its way south, and he wondered if anyone would survive its frigid waters. A dirt path followed the water's edge, a bit too close for Charlie's comfort. She kept peering at the water; it splashed off rocks and sprayed white foam.

Thick vegetation enveloped downtown Fort Defiant and buried it. Like gravestones, a bit of concrete, stained by orange rust, emerged from the dense undergrowth. Jake tried to guess the structure, or where they were, but it was impossible. It was then that he noticed Brother Henry. The wizard moved his right hand to his face and drummed his lips. "Not right," Henry mumbled. "Not right at all." He turned in the saddle, perplexed, eyes searching for a familiar landmark as if he searched for his parked car in a vast lot. "It should be here." Jake was about to question him when Brother Henry tapped his heels and rode away.

The travel ponies knew the path and could walk it in the dark. When they emerged from the trees, the Black Mountains reached into the skies. White plumes blew from the snowcapped peaks and sliced through passing clouds. Craggy rock faces and sharp folds rose up to the highest peaks in the world. Jake tilted his head and his sparkling blue elvan eyes admired the grandeur.

The smallest peak in the mountain range was taller than Mount Everest, and when these peaks suddenly appeared, they crushed the earth and reshaped the face of the land across the globe. Like a rock thrown into the middle of a bed, it wrinkled the land with flowing hills, created deep canyons, twisted land, ripped asunder east and west North America along the New Madrid Fault, and triggered the San Andreas fault, sliding California into the sea. Bedrock jutted from the earth as if broken bones. All this created massive tsunamis that washed across continents and destroyed what remained.

The ponies climbed trails as if on level ground, their hoofs gripping the loose gravel. After rounding a swayback, they continued up the trail. Charlie crossed her arms and shivered. She gazed past the edge of a sheer cliff and searched the land for something familiar, some hint of home. However, nothing remained of Fort Defiant. She was cold, weary, and sullen. She had no home, no warm hearth, no pictures of loved ones, and no soft bed.

"Hey baby girl," Thor said, "you finally got that chance to go riding in the mountains."

A smile brightened her face. "You're right, dad. It's great." Her father was back in her arms, and that made all the suffering worthwhile.

The trail weaved through patches of gray and white, and it disappeared somewhere in a white cloud. The wizard turned back to the others and said, "When climbing an icy mountain, care is required. If you stumble or slip on ice, you could tumble off a ledge. Let your pony determine the pace; he knows the way to our destination."

Jake rode up to Henry' side and asked, "If I'm an elve, how come I'm cold? My nose feels like something is biting it. Shouldn't I be immune to the cold or something?"

"Elves don't age, but they can die from accident, injury, or violence," Henry said.

Jake waited for the rest of the answer, but none came. Henry appeared satisfied. He rode in silence a while and pondered the answer. It satisfied Jake's intellect, but his face still stung from the cold, and the saddle made his bottom sore. "If you really are a wizard, can't you make it a little warmer?"

Henry rolled his eyes and shook his head. "Snow in the winter, rain in the summer, all things in their season," he said. Hot breaths jetted from his nostrils. "I know you are a newborn, but try not to plague me with questions."

"Newborn, who's a newborn?"

The wizard stopped and faced Jake. "You are newborn to the Elven race. The weather, the land, the insects, and the animals are ... well ... they are what they are. I cannot change all of nature to suit you. What exists in the temporal world exists in the eternal world. Now, I need to concentrate." He turned and continued their trek.

"But there is no such thing as elves. I mean, I never thought there was," he replied and looked off into the distance. Looking through the valley between two mountains, he saw a fertile, green forest and deep blue rivers that snaked through it. "This place is beautiful, but there's nothing like I remember. Do the other worlds look like this?"

"There are other worlds, other dimensions, other times," he said. "The temporal lands are a composite of all terrains."

"I guess that makes sense," he mumbled.

Henry noticed Jake's contemplative expression and said, "What?"

"Are you a real wizard or one of those make-believe wizards?" asked Jake.

The wizard pointed his staff at a boulder, and a pulse of energy jumped from it. It blasted the rock, sending sharp shards flying. "My power is real, and so is that of our enemies."

Silence settled back upon the group, and each person contemplated Henry's words in silence. When they neared the clouds, Henry extended his staff and blocked their path. When he dismounted, the others joined him. "My butt hurts," Reggie said. When she caught Brian and Bain staring at her bottom, she turned toward them and glared. Their gaze shifted to her chest.

"Wait here. There's trouble ahead." He gripped his staff with both hands and entered the clouds. Jake searched the wall of white mist and drew his sword. It seemed a feeble display since he knew little of sword fighting, but what other choice was there? The others then drew their weapons and joined him at the mist's edge.

"Come, but walk your horses," Henry said. "This battle ended long ago."

After returning his sword to its sheath, Jake entered the mist. The heights, the cliff's edge, the trail beneath his feet, a blanket of white covered everything. He minced along the trail with his arms extended and tried to feel his way through the emptiness. "I can't see a thing. Where are you?"

"Over here."

One careful step after another, he climbed the trail. "I've never seen fog this dense. It's like I'm blinded."

"An apt description," Henry said. He waved his staff and the cloud dissipated. "There is nothing natural about this. There must be … ah, there it is."

Something struck a rock to Jake's right and shattered. The cloud began to fade, and sight returned to his eyes. On the trail up to his right, he saw Henry squatting beside something. Jake hurried around the swayback and moved to the wizard's side. Two corpses, rotting cloth wrapped around bones, lay upon the ground.

"Some daemia placed a totem here. It increased the cloud density, blinding travelers. They attacked and killed these two." Henry released a belt buckle and handed two sheathed swords to Jake. "I don't see anything to identify them."

Henry removed a bow and quiver from the second victim. Jake drew the one of the swords: light as a feather but strong as steel, elegantly curved, adorned with black scrollwork, sharp as a scalpel, medium length, the blade seemed a part of him, an extension of his arm. "Don't go waving that thing about. I don't want my head cut off. That blade is sharper than a surgeon's scalpel."

He sheathed the sword and strapped one of them around his waist. After he had slung one of the quivers over his shoulder, he handed the second set of weapons to Reggie. When Henry handed them a matching knife, he asked, "Why kill them and leave their weapons?"

"Elvish weapons cause daemia pain. They are of the light, as the elves are. The same is true of daemia weapons. If you were to touch one, it would cause you pain." Henry pointed to the missing legs, cleaved off with a hacking blade. "The daemia were hungry. They cut off the elves legs for food, probably while they were still alive. Daemia like the meat fresh, with the blood still in it." He opened one of the shirts and saw a long gash. "They gutted them too. Gruesome business," he said. He pointed at two more bodies up the trail. "Someone killed two daemia."

"That's disgusting," Charlie said.

Thor and Gunner drew their weapons and searched for threats. However, Brian and Bain marched up the trail to see if the way was clear. Jake and Reggie approached the daemia. It was humanoid. Rough leather covered its powerful limbs, and its face was hideous. Eight spider eyes covered its forehead, jagged teeth jutted from its wide mouth, and ten horns covered its knobby head. Reggie's face contorted, she said, "It stinks." Lacking a stick, she poked the carcass with a sword. "Why isn't it rotted?"

"WAIT?" Henry shouted.

The daemia roared and scrambled to its feet, weapon in hand. Jake and Reggie leaped backward and drew their blades. The second daemia also rose to its feet. They growled and rushed at them. Jake slashed and jumped aside. A bolt of energy leaped from Henry's staff, and the first daemia exploded into chunks of black, bloody flesh. Five more leaped down from the upper road. Thor and Gunner traded blows with the frenzied creatures.

The second daemia was almost on top of Henry when Jake stabbed it in the back. The wounded creature cried out in agony. This delay allowed Henry time to fire another bolt. The daemia exploded into a wave of black gore and splattered Jake.

The sound of battle raged up ahead. Daemia surrounded Brian and Bain. They fought back to back, trading blows with the daemia. Reggie slotted an arrow in her bow and let it fly. The arrow hit the daemia in the right butt cheek. The hysterical creature leaped about and pulled it out. When it turned around, Reggie released another arrow. It hit the daemia in the groin. It shrieked and stumbled backward, falling off the edge of a cliff. Jake released two arrows. They hit the mark and struck down two daemia.

Thor and Gunner rained down blows on the daemia. Gunner deflected a blow and brought his sword down on the back of the daemia's neck, decapitating it. He swept around and cut through the back of a daemia's leg. The daemia hopped around on one leg, its wounded leg partially detached. He then thrust through the daemia's heart. When a daemia attacked him from the rear, Thor blocked the blow and shoved it backward. The daemia lost its footing and stumbled backward into a flat rock. Thor smashed its head, and the headless corpse lingered on its feet for a second and then collapsed, black blood and brains splattered on the rock.

Linda and Charlie led the horses back down the road, away from the fighting. Meanwhile, Brian and Bain were overwhelmed. They hacked, chopped, and bashed in a wild frenzy. Arrows flew past them and struck down the daemia. Jake sprinted up the road and leaped into the battle. A staff blast exploded the daemia, once again splattering him. He opened one eye and glared at Brother Henry.

Reggie fired arrows with a variety of effectiveness. Some hit their mark, but many whizzed past the daemia, making them duck. After Gunner and Thor had finished off their foes, they charged up the road and joined the attack. The remaining daemia fled.

It was then that they heard screams. When they looked down at the lower road, they saw Linda and Charlie fighting a pair of daemia. One of the daemia drove Linda back to the cliff's edge. Jake slotted an arrow and let it fly. It hit the daemia in the back of the neck and jutted out its mouth.

A huge daemia bashed Charlie and knocked her to the ground. Thor scrambled down the rocks like a ranger. He leaped and tackled the daemia. The pair rolled down the road, holding back each other's knife. Thor broke the creatures grip and stabbed it in the gut. The wounded creature fled the battle. Brother Henry used his staff to lift and fling the daemia over the edge. It cried out in rage as it plummeted to its death.

Frozen in place, lips pressed tight, eyes blinking, Jake tried to grasp the moment. He grimaced as he wiped the black blood from his face and spit. "Aw man, this stuff stinks."

"I was careless," Henry said. "I should have checked the daemia first. I'm getting senile in my old age. I never would have fallen for that trick a thousand years ago."

Combat left them shaken. Reggie's hands trembled; her legs were weak, and nausea twisted her stomach. She sat upon a rock, and Jake sat next to her and wiped the black blood from his face. "I can't do this," Reggie said.

"Do what?" asked Henry.

"Any of it," Reggie said. "I want to wake up in my bed. I want to forget all of this like a bad dream. I want my life back. I want my family back." She broke into Spanish and raged at the injustice.

Henry sat on the rock beside them and removed a silver flask from a large pocket. He took a swig and handed it to Jake. After he had taken a swig, he handed it to Reggie. "It's ambrosia. It'll settle your nerves." Reggie took a swig from the flask, but instead of bitter alcohol, vitality water filled her with radiant joy and warmth. She took another swig and imagined herself under the blankets and watching a roaring fire in the hearth. "That's enough." Brother Henry snatched back the flask before Reggie could take a second swig. "Medicine must be administered in the proper dose." He took another quick swig and screwed down the cap.

"I'm never going home. Am I?" asked Reggie.

"No," replied Brother Henry. "Even if you could go home, it would never be the same." He parted his lips to offer sage advice, but the sadness of many lifetimes pressed down upon his soul. "I hate partings, and I have lost many homes and loved ones dear to my heart."

They lingered in silence a while, consumed by private grief. The frigid winds swirled the snow in a frenzied dance upon the mountains. Beyond the mountains, in the valley below them, lay a trackless forest of green, and beyond the forests, the Misty River flowed southwest on its way to the sea. "It's a beautiful world," Jake said.

"One of many," replied Henry. He groaned as he lifted his bulk from the rock. "I used to be skinny, thin as a bean pole, but after more grief than I could bear, I found comfort in food. Now my weary body resents my gluttony and punishes me. But we must continue our journey."

Jake rose to his feet and gazed skyward. "It has to be late in the day. When is sunset?" Turning this way and that, he searched the sky for the sun, and it was passed noontime. "Will we arrive at our destination before dark?"

"We must. It's not safe in these mountains after dark," Henry said.

"Maybe we should turn around," Linda said.

"I'm so sick of violence," Charlie said. "Why do those things keep attacking us?"

"We cannot turn around. It would be farther back to Crow Valley than ahead, and as to daemia attacking us, it's what they do. The men are food, and the women are for breeding."

"Sex?" asked Reggie.

"Yes, unlike haugr, daemia have females, but they still reproduce by rape. We will need to purchase maiden's belts for the women when we arrive. I checked with Marta, but they had none to spare."

"What's a maiden's belt," asked Charlie.

"It's like a chastity belt, but one you can remove as you wish. It keeps you from being raped by daemia or haugr," Henry said. None of the women were happy to hear this news. "Normally, I don't travel with unprotected females, but we had no choice. We must keep moving," Henry said and continued his upward trek. The women grumbled and swore they would never wear such an offensive item.

Thor and Gunner retrieved their armor from their horses and changed into it. They assume that a well-traveled road up the mountain would be safe. However, they now realized that there is no safe place on the planet. After they wore the armor gleaned from the fort, they led the way up the mountain.

The road zigzagged two more times and then skirted around a butte, passing through a steep canyon. The enemy sought out such places: both the darkness and the strategic layout pleased them. Henry rubbed his chin and considered their options. A narrow, dangerous trail passed deep into the heart of the mountains, but it would take them out of their way, through the dwarven mines of Mareck.

They neared the flat top butte and the fork in the road. The broad way traveled into the narrow canyon with high and tight walls. A child could throw down rocks and injure them. The other road, if one could call it as such, led up and around the butte. Random worn patches and loose gravel marked it. He took a swig from his canteen and pondered the matter. Jake looked about, trying to understand why they paused. When Henry glanced at the path leading to darkness, a chill swept over Jake and he asked, "Why do I feel such foreboding about going that way?"

Henry hummed and shook his head. "You have good instincts. Always listen to them and heed their warning. We go up." He turned right toward the high road.

Chapter 28

The road narrowed into a trail. It skirted a sheer rock wall, little more than a goat path and very hard on Linda's nerves. The narrow ledge forced them to travel single file. When Jake looked to his left, a fertile valley lay far below them: square plots of tilled land, checkerboard plots of land, cattle appearing like white dots, and farm buildings no larger than a child's toy. A small town lay at the junction of three rivers. The main river turned mill wheels, and shoppers wandered the streets.

Sudden gusts buffed Jake and shoved his pony toward the ledge. He touched the cool rock wall with his right hand and looked over the precipice. The Misty River appeared no more than a thin blue line, and hills appeared like bumps on a relief map. Brother Henry was already far up the trail, and they followed the relentless old man.

Their ponies plodded up the trail as if it was just another day. When they looked up at the trail, it skirted the S-shaped wall and ended at a plateau. Brother Henry crested the top and never looked back. Jake quickened his pace, as did the others, and they hurried around the curved wall, eager for the rest of flat land.

As the top neared, their hungry eyes searched for a place of rest. Brother Henry sat up a rough stone bench carved out of a single boulder. He ate a bit of bread and took a swig from his canteen. As the edge of the cliff gave way, they also saw three dwarves seated beside Henry. They chatted like workmen on lunch break.

When Jake dismounted, his bottom ached in complaint and legs felt like rubber. They led their horses over to him. "There you are," said Henry. "I'd like to introduce you to Master Brondril, and his two associates: Nog and Orie. They're going to lead us through their mine."

Master Brondril acknowledged Brian and Bain, but he treated the others as if they did not exist. "Yes. We are pleased to guide you and give aid to your journey. I am sorry to hear of your great suffering." He stuffed the last bit of food in his mouth and walked toward Brian and Bain without saying another word. Nog and Orie copied their master. Orie glanced back at Jake and spit a wad of chewing tobacco.

Brondril took Brian and Bain aside, out of earshot of the others. "Brothers, why do you travel with these elves?" whispered Brondril. "Surely there must be dwarven caravans."

Brian understood the dwarves disdain. "You're the first dwarves that we've ever met. We've had a bad week.

Page 229

Besides, we grew up with them. They're not so bad once you get to know them."

Brondril scanned the others and snarled. "Really? Do they treat you as an equal? Will their women share your bed? When you try to make a profit, do they treat you like a dog?"

"Yes," Bain said. "Our father owned a construction company before he passed away. Every single day someone in our town made fun of us or criticized us for our father's success. The girls would never go out with me, and if they did, it was just to make someone jealous. Even in Crow Valley, they treated us with contempt, but our Elven friends they honored. I'm sick of it. But it was never Jake, and it was never the Vakhal family. Jake's parents treated us like sons. They are true to us, so we are true to them."

"I see." The dwarven master stroked his beard and nodded. "We will assist all of you. You have my word."

Henry rose with a groan and wiped some crumbs from his belly. "You must forgive them. They have a strained relationship with the elves. Neither group approves of the other." He patted Jake's back and led him up the trail. "Ignore their contempt and be on your best behavior. We require their lodging and their protection."

A gradual slope across the plain led to the crescent shaped mountain base, and the entrance to Mareck lay in the center. It appeared small, barely a mouse hole and tiny figures entered and exited it, traveling on a large ramp. A small town of rough buildings with thatch roofs lay before it. The smoke from many chimneys rose into the sky where a powerful crosswind swept it away. The main road followed the curve, going north and south. Many traveled it: wagons filled with food, merchandise, and treasures.

"The town of 'Trader's Hold' is a treacherous place. Many an unwise traveler mistakes it for a safe haven. The Merchant Association tries to maintain order, but the swindlers, thieves, whores, and drunkards are too numerous. That is why we will stay in the mine; the dwarves bring swift and sure judgment down upon scofflaws."

Endless blue skies stretched off to the horizon, yet with every step, they entered the shadow lands. It was subtle at first, as though Jake put on a pair of sunglasses. However, as the mountains grew large, the light faded, and shadows grew long. The surrounding rocks transformed into grasping monsters, and that which was good, decent, or beautiful fell behind them. As they neared the town, street lamps maintained their eternal vigil. Even so, the darkness ate the light and plunged them into a twilight world; shadows reached out to block their path, and dangerous men loitered about, hoods drawn, faces hidden. They caressed knife handles and searched their prey for weakness. Bawdy women spilled out of taverns, their breasts bulging in low-cut gowns, and foolish men pawed at them, losing what little they owned and risked disease. Raucous music, tinny and sharp, the aroma of cooking meat, the din of conversation, and the roar of laughter beckoned them to partake.

Jake spotted a foolish young man, handsome with golden hair. Two women fell upon him and flattered him. In an instant, he gave way, an ox to the slaughter, and entered the chambers of the damned. "It pains my heart," said Brother Henry. "A young man throws his life away, and for what?"

"What will happen to him?"

"Happen? Lust has him trapped. When his coins runs out, he will abase himself, and do things he never dreamed. But hope remains." As they passed along the cobblestone street, Brother Henry's mind drifted back in time. "If you walk in the shadows too long, you look like me. The eternal battle between the light and darkness weathered me. I need rest and renewal, but there is so much to do – no time for rest."

A pair of girls, one dressed in crimson lingerie and the other in shimmery blue, rushed out of a tavern. They fell upon Jake. "Do you want to party? I can get you a free bottle of whiskey, and our master will let you have to two of us for the price of one." She caressed his body and whispered in his ear, "I promise you such a memory."

Brother Henry stopped but remained silent. Jake felt the weight of Henry's gaze, and the ache in Henry's heart; yet it was not his place to interfere: men must choose the light. His mother, on the other hand, flew into action. She drove the girls away and glared at them. The girls shifted to another man and wooed him into their lair.

Sensing Jake's regret, Henry said, "No sane woman chooses to be a prostitute, and there are some female prostitutes who used to be men." When Jake furrowed his brow and snarled. "It's true, magic is real. When that handsome young man back there is deep in debt and can't pay his bill, they seize him and sell him as a slave. "Shadow Land" slaves seldom escape their human masters and work to their death in the mines. But this is not the worst fate: some men sink into the darkness and transform into daemia, a ravenous beast, twice damned."

A single beam of sunshine found its way between the craggy peaks. Master Brondril stopped and said, "Behold Mareck, the symbol of dwarven power. Tunnels and shortcuts riddle these hills. The dwarves do business with men and leave." Nog and Orie rushed rode past them, bundles upon their animals.

Two streams of dwarves, from the north and south, merged into a single river and entered the tunnel entrance. They drove wagons filled with food, cloth, furniture, and other goods. They merged with the swell of the crowd and joined the slow procession into the Mareck.

The procession slowed to a crawl and climbed the stairs. The drivers struggled to scale the steep ramps in their wagons, heavy cargo multiplying their woes, but the dwarves are a hearty folk; and they heaved and pushed their carts to the top. With every step, the mine entrance yawned, gaping like a giant maw. The dwarves appeared relieved, but Jake felt damned, a prisoner consigned to the underworld. As he entered, he imagined green fields and sparkling lakes. Just when he was about to turn and leave, Henry laid a hand on his right shoulder. "It's going to be all right." His words brought comfort to Jake and shored up his courage.

When they crossed from the light to the darkness, Jake smelled baked goods. Arched entryways led to intimate taverns and warm hearths. Smiling faces greeted one another, and long parted friends embraced. Weary dwarves dropped their heavy packs, assured by the presence of peacekeepers, and entered the taverns, thirsty for ale.

"Do we have any money?" asked Reggie.

"Why?"

"I could use a drink. It's been a long day."

Gunner chuckled and said, "Me too."

"Later," said Henry, "we need to locate our lodging and stow our gear. Our hosts will provide us with free ale."

Linda liked free things; free was good. The gold coins from they obtained in Sterling had to buy a home and food. "Do you know what we can do for work? Gunner is an experienced merchant, and I have nursing training."

"Work? Elves live communally. Every person contributes and all reap the benefit. I wouldn't worry about that. All of your needs will be met. Trust me on this," Henry said. "I need all of you to remain silent about the Dragon's Eye Pendant that Gunner carries. If others were to learn of its existence, the dwarven authorities would seize it."

Chapter 29

After they returned the ponies to the travel service, they leaned against a wide, stone railing and admired the view. The dwarven city of Marek, translated the "golden bastion," staggered the mind. Rhunite lanterns illuminated the labyrinth. It sank down so far that Jake's elvish eyes failed to see the bottom, and, carved out of the mountains, the network crisscrossing spans, roads, and buildings dizzied the mind. He combed his fingers through his flaxen locks, uncertain whether to shout or sing. He wanted to see it all: travel every road, drink in every tavern, and search its hidden depths. "It's impossible. This has to be a dream."

"No. The world you knew is the dream. This is reality." Henry patted Jake on the shoulder. "Come, we should be going."

"That statue," Brain said and pointed. "It's bigger than the Colossus of Rhodes." Twelve titanic statues lined the exterior walls and continued out of sight. The empire state building could fit inside any one of them. "It staggers my mind to think how long it took to excavate it."

"Come," Henry said and led them off the balcony. "We have a long journey ahead of us. Mareck is a vast city inhabited by millions." The dwarves waited with crossed arms and tapping feet. When they exited the balcony and stepped onto the main path, the dwarves turned and walked away, speaking to one another in dwarven whispers.

The trek led them over an array of bridges and tunnels that left them disoriented. Each new wonder exceeded the one before it. From the glow of the depths below to the soaring heights above, the grandeur of Mareck left them overawed. However, they welcomed the day's end, and the dwarves offered them accommodations.

Master Brondril held open the door to his home. The spacious interior took them by surprise. Tapestries hung on the wall; plush leather furniture, oak end tables, and area rugs lay in a sunken living room. Charlie and Reggie hurried onto the terrace that overlooked a vast chasm. As far as the eye could see, balconies and terraces covered the cavern walls. At different levels, bridges spanned the gap; shopping districts rose high, and merchants' street bazaars filled plazas with wears.

"I would like to go to my room and rest," Gunner said. Brondril led Gunner and Linda through a maze of hallways and interior rooms. Gunner never imagined dwarves to possess such grandeur. Archways spanned the rooms, meeting the center; the stonework was the finest he had ever seen.

He opened a heavy oak door with a rounded top, and said, "This is your room. It has a human and Elven size bed in it. The dining room is down the first hallway to your right. My wife will provide a buffet of food."

"Thank you for your hospitality," Linda said. After the door had closed, Gunner collapsed into a padded chair and stared with empty eyes. She sat down beside him and touched his arm. "What's the matter?"

"Everyone we ever knew is gone. Hell, the world we knew is gone. Just days ago we were fighting for our lives in Fort Defiant, now we're here. I keep thinking about all those poor people: how they died," he sighed.

"There's nothing we can do for them. All of that happened 3,000 years ago," Linda said.

"No. It was yesterday, and I have a magic amulet to travel in time. But … even if I was to return, what could I do? It would take an army to save them, and no one was prepared." He rubbed his face. "It's just the fatigue talking. I need some rest." He trudged over to the bed and collapsed upon it. The second his eyes closed, he fell into a deep sleep, which was unusual for an elve.

Gunner submerged into a vivid dream: arms outstretched, he flew over Fort Defiant. The morning sun reflected off steel and glass buildings, and the world awoke to a new day. Far below, men and women hustled here and there, the normal stuff of life. Children waited at the bus stop, wishing for an early snow to cancel school. Pocket watches – some as large as swimming pools and others the size of dinner plates – were limp, flaccid, and draped over roofs, branches, and streetlights. A wide-eyed man, stroking his beard, replaced the sun; he looked down upon the earth with unblinking intensity.

The wide-eyed man began to weep, and his tears rained upon the earth. Flood waters rose, at first flooding the streets and then covering rooftops. Men and woman clung to branches, and children climbed to treetops. The limp pocket watches swirled in the turbulent waters, and black blocks streaked through the flood waters, destroying homes and businesses. A monstrous creature climbed to the top of a tower and ripped away his clothes, revealing a hideous body, the embodiment of war. The monster threw back his head, spread his arms, and released a primal roar.

"You can save them," a still, small voice whispered.

He began to fall. Gunner tried to fly, but his body became heavy as lead, and the world began to spin. He cried out for help. "SAVE ME!"

Gunner sat up in bed: grasping air, blood rushing in his arteries, his eyes searched for danger. The bedroom door opened, and light flooded the room. Linda entered, and worry marred her beautiful face. "Are you okay? I heard you from the parlor."

He pushed aside the blanket and sat on the edge of the bed. "I had a nightmare." The details began to fade, but the theme remained. He took a drink from a glass of water beside the bed and struggled to steady his hands. He fixed his gaze on her and said, "We have to save them. If we don't, we will all be destroyed."

Chapter 30

"We registered as apprentice miners, and we found jobs five minutes later," Brain said. "They're going to teach us a trade."

"And they let us stay in the bunk house," Bain added.

Heaviness overshadowed Jake, and he sat on one of the bunk beds. He rubbed his face and rested his elbows on his knees. "I hoped … well … I hoped we would live together. The two of you are closer than brothers." When his eyes began to water, he rose to his feet. "I'm gonna miss you, but it sounds like a good opportunity."

"We'll see each other," Brian said. "I'm told it's a half day's journey up to Lentel."

"Yeah, it's not like the moon," Bain agreed.

"Lentel … I guess I'll live. That's where elves go, right?" Jake rubbed his face and trudged away. He lingered in the doorway and took a last look at his friends. A heavy sigh escaped his lips as he turned and walked away. When he reached the parlor, Charlie asked, "What's up?"

"Brian and Bain found jobs and a place to stay." Jake collapsed onto a sofa next to her and laid his head on her lap. She brushed a flaxen lock from his face and tried to make sense of it all. "I want to be happy for them."

"But?"

She sighed, "It's great that they found jobs, but this isn't their home, and Lentel isn't our home." He sat up next to her and put his feet on the coffee table. "We should find a place together by some river. Each of us would have a cottage, and every morning we walk to work together."

"Doing what?" asked Charlie, her head cocked.

"I don't know, farming, running a flower mill, something like that."

She chuckled. "What do you know about running a flower mill? You barely know how to make instant pancakes."

He snapped up to his feet and began to pace. "I know that. We could run a general store. We would be ... we would be a family." He sat down again, his head in his hands. Drawing in a deep breath, he repressed the disappointment and said, "I suppose this is for the best. All of the dwarves look at us like we're criminals."

"I've noticed," Charlie said. "I wandered out of the house and scarves caught my eye. I was looking through the merchandise when I sensed anger. The female dwarf who owned the cart glared at me, her arms folded, daring me to say something. I had to leave."

Brian and Bain strode into the parlor. Master Brondril gave us these boots and jackets. They appeared very dwarvish: barrel-chested, broad noses, and sporting thick beards. Bearing tan canvas backpacks and scared helmets upon their heads, they displayed their new mining hammers for admiration. "What do you think?" asked Bain.

"You look very dwarvish," Charlie said and scrunched up her nose. She gave them a hug and grew glassy eyed. "I'm going to miss you."

They stared at their toes and shuffled their feet. "We're going to miss you too," Brian said, "but this is for the best. Once you get settled, we can get together."

"We're starting a new job," Bain said," so we won't have any vacation time for a year."

"You don't know that." Brian crossed his arms and frowned. "We might have some time off. You never know."

"Please, no one gives new people time off," Bain replied.

"Guys, I'm sure I'll see you soon." Charlie gave them another hug and sniffled. "We've never been apart." When she began to tear up, she hurried from the room. The brothers looked at one another and their hearts felt heavy as lead.

Jake shook their hands. "I'm sorry to see you go, but I'm glad you've got a career. It's more than I have. I'm not sure what elves do, prance in the woods and play the flute. Are there any elve trade schools? Would we make toys for Santa? No idea." Both brothers grinned and said their final farewells.

When they departed Brondril's home, a throng of dwarves swelled in the city streets and pushed them against brick walls. The crowd parted as dwarves pounding heavy drums passed, and priests followed, swinging censers that billowed white incense. Another group of priests shook racks that were covered with bells, and the next group shouted praises in an ancient dwarven tongue. Dwarven virgins danced in wild steps, with leaps, and in high pirouettes; and they flung flowers from wicker baskets. Floats bearing statues of dwarven demigods, heroes of old, servants of Tsuur, the Most High God, rode on the shoulders of Dwarven bearers. After the floats had passed them, bare chested dwarven males chanted in deep throaty groans and whipped their backs with scourges until blood flowed. An army of dwarves, gleaming with polished armor and bearing deadly weapons, followed the procession.

"Is it some sort of celebration?" asked Bain.

"How would I know," Brian said. "Let's get going. We're supposed to report for work."

As they pushed through the crowd, Bain had an epiphany: everyone was the same as him. Short, stocking, bearded dwarves swarmed around him. There was a sameness to them that declared, "You're home." The strange world of men, the home of his youth, the world of men, seemed like a dream. Had he ever walked among such people?

Brian cut down a side alley to avoid the crowd, and Bain chased after him. The twins happened upon a bank of elevators. Formed in a cluster of six brass tubes, there were six groups of these clusters. Each tube had an oval doorway, which when opened allowed one to enter magnetic-lift cars. A grim-faced attendant avoided eye contact and stood with his arms crossed. Brian asked, "Which elevator do we take for the Ingot Mine."

The dwarf rolled his eyes and said, "The sixth bank all go to the Ingot. It's only the largest mine in the mountain. Which level are you going to?"

"Um ..." Brian retrieved a note from his pocket, "we want the 10th level."

"You grubbers gonna gopher the tailings, huh?" asked the dwarf.

"Um … I guess," Brian said.

The dwarf chuckled and led them to the correct elevator. He pressed the lift summons and gave them a sideways glance. He shook his head and said, "Say hello to Millot for me. He's gonna love meeting you two. He'll probably have you mucking."

"What's mucking?" asked Bain.

The dwarf threw back his head and roared with laughter. "You two really are raw. Even a nipper knows that. You must be castoffs." When they failed to respond to his insult, he shook his head. "You are about to have the worst day of your life, and every day after that will be the worst day of your life. Take the advice of someone who has mined that shaft: go back to the celebration. Get drunk, and ravish some beauty. Forget about mining and dreams of riches. It only leads to misery. Anything you find will fill the purse of another dwarf. None of the glory goes to the likes of you and me. Ours is to bend our backs and be replaced when we break. You're nothing more than a tool."

The doors slid open and the brass interior bid them enter. After they had entered, the operator stood in the doorway and prevented its closure. "Take my advice; seek out Kairn. He runs a mining school. He trains you with the understanding that you will venture mine in virgin territory. That way he builds up the Alliance of Independent Miners and bolsters his influence with the Great Counsel. He will treat you square, no short tailings."

"Where do we find Kairn?" asked Brian.

The operator pressed the button for floor 11. "Go off and ask for Kairn. They'll send you on your way. Best of luck," he said and exited the elevator.

After the doors had closed, Brain reached out to press the 10th level button, but Bain said, "Wait a second." Bain pressed the hold button. Brian furrowed his brow and looked for some explanation. "Dad's earthmoving business hired shovel idiots all the time. He used to chuckle how he conned people. He promised to teach them to operate the heavy equipment, but he never did. When they got frustrated, he hired someone to take their place. That guy called us 'grubbers'; it sounded a lot like shovel idiot. I want to check out Kairn first. If he's running a free mining school, that interests me."

"Okay brother, we'll give him a try. If it's bogus, then we can always report for our mucking jobs." Brian said and released the hold button. The elevator jostled, and the car moved. They plummeted farther than one might suspect and watched the display change.

When the elevator doors opened, the deep throb of heavy equipment impacted them with heavy blows. They stepped out of the elevator and grinding squeals began. The rock beneath their feet shuddered and chunks of debris spewed from a dense cloud of steam. The vague form of dwarves lingered in the mist: specters that made their courage melt. Brian took a step and rubbed his face. The intense heat and steam caused a fine sheen of sweat on his face and prickles beneath his clothes.

The roars ceased and the ground became still. As the mist began to clear, they saw a long yellow machine. It crawled upon tracks and twin arms carried a drum studded with hooked teeth. Steam hissed from various hose fittings and water coated the cavern walls. Kairn said, "Excellent job, Gladgrac, but you were a bit too aggressive. Let the teeth do the work; they will lead you through the different gauges of strata …."

Bain spotted simple picnic tables covered with food: roast meat, sweet potatoes, vegetable dishes, barrels of ale, and other unknown delights. His stomach rumbled with approval. His mouth watered, and his feet carried him toward it. As he reached out to sample a turkey drumstick, Kairn said, "Who might you two be?" Dwarves on top of the yellow machine and others performing various tasks paused and stared.

"My name is Brain, and my brother is Bain. We are interested in your mining program. Is it open to new students?"

"Perhaps," said Kairn. "But there is much to discuss before I would grant you admittance."

"What is the food for?" asked Bain.

"We encountered a celebration in the city, but we don't know what it was about," said Brian.

"You don't know the Celebration of the Fallen? That is peculiar." Kairn said to the students, "Leave your tasks. We will feast, and these strangers will tell us their story." The dwarves climbed off the machine, ceased their tasks, and rushed for the empty tables. After Kairn had prayed for their food, they filled plates and mugs.

"A proper story starts at the beginning ...." Brian was always a good storyteller. He included salient details, used varying voices, and embellished where appropriate. The dwarves listened with rapt attention.

"That is quite the tale, said Kairn, "and a bit unbelievable. Yyyeeettt ... I can see the truth of it in your eyes." He stroked his beard. "It must have been awful to live with humans."

"Yeah, it was." Bain slurped his ale and belched. "The women thought we were weird, and the men never understand our fascination with the earth. I always felt at home in our underground bunker. Our dad built it in case of a nuclear war."

Kairn rose to his feet and raised his mug. "All those who wish to admit Brian and Bain to our Association join me in a toast." Everyone, except Og, who never approved of anyone, raised their mug. "Then let's drink to our new provisional members." They tilted back their mugs until rivulets ran down their beards. Not wishing to be left out, Og chugged his ale. Afterward, hearty belches erupted.

He slapped Brian and Bain on the back. "You are now provisional members. After a year, you will become apprentice miners, and at graduation, you become journeyman miners. After several hundred years work, you too may become a master miner like me. Come and greet your new brothers, born to us this very day." Chairs slid and the dwarves crowded around Brian and Bain, shaking hands, slapping them on the back, and tugging their beards, a gesture of goodwill and kinship. Both Brian and Bain wore irrepressible grins.

A siren blasted: shrill as fingernails on a chalkboard, powerful as an explosion. The smile disappeared from each dwarve's face and the mugs slipped from their hands. When they faltered, Kairn shouted, "TO ARMS."

Pandemonium ensued. The dwarves sprinted into the weapons locker. Some handed out armor while others distributed weapons. They slapped sets of armor and weapons onto the twin's arms, heavy chainmail and plate armor, piled high. Brain dumped his armor onto the table and asked, "What's happening? Is this some sort of training exercise?"

"Training? Nay, we are under attack. Put on your armor before they fall upon us. "Get ready for battle," Kairn said and rushed past them.

Bain examined the chainmail, turned it this way and that, and debated how to wear it. Seeing their disorientation, two dwarves helped them dress in the battle gear. When they finished, they slapped a weapon Bain's hands. Bain examined the notched and scared battleax. He wanted to believe they resulted from weapons practice, but he knew better.

The main lights flickered, grew very bright, and then extinguished. A few seconds later, the red emergency lights illuminated. "Everyone is at the Celebration of the

Fallen," Gladgrac said. "We should load into the lift and ride to the lower shafts?"

"Nay," Kairn said. "The dwarves down there are already dead. Besides, the lifts require an emergency key during an alert."

Howls and screeches echoed in the main shaft. They ran up to the shaft and peered through the chain-link fence, designed as a safeguard against falling debris. "I saw something," Og said and pointed. A fleeting shadow raced up the mammoth shaft and disappeared in mere seconds.

A chorus of howls sent shivers up Bain's spine and made his feet tingle, and senses come alive. Then he saw it: a creature with the face of a bat, a humanoid body, clad in armor, razor sharp claws, and crude weapons strapped to its back. It scrambled up the shaft and leaped across support beams. "What is that?"

"Haugr," Kairn whispered. When he looked over the ledge, his heart skipped a beat and a shudder surged through him. Haugr beyond number climbed up the access shaft. He jogged backward and then turned to run. "Run for your lives!" The dwarven students faltered and then chased after their master. "We make for the emergency shaft."

A few seconds later Brian and Bain were alone. A multitude of screams and countless scrapes of claws on rock echoed up the shaft. A great thunderous tumult made their hearts beat in their throats. "RUN, YOU FOOLS," shouted Kairn. Both Brian and Bain sprinted into the darkness. A moment later, haugr beyond count raced up the sides of the main shaft, covered every access shaft, every surface boiled with them, and they kept coming.

The twins ran with reckless abandon. They saw the other dwarves gathered inside a crude shaft. They waved and screamed for them to hurry. Brian and Bain raced toward their new comrades and passed through a section of smooth rock. The moment they reached rough rock again, Kairn ordered, "Knock out the keystones." Two dwarves with massive hammers swung high and brought them down on two round segments set in vertical columns. The two breakaway segments, set at 45-degree angles, were located in the middle of the columns. Blow after blow rained down upon these breakaway segments. When a dozen haugr sprinted toward them, the dwarves readied themselves for battle.

The first keystone cracked and then tumbled. The column collapsed into rubble. "HURRY," Kairn shouted. He gripped his battle ax and readied it to cleave a haugr skull.

The haugr were almost on top of them. The column cracked and then shattered. It tumbled as two haugr entered the smooth section. A 30-ton block-stone collapsed, crushing the haugr, and black blood sprayed them.

Absolute darkness swallowed them. There in the darkness, it seemed to Bain that the walls closed in around him. Panic welled, and he was a second away from fleeing like a terrified beast. Then he saw a spark and a headlamp blazed brightly. One by one, the dwarves lit their lamps and light flooded the shaft. They showed Brian and Bain how to light their headlamps.

"We should have stayed to fight," Og said.

"We'd already be dead," Gladgrac said. "What good would that be?"

"We'd have died heroes. Our souls would have joined the fallen in the halls of our ancestors," Og said. "Now we're just cowards."

"Our heroes of old were courageous and wise. They fought for our people, and yes, they died in battle; but they did not throw away their lives. They fought for our people in a noble defense of our lands. They had no use for false displays of bravery. By this time, the city guardians have closed the access routes to the city and to other mines. They have locked out the haugr and are preparing to wage war. It is our duty to return to the city and join them." The dwarves grunted and nodded. "Now, let's find the quickest route back to the city."

Chapter 31

"We cannot stay," Henry mumbled as he paced. Master Brondril crossed his arms and raised an eyebrow. When he noticed Brondril's inquisitive stare, he said, "I do not wish to offend, but my need is most urgent. In fact, you and other dwarves should attend."

"Attend what?" asked Brondril.

Henry leaned close and whispered, "Lord Ceven of Lentel has called a war council. The daemia are on the move."

Brondril's arms slipped apart, and he leaned forward. "I've heard nothing of this. How many are there? From whence do they come?"

"I have few details, except that they come from the north," Henry said. "The Great Counsel of the Dwarven People must appoint representatives to attend. We must unite and fight as one."

"Agreed." Master Brondril mumbled about the elves and their lackeys, men, "A war comes and they say nothing … damn elves." A siren ripped through the city and shattered the peace. "That's the defense siren. The city is under attack." He bolted from the room and shouted, "Orie, Nog, ready my gear. We are under attack."

Linda lounged upon a plush sofa and gazed through the threshold and the balcony railing. The siren shattered the festivities, and the crowd stampeded through the streets in a complete panic, blocking the path of the city defenders. Great slabs began to move and blocked off main thoroughfares, blocking the path of invaders, but also blocking the reveler's escape. Linda scrambled from the soft and hurried onto the balcony. Screams and shouts came from all directions.

Back in the bedrooms, Jake and Reggie lay in bed. Charlie sat on an overstuffed chair, a blanket on her lap and a cup of tea cradled between her hands. "Two hours and I am awake," Reggie said. "I want eight hours sleep, damn it. And what is that whining noise? How are we supposed to sleep?" She crossed her arms and glared at a mantel clock.

They heard the thump of running boots, and then the door burst open. Gunner rushed into the room. "The city is under attack. We have to go. Gather your belongings and get ready. Henry insists that we leave with him. He has an important meeting in the Elven city of Lentel, and we have to go with him."

"Who is attacking?" asked Linda.

"Some creatures called haugrs. Thor is standing guard. You have to hurry. We need to reach the Elven city." Gunner rubbed his face and debated his next words. "We have no word on Brian and Bain. They were trapped inside the mine when the haugr attacked."

All eyes turned to Brondril when he returned. "The city is in chaos, and our defenses are used against us. The guard captains are working to open the barriers so that we may battle the haugr, but they say it will take a while. I found only one council member and I explained our situation. He asked me to accompany you to Lentel."

They departed in silence: a sense of doom settled upon them. Conflict chased them since this odyssey began, and now it chased them from the dwarven city. However, their destination encouraged them. The elves were generous to a fault, and Brondril made it clear that the Eleven city was safe. Their kin would welcome them. Jobs, food, a new life awaited them at the end of the trek, yet each step came with difficulty.

The great spires, the towering statues, engraved artwork many stories tall, and magnificent architecture failed to register in their troubled minds. They hiked for hours, but without the sun to mark the time, they could only guess how long. When the first shaft of light beamed through the tunnel entrance, joy filled their hearts. Their pace quickened and a smile returned to their face.

After they had exited the tunnel, they stared in awe as if they entered paradise. Waterfalls cascaded from the mountain heights and thundered into the fertile valley. Four point arches reached into the sky, erected for no other reason than for beauty, and they stood on either side of a cathedral, as grand as in Europe. A circular stained glass window gleamed with blues and white. Elves clothed in white walked the ancient, golden path.

"This way," Brondril said and walked away as if it was nothing. They followed the elves, but when the elves followed the path up to the pinnacle cathedral, they turned left and circled around it. Vibrant blue, purple, red, and yellow wildflowers adorned rolling hills of green, and beyond it, they saw lush forests and sparkling blue waters. Charlie sank down to her knees, overwhelmed at it all: all of nature sang to her in perfect harmony, music only her Elven soul could hear.

"Is there something wrong with her?" Hands on his hips and a frown on his face, Brondril said, "This is no place to stop and rest."

Brother Henry touched Charlie's shoulder and helped the girl stand. He noted that the others were in little better condition. After a brief rest, they continued on the golden road that weaved around the rolling hills. Their steps grew lighter and the hearts merry. The sun shone brightly upon them, and mountains formed a protective ring around the land that was fairest.

After they had circled around a grove of maple trees, they happened upon a village nestled along the bend of a gentle river. They crossed a bridge of stone and entered the dreamy village. The quaint buildings of dark brown beams and tan walls sparked a memory. *Ah yes, this is home. This is where I belong.* The Elven people, fairer than all the sons and daughters of men, strolled about on their business. Mothers shopped at outdoor markets and children scrambled about on a quick game of tag. The fathers paused from their labors to watch these strangers pass, but their eyes radiated warmth as if long lost loved ones now reunited. Music from a beautiful chorus and spiced incense floated in the breeze: a sense of the divine overshadowed all. Even Brondril succumbed to the bliss and lost his irritated edge, much to his annoyance.

They passed through the village as if on their way home. Linda thought, *it should be just around the corner.* She was certain of it. She waved to lovers stealing a kiss in a second-floor window, and they returned her wave as if old friends.

The trail led them through worshipful forests, along gentle fields of wildflowers, beside still waters, crisp and cool, and through golden fields of golden wheat. Produce seemed to spring from the ground as if touched by the hand of God. After climbing a tall hill, they saw it, a castle of such rich beauty that it made them feel that they wandered into a dream.

The winding road met a bridge that spanned a deep gorge. It then weaved up the hill to reddish walls framed by gray granite blocks, and circular gray towers marked each corner. Behind the walls, white towers – that gleamed like freshly fallen snow – thrust into the sky, their pennants caught in the brisk wind. White buildings with scores of windows, framed by rich red curtains, and balconies looked out upon paradise.

They walked swiftly, then jogged, and then ran. Brondril lagged behind, annoyed to be last but refusing to be excited. They ran up the road and never grew tired. It was as if they strolled on a cool spring morning. Brother Henry, however, gasped and sweated as he waddled up the road. When they approached the gate, the guards, clad in gleaming silver and white uniforms blocked their path. "I am summoned to a meeting of the War Council, and these are with me." The captain of the guard checked his entry list and nodded. The guards stepped aside just as

Brondril caught up to them. The master dwarf growled at them as he passed.

When they reached the courtyard, Brother Henry said, "The attendants will show you to rooms. Refresh yourself and eat. The meeting will begin in two hours. It is most urgent that I attend, and they may have questions for you."

Chapter 32

Brother Henry strode past the guards, with Gunner, Thor, and Brondril following him, and all eyes turned toward them. "I have the latest charts and news from Denver." The assembled generals, nobles, and kings looked up from the map table: a three-dimensional table that projected a topographical map of the Black Mountains, the great plains between them, and The Rocky Mountains. He touched his Oracle Scroll to the table. The leather scroll contained data stored at a quantum level and transferred it automatically to the table. The map shimmered for a moment and then displayed the revised troop estimates.

Five triangles represented cavalry battalions: 7,500 daemia troops. They preceded ten black rectangles that represented divisions: 125,000 daemia troops. They are moving south through the Plains Gap, which grew most of their crops. "The drathva Dagon is going to take all the land north of Denver, cutting us off from our food supply. He can afford to wait the winter and feed his daemia troops off our stores like a plague of locusts. They will capture humans and dwarves. They will eat the males and rape the females, breeding more daemia troops. Every month that passes, we will grow weaker, and they will grow stronger."

"Our women would drink their death vial rather than submit to a drathva," said General Degar. "They are loyal to our people and land." A death vial was a lethal poison that all women wore on chains around their necks. Most carried enough for themselves and their children.

"They won't have a choice. The cavalry will sweep into villages and release their stun-gas. They won't have a chance." Henry grabbed Gunner's left arm and drew him up to the table. "This is Gunner Vakhal. Three thousand years ago, when the last age ended, he found one of the Dragon's Eye Pendants. He traveled through time and rescued his family. He was there when Fort Defiant fell."

The King of Denver, Edward Mountbatten III, stroked his calico beard and scanned the map. "I know of no such town, and I am King over all the Plains Gap. You say it fell 3,000 years ago. How is that relevant?"

"I'm trying to tell you. I saw shadows of a great city, the strong defense of all freeborn people. Fort Defiant was the most prosperous city in your entire kingdom. They carved a broad highway into the mountains; they sailed up and down the Misty River in barges filled with goods: wine, grain, livestock, and other merchandise. Their battalions alone could route any daemia army. They were the fiercest warriors in all the lands. They vanished, and all of you have forgotten them like a dream upon waking, but not me: I remember them. They haunt my every waking moment, specters that demand birth." He patted the medallion beneath his robes. "I am protected from time shifts."

"Then you theorize that Dagon has the other eye medallion," said the Elven Lord, Ceven. He stroked his chin and stared at the Misty River. "These past few nights my sleep has been fitful and filled with trouble. I dreamed I stood in the middle of a great city as the daemia attacked. Their great towers burned; death was all around me, and blood turned the Misty River red."

"You have seen his plan," Brother Henry said and pointed at the strategic cities. "He has the other medallion, and he is traveling into the past to wage his war. The elves are safe, but humanity, our first line of defense, is set for the slaughter. We must act now to save them."

Brondril said, "We have been troubled about our western access. We often wondered why our ancestors never created a route to trade with the west. It turns out that they did, but our memories have a hole. You are to blame for this. If you had warned us about the invasion, our wizards would have foreseen this calamity. Now Marek is under attack, and you could have prevented it."

"Your priests and military advisers knew of the threat. They dismissed the danger as the peril of men and elves," said Lord Ceven. "You're King knew of the invasion months ago. You should have warned us."

"Warn you?" Master Brondril, "We knew nothing of this. Would we hold a feast while the enemy is on our very doorstep?"

"This argument is pointless," Henry said. "We may have already planned our defenses on another timeline. We cannot say. Elves, men, and dwarves may have stood side by side to defend our homelands." Henry rubbed the back of his neck and snorted. "We must act. Our troops must depart now and save Fort Defiant."

"Our forces are committed to defending the six cities. They must defend our lands and safeguard our industry." King Edward sniffed and then shook his head. "We have only a thousand troops to safeguard the pass, and 25,000 troops to deal with this invasion, a paltry sum. We cannot do it. Perhaps Lord Ceven can assist you."

Lord Ceven raised an eyebrow. "May I see the pendant?" Gunner reached behind his neck and drew the gold chain from around his neck. All eyes turned to the Dragon's Eye Pendant, and it stared back at them in reply. In a hushed voice, Ceven quoted "The Dragon's Eye Prayer".

One eye is virtuous.
One eye is evil.
The dragon's heart is fire,
The dragon's wrath is dire.
One is Righteous.
One is the Devil.

Lord, deliver us from the terror by night.
Lord, protect us by your heavenly light.

"This prayer flows from every mother's lips when she sees a shadow or hears the hoot of an owl, never giving the true meaning a second thought. Now we know. The Dragon's Eye is found, and it will be the ruin of us all."

"We must act," said Prince Reeve Mountbatten. "This medallion gives us a single chance for salvation. We should save Fort Defiant."

King Edward shook his head and crossed his arms. "We simply do not have the resources. If we send troops to the past, we will be without protection. No, my son, this is a fool's hope. The enemy wishes for us to squander our precious resources on pointless battles. Those who died in the past are beyond our aid. We must deal with the world as it is, not as we wish it to be."

"That is your plan?" asked Callon, Lord Ceven's son, "to wait for our doom as sheep for the slaughter."

Henry pointed at the map. "A thousand troops to the north of the ruins may turn the tide of battle in the past and perhaps this will deliver us in the present. Gunner and I will return to them. He will use the Dragon's Eye to open a pathway back to the battle."

"'May,' 'Perhaps,'" Lord Ceven said and shook his head, "those are feeble words, full of weakness and dread. Those defenders guard the entryway to our lands. If they are lost, we will be defenseless."

Henry looked them in the eye and said, "If we fail to save Fort Defiant, our defeat is assured. None of our lands will survive."

———

The fact that he was about to die made little difference to General Leland McCloud. He began his day — as he had every day of his life — with calisthenics. Deep knee bends, jumping jacks, pushups, squats, and a short run primed his body for the day's rigors. When he finished, he put on a clean white dress shirt, a clean jacket, and strapped a cavalry sword to his side, a symbol of his regiment.

The camp buzzed with activity, anything not to think. The enemy army paid them little heed, the ultimate insult. The advance daemia guard of 7,500 troops camped across the field. It was to their enemy's advantage to wait; the main force of 150,000 troops would arrive in a matter of days. If General McCloud moved to attack, they withdrew, only to return when the general returned to his camp. The enemy force had one goal: to shadow them, to report on their movements.

Fists on his hips, he surveyed them and contemplated his options. Mounted cavalry rode behind him on their daily patrol, and a platoon of foot soldiers jogged along the dirt road through the camp, raising a cloud of dust. The general tried not to look at his men because of the pain in his soul. They need him to be strong, to assure them that they might survive the battle, yet in his heart, he knew defeat and death awaited them. He contemplated writing a last, farewell letter to his wife.

"Sir," said his adjutant with a fist bump to his chest. "Your presence is requested for a conference with headquarters." The general followed the junior officer to the command tent and noted the grim faces of his officers.

A miniature holographic image of King Edward appeared on a communication crystal. The crystals were the size of a paperweight, flat, an octagon, transmitted using gravitons, and was one of twelve. The king clasped his hands behind his back and said, "I just informed your junior officers. There will be no reinforcements. The haugr just attacked Mareck, and the dwarves are defending their homeland. This attack has prompted our Elven allies to reinforce their borders so no troops will arrive from Lentel. I'm afraid you are on your own."

General McCloud paused to collect his thoughts. "Your Majesty understands that we cannot hope to resist the enemy forces. Our defeat is a certainty, and it will take very little time. Do you still wish us to stay, or should we retreat to a strategic position?"

The king's face grew red and the veins on his forehead bulged. He surveyed the map and pondered in silence. "We shall have to adopt a strategy of harassment. Avoid a direct confrontation; slow their progress. When they arrive at the foot of the mountain, reassemble and delay them as long as you can."

"Yes sire," he said, "and what of the reserve brigade?"

"They are stationed so as to safeguard the passage into the mountains, but when you defend the pass, they will supplement your forces as required." The image dissolved and left them in brooding silence. The general addressed his staff. "You have your orders. We will break up into five bands of varying size. Your orders are simple — harass the enemy: burn fields, drive away cattle, leave them nothing to eat, attack them by day and night, but quickly withdraw. When they reach the foothills of the Black Mountains, you will reassemble here for a final battle. Dismissed."

Captain Posner lingered after the others left. He knew his commanding officer too well. The general stood next to the planning table, index finger tapping his lips, and studying the map. "You're not leaving, are you, sir?"

The general raised an eyebrow. "No. There is an army of daemia camped on the other side of the field. We must see that they stay there, have unmarried and childless warriors assigned to my unit. If our position collapses and the enemy takes the mountain road, then you are to retreat to the nearest base and join the resistance."

"Yes sir," the captain said and saluted. "And sir, it has been a pleasure serving with you. I will see you again in the undying lands, and we will share a pint." The general returned the salute and returned to his maps.

Chapter 33

Rivulets of sweat trickled down Bain's forehead and stung his eyes. Beyond the light of his headlamp, the ever-present darkness threatened to engulf him. The smallest comfort – cool air, the kiss of the wind, or the warmth of the sun – seemed a dream. The boulder upon which he sat, the cave wall, and the very air were damp, and acidic air burned his nostrils. His soaked clothes hung heavy upon him and chaffed. Every so often, he and Brian exchanged sullen glances. Their great adventure turned into a marathon hardship.

Kairn rose to his feet and wiped the sweat from his brow. He touched a blue stone set in a silver bracelet, and a blue holographic display illuminated. It showed their location in the emergency escape tunnel. Sixteen kilometers of twisted tunnels filled with jagged rocks, underground rivers, and sheer walls lay behind them, and another 5 kilometers lay between them and the exit. "Enough rest. It's time to press on."

"We should turn back and try another tunnel," said Og. "This passage hasn't been used for over 800 years. My grandfather was the last one to survey it. It could be blocked or underwater. We won't have the provisions for a return trip."

"The escape passage is a known safe route. If we leave it, we risk losing our way or encountering a haugr patrol. No. We will follow the escape route, and then we will return to the city above ground." Kairn put his hands on his hips and said, "Get moving!" The dwarves grumbled and rose to their feet.

Rotted navigation ropes, partially blocked passages, and flooding slowed their progress. Bain and Brian lost all track of time and the oppressive heat and humidity grew worse with each step taken. When they encountered a collapsed wall, they climbed the sharp rocks to rejoin the passage. At the top of the pile, Bain turned his head and happened to see a flash of red tile. He looked back and saw more red and white tiles.

"Bain, where are you going?" asked Brian.

"I saw something." Bain scrambled down the pile and crawled through a rough opening in the wall. When he stood upright, he found himself in a domed cavern. Then his light fell upon a huge figure. He shouted and scrambled backward.

"Are you okay?" asked Brian. "What's happening?"

Bain's heart hammered as he studied the threat. A giant wore a cowboy hat, and it stood upon bowed legs, a thumb pointed to its chest. He knew it. How?

A memory sparked in his mind. Blue skies, cars whizzing down a country highway, oak trees waving in the wind, a crowded parking lot, and a cowboy sign, his father took the family to the "Chuck Wagon Grill" when they visited Colorado. How did it get inside a mountain? Then his face lit up with understanding. The Black Mountains shifted from Eden to Earth, crushing many of those beneath them. The cavernous dome protected the restaurant from annihilation.

When he turned his head, the light illumined a pickup trick. Thousands of years turned it into a grimy mess. Its aluminum body resisted the slow decay of time. He rose to his feet and walked toward the restaurant. The filthy building, the long silent rectangular clock tower, and the gas pumps were mere shadows of the new facility in his memory. When he pushed through the plate-glass doors, his light fell upon a gaping skeleton, bits of clothes and dried fragments of flesh on its bones. A dozen more patrons still sat in rotted vinyl booths, and the bodies were slumped over the tabletops, the back of their skulls missing. Why? Then he saw the body of a state police officer and the gun still clutched in its bony hand. They committed suicide.

"What are you doing?" asked Brian.

Bain jumped and spun around, his heart beating in his throat. "Don't do that. You scared me." He wiped the sweat from his face. "Dad used to bring us here as kids."

"It's gone downhill since then," Brian said. "The corpses ruin my appetite."

"Be serious. A lot of good people died here." Bain picked up a menu, but it fell apart in his hands. "I wish we could have saved them."

"We need to save ourselves," Brian said. "Now let's go."

"I can't imagine their terror. They were eating, talking, and laughing, and a second later they were trapped beneath a mountain. It must have been a nightmare." Bain picked up a quarter from a table and slipped it into his pocket. He sighed and walked past Brian. "It's so sad."

Brian rubbed his face and took one last look. He never allowed himself to think of it: the death of a civilization. Everyone he ever knew was dead. He brushed away the melancholy and followed his brother from the restaurant.

"What took you so long?" snapped Gladgrac. "We must be going."

"I saw some ghosts from the past," he said and walked past them. The others peered back into the chamber and saw the restaurant. With a shrug and mumbles, they followed him.

Chapter 34

Jake, Charlie, and Reggie wandered through the palace as if in a dream. The girls wore long gowns and luxurious robes, making both feel like a princess. Their heels clicked and clacked on the white marble floor, which echoed off the cavernous structure. Their eyes drank in the wonder of it: the sweeping stairs, the red carpet, the high walls with two story windows, immense frescos bordered by gold friezes, a chronicle of sweeping scenes of Elven lore, crystal domed halls, ribbed vaulted ceilings and sparkling chandeliers. Each new room left them wonderstruck and hungry for more.

When they entered a great hall, two elves emerged from a concealed door. Large braziers outside the hall provided subdued lighting, which beamed through towering windows and stretched across the brown marble floor. The elves moved with feline grace and decorum as if in some solemn ceremony, their silver robes embroidered with gold thread trailing behind them. "It is fortuitous that our paths have crossed this fateful night. I am High Priest Golradir, and this the King's Viceroy, Amras."

"Hello," Jake said and crossed his arms, "you were looking for us."

"Actually, we sought the two elvas, but a star shines upon the hour of our meeting. We were informed that ... um ... Reggie and Charlie were never given the rite of inclusion." The corners of his lips curled into an evasive smile, and Golradir gestured with his right hand. "If you ladies are ready, we would like to begin the ceremony."

"Does it take long?" asked Charlie.

"No, not long," Golradir replied. "Please," he said with a sweep of his arm." As the ladies walked away from him, a twinge of suspicion pricked Jake. However, he dismissed it. Everything he witnessed and experienced since entering these lands had a wholesome and virtuous quality.

"If you don't need me, I would like to return to my quarters," Jake said.

"Of course," Golradir said.

Jake watched them depart and then retraced his steps through the palace. Unlike human palaces, the elves preferred subdued illumination, and the palace took on an ancient, storied ambiance. As he strolled through the halls, the spirit of the elves radiated like the warmth of a fire, full of memory, and made him feel one with these ancient people. He paused to study the ancient frescos: broad battle pictorials displaying heroes of old and ancient demons. They belonged to him; they were his heritage.

When he walked past a balcony, he saw an elva, clad in a chiffon gown, silhouetted by a silver moon. Although she was a stranger and the balcony unfamiliar, it sparked a vague memory, so he paused. Out of impulse, he turned to speak with her and stepped between the columns, entering the balcony.

When she turned toward him, half in shadow and half in light, her beauty took his breath away: timeless features, hair fixed up behind her head, pointed ears adorned with jewels, and youth that belied her ancient wisdom. He started to introduce himself when he recognized her. "Juliana, is that you?" He took a step toward her and joy radiated from within. "I can't believe I found you. Where have you been? What happened?"

Her lips parted to speak, but she paused. She cocked her head, narrowed her eyes, and studied him. Then recognition brightened her eyes and caused her to rush into his arms. "Jake!" She held him tight and buried her face into his neck.

Her perfume intoxicated him, and the softness of her body soothed his troubled mind. "I thought I would never see you again." He recounted an abbreviated version of his tale. She listened with interest, but every often, she scanned the hallway and grounds to make sure they were unobserved.

He asked, "What happened to you?"

She caressed the side of his face and saw youthful innocence and passion still burning in his eyes. "It's been over three thousand years since I lost you. After the earthquake and the Black Mountains appeared, I was back in my bedroom in Golden Colorado. I wanted to find you, but we had no power, no cars: everything was broken. I wanted to return to Fort Defiant, but we heard reports that daemia destroyed the city. I joined the civil defense forces, and 26 years passed before I returned. There was nothing left but ruins. I thought you were dead."

"We almost were," Jake said. "At first, my heart ached to find you, but then I was glad you were gone, safe somewhere else. When I close my eyes, I can still see the daemia attacking the fort. But for me, it has been less than a week. Travel through time is disorienting." He held her hands and studied her face, trying to memorize every feature. "You look the same … well … except for the ears and that … Elven quality."

"Same for you," she laughed. Then she narrowed her eyes, looked upward, and searched her memory. "But you always did have an elvan quality that drove the girls wild." She drew in a deep breath, released his hands, and turned away from him. Head bowed and eyes lowered, she said, "I'm married."

"Married?" he echoed.

"For over two thousand years," she said with a sad smile. "If only —" but she drifted into silence. "My life is so much different than I imagined it."

He caressed her cheek and turned her toward him. "I'm thrilled you're alive, and I'm happy you found someone to love. I … I just wish it could have been me. My heart is aching but happy. Did you ever have children? I know how much you love them."

"No. My husband is ambitious. Children make demands for time and attention." For the first time, a bitter taint marred her great beauty. He wished to comfort her, but he was at a loss how to do so. Juliana glanced back at the hallway, crossed her arms, and narrowed her eyes. "My husband is a member of parliament. They called an emergency session, but it may adjourn at any time. We should walk."

They wandered through the castle and then through a garden. Juliana shared some of the high and low points of her life. Whenever they heard voices, Juliana sucked in a small gasp and tensed. When they were alone again, she relaxed and continued. They followed a winding path and paused in the middle of a wooden bridge. The moonlight reflected off the rippling waters.

Jake wanted to be the one who shared her life, and melancholy overshadowed him. He turned toward her and held her hands. "I want to say my goodbye now. You're married, and —" He cleared his throat, "— I lost you." She wanted to object, but his words had the weight of truth. He moved toward her and took her in his arms. The softness of her body, the sweetness of her perfume intoxicated him. They kissed, and for that moment, the universe made sense; but too soon they separated, and the light extinguished in his heart. "Goodbye, I wish our lives had been different." He turned away and left her alone on the bridge.

Jake wiped the tears from his eyes and tried to extinguish the pain. When he entered the parlor that led to their private quarters, he encountered Brother Henry. "Fools, idiots," Henry muttered as he paced. "We should go now. Every minute delayed puts us in greater jeopardy. Never was there a noble who made a decision without a committee."

"Well, I don't —" Jake started to say and sat upon a burgundy plush chair.

"Now is the time to strike." Henry crossed his arms and glared at a bowl of fruit. "Pompous idiots, it is clear what we must do."

The chamber door burst open and Reggie strode into the room. "Look at this." She pointed to her neck. A silver choker necklace: beautiful, ornate, and magical circled her neck. Although various embossed characters adorned it, the front oval was a void, smooth surface. "I thought Golradir wanted to give me some strange jewelry. I was being polite." She paced the floor. She growled and grabbed at her neck. "There is no way to get rid of it. Whenever I take it off and walk away, it reappears around my neck." Her hands slid around the choker and released it. She threw it across the room, but it reappeared on her neck.

"I did tell you about this back in Crow Valley," Henry said.

"This necklace is a patriarchal attempt to subjugate women and to remind them of their inferior status. Men should wear our necklaces, and women should wear the signet ring to control men. You don't see women starting wars or dropping bombs on innocent people." She glared at them and growled, "How do I get rid of it?"

"You can't," he said. "It bonds to the flesh and life force. All Elvas wear one: it marks their birth clan. When you wed, your wedding ring will bear your husband's coat of arms. It joins the two houses. Thus the saying, 'The elvans build the houses, but the elvas build the community."

"What? A man will never claim me with some magic ring. I am a free and independent woman." She crossed her arms and pouted. "I can't believe this."

Jake said, "It's very beautiful."

"I don't care. I don't want to wear one, and I sure don't want to wear a corset. I feel like a tube of toothpaste squeezed in the middle, and I hate this damn maiden's belt." She wiggled her hips and fussed with the thong-like belt beneath her clothing. "They can't do this." She stormed out of the room and slammed the door.

"Some females are resistant to the necklace at first, but it will adjust her to it. She'll be fine. By morning, she won't remember what the fuss was about." Henry selected a shortbread cookie and nibbled on it.

"The necklaces affect the mind?" asked Jake.

"Yes. Both the ring and the necklace do so. A great deal of evil magic attacks the mind and makes one prisoner to the caster. The necklace protects against such attacks, and it prevents depression, anxiety, and such the like. It also provides robust health, blocking infection and curing various maladies. As a matter of course, it works to create harmony in marriage: it gives the elva enhanced empathy, sensing her people's emotions and sharing in their strength. True, it does exercise reasonable control over her, limiting her travel to safe regions and prohibiting unhealthy relationships. It's all for the best."

Jake squirmed, struggling with this revelation about Elven culture, and asked, "Such as a former suitor?"

Henry nodded, "Yes. That would certainly be a legitimate use. No husband wants a former lover around his wife. But the wedding ring, not the necklace, would do that." He furrowed his brow and looked up at the ceiling. "What was I talking about?"

"Our delay," Jake said and brooded in silence. Juliana's behavior made sense. If her husband saw them together, he could prohibit her from seeing him again or even being near him. She was lost to him. The room pressed in on him and his stomach churned. Rubbing his face, he agonized over her loss.

"Oh yes, the council hasn't an ounce of sense between them ...."

———

Gunner and Thor walked the castle wall and the frigid night wind blasted them. Although they sensed the cold, they were warm as if a summer's day. Every so often, they passed by torch lamps made of brass and hand-blown glass. The nearby guards searched the surrounding forest for threats and eyed these strangers.

Turned toward one another, speaking in hushed voices, a pair of strangers lingered in the shadows. Gunner and Thor slowed their pace, and their hands grazed their swords. Prince Callon and Prince Reeve turned and stepped into the meager light. The sharp contrast between light and shadow made their faces appear ancient and grim. After an exchange of glances, Callon said, "Our fathers have decided against Brother Henry's plan. They say, '... our western borders must be defended.' Yet they know our defenses will fail."

Gunner searched their faces and said, "You do not agree?"

"Well, we are of a different mind –" Callon started to say.

"No, we do not agree," Reeve said. Although small in stature, he was an imposing figure: clothed in black fur, armor plate beneath his coat, a broadsword upon his left hip, a trimmed beard, and an iron crown upon his head, the embodiment of a barbarian king. "If Brother Henry is correct, we have one chance to win this conflict. Otherwise, well ... our chances are slim."

"You want us to defy both of your father's orders," Gunner said.

Callon bowed his head and turned away. Reeve drew in a deep breath and stroked his trimmed beard. "Your family has no standing in the court or either kingdom. You could act without fear of reprisal. We, on the other hand, must be circumspect. We have obligations: our legislative bodies require our administration."

"That means yes," Thor said. "If we fail, it provides the two of you with plausible deniability. You disavow us, and your position is secure."

"Well said," Reeve replied. "You're family must go with you. Once your actions become clear, they would arrest and imprison them. However, if you succeed, our fathers would pardon your actions. I'm sure of it."

"If you are so sure, then you can write us a pardon in advance," Thor replied.

"No," Callon said. "You must bear this risk alone. We will help you as we are able." Gunner very much doubted that they would provide any assistance, yet what other choice did he have?

Chapter 35

"I wanted to stay." Reggie rode a horse through the darkness. "I'm just saying; it would be nice to actually spend more than one night at a place. I felt safe." She fussed with her maiden's belt.

The protective garment included a wide silver belt, secured around the waist, and a silver metal thong, attached to the belt at the sides. The manufacturer keyed the bio-locks to biological signatures: family, friends, and comrades – it was not a chastity belt – and included lavish adornments; but this failed to assuage their insecurities. Civilian females wore them underneath their clothing, but since all of the group wore armor, the belt was on the outside of their glossy black slip-suits. However, their silver scale-mail tunics fitted them like micro mini-dresses and provided some marginal covering.

Reggie said, "Why do I have to wear this maiden's belt thing?"

"It keeps you and all of us safe. Daemia possesses crude telepathic abilities. They can sense prey, enemies, or available females for miles," Brother Henry replied.

Although Charlie and Linda remained silent, they agreed with Reggie. Maiden's belts were an uncomfortable and embarrassing nuisance.

Jake found it difficult not to stare at Reggie. When Reggie felt "the weight of his stare," she snapped her head to the right and glared at him. Jake looked away as if admiring the stars. "I don't see why I had to go. My family is all in Houston."

Although still in safe country, Gunner feared that the Kings would discover their plan and send riders to arrest them. However, he heard only normal night sounds: the hoot of an owl, the drone of crickets, the clip-clop of hooves, and the distant bark of a dog. He regretted bringing the children and Linda, but they had no choice. They faced arrest and imprisonment. "Reggie, I know it has been hard, but could you go five minutes without complaining?"

"I guess," she said. "To think, I read all those adventure novels and wished I could have one. This sucks."

Master Brondril brought up the rear and road a mountain goat. The surefooted animal could scale the highest peak but offered little benefit on a cross-country ride. The goat moved with a seesaw action that made his bottom sore. "I don't see why the elves have to be so damned unreasonable. They are the ones that blocked the rescue of Fort Defiant. The humans always agree with the elves. Puppets, they are nothing but puppets."

Dawn broke over the mountains and painted a sherbert sky, vivid ripples of crimson and orange set in a field of blue. A white shroud of mist clung to the ground, making it appear like winter, and birds darted about in search of a morning meal. A lake appeared smooth as black glass and reflected the vibrant sky. A fish leaped from the tranquil waters, snatched a dragonfly, and landed with a splash. The broken remains of a wagon and toppled blocks penetrated the mist. "A great battle was fought and lost. The fortress of Vahva Pulous and the city of Lansipour fell."

The ancient road skirted the western side of Mareck Mountain. Paving blocks, bridges carved from mammoth boulders, and street lamps on the road's edge marked the proud Dwarven Highway. It had a timeless, rugged quality that mirrored the people who built it. Even tunnels, bored through granite, reflected Dwarven aesthetics, and rough rock bore rune inscriptions.

When they rounded a bend, Jake peered over the shoulder of the road. It snaked down the mountain, a thin ribbon of gray, and traversed a crescent-shaped valley. In the center of this depression lay the town of Trader's Hold and the Mareck mine entrance. The sun cleared the mountain peaks when they neared the city. The trip was much shorter, and that perturbed him. "Why didn't we come this way to start with?" he asked Henry.

"Hmm, what? Oh, well, Master Brondril and the dwarves had a right to understand the threat and to attend the meeting, so we made a quick detour." He turned and noted the impatience in Jake's eyes. "The shortest path is not always a straight line. You must be strategic in your thinking …." Henry continued his monolog and made Jake sorry he asked.

They skirted around the north city limits of Trader's Hold, to avoid entanglements. Armed troops cleared the Narrow Gap Pass, which also sped up their trip. As is the case with most travelers, the trip down the mountain seemed to go much faster, and by the time the sun sank behind the Rocky Mountains in the west, they reached the valley floor.

They camped in the ruins of the dead city, but like most elves, sleep came in a short burst, if at all, and filled with turbulent dreams. The tent flaps burst open and Jake stepped into the night. His eyes adjusted to the darkness and a monochrome world took shape around him. A full moon hung in the sky like a shiny new dime, and he wondered if it was the same moon. How could it be? So much had changed, yet heavenly bodies endured while man perished.

He buttoned his jacket and strapped on his weapons. The nighttime forest beckoned him. He broke into a jog, then a run, and then a sprint. He dashed through the forest quieter than a cat, and he bounded from shadow to shadow. He scampered up a fallen tree and leaped into the branches of another. His breathing calm, he surveyed his surroundings. A slight movement by the river caught his eye. He slotted an arrow, but he paused: better to not shoot at an unknown target.

After he had scampered down from the tree, he raced between the trees and approached the river. A small figure wore a cloak, the hood raised, and stood next to a bend in the river. The moon and stars reflected on the ambling waters. The figure turned, red locks emerged like a red flame; they framed a pallid face with eyes black glass. He drew in a gasp and reached for his sword. She cocked her head and said, "What's the matter? It's just me."

Jake narrowed his eyes and studied her face. "Charlie?" asked Jake. "You scared the crap out of me. What's with the whole spooky girl by the river routine? Are you feeling okay?"

She cocked her head and without expression said, "I'm fine … I think. Perhaps not, but I'm not sick either." She scanned the shore and the woods beyond. "I see them."

"See who?" asked Jake.

"The ones that live here, or used to live here until … until the drathva Dagon snatched away their lives: never born, never sung, never kissed, never wept, lost in the mists," she said.

"Yeah, okay, there's nothing spooky about that." Jake rubbed an itch from his nose and studied the mist rising from the river. Figures arose in the wisps and turned into ghostly men. They mounted steeds, formed ranks, and marched before them. Black holes for eyes stared at him, demanded action, demanded birth.

"We have to save them," Charlie whispered.

Chapter 36

"Why do I always get sentry duty?" asked Grindal. "My feet hurt; my back hurts, and my ass is on fire."

"Your ass is on fire?" asked Brunt.

"Yeah, I had the doc look at my hemorrhoids, but he just gave me some cream. It works for a while, but it always comes back after I use the toilet." Grindal stamped his feet and blew into his hands. "It's cold."

Brunt shook his head and gazed down the dirt road. The road entered a grove of trees, turned around a bend, and disappeared from sight. He hated being so close to the tree line: an archer could reach their position. They were the first to die in case of attack, and Grindal complained all the time. Brunt cast a sideways glare at Grindal and shivered.

"… And my wife refused to send me a warmer coat. Can you believe that?" asked Grindal.

Brunt raised his hand and squinted. Riders emerged from the woods and then several more. "Rider's approaching," he shouted. The captain of the guard rode over to their position. "Elves and a wizard approach, Captain Rowan."

Captain Rowan retrieved a pair of binoculars from the horse's saddlebags. He knew Brother Henry, but the elves were strangers to him. He trotted his horse past the sentries and greeted them. "Hail Brother Henry, we did not think that we would see you. Is all well?"

"I bring orders and counsel," Henry said, "but I require a private audience with your commander. Who is he?"

"Colonel Briggs," Captain Rowan said. "I will escort you to his tent."

"My companions and their mounts require food and rest," Henry said.

Rowan signaled two of his men. "Show them to guest quarters and see to their horses. Please follow me," he said.

No matter what the age, military camps have the same atmosphere. Tan tents, erected in a grid pattern, lay in the center of a pasture. A palisade of sharpened logs, followed by a ditch, then a berm, and then a parapet with angular spikes protected the camp. The defensive measures had a crude and hasty appearance, but they appeared effective. Aggressors would be reluctant to assault the camp.

Even at the precipice of war, the routines of life occurred: a group of men drilled; a smithy shoed a horse; a chef stirred boiling pots, and other men polished their armor. The group rode to the center row and then toward a large tent in the center of the camp. Red pennants embroidered with silver steeds flapped in the morning breeze. When they reached the command tent, a pair of youths tended to their horses.

Sentries drew the tent flaps open at their approach. Colonel Conrad Briggs and his staff stood around a mapping table and studied the defenses for the surrounding area. The colonel glanced up from the map and raised an eyebrow. The captain said, "Brother Henry comes bearing news and orders."

Henry handed the colonel a message tube. "It's been a long time. I did not think I would see you again after the battle of Dead Fork. You look well, a bit gaunt and weathered, but fit."

"And your girth is even greater than I remember, and you have less hair." The colonel's scowl turned into a warm smile. He shook Henry's hand and patted his arm. "It's been too long, my old friend."

"Yes. It's a shame that war brings us together," Henry said.

The colonel examined the tube. The wax seal bore the king's signet. "It's about time we received orders. We've languished in this pasture for months." He broke the seal and tossed aside the tube. After unrolling the documents, he lay them on the table and read them. The officers were fixated on the documents and failed to see the seal turn to ash, but Henry noticed: there was no turning back.

"What is this Dragon's Eye Pendant?" asked Colonel Briggs.

"An elvan, Gunner, possesses it. It is he who will open the curtain to the past," Henry said.

The Colonel leafed through the documents and shook his head. "There is no map of the city and no indication of our enemy's location or troop strength. Riding into battle under such conditions would be a disaster."

"I can help with part of your need." He searched through his leather satchel and pulled out a map. He unfolded it and spread it on the table. The colonel held down one side and studied it. "This is an ancient map that details the exact layout of the city." He pointed at the Fort Defiant State College and said, "The campus is set upon a hill and has a nominal wall surrounding it. It would make a good command headquarters." He moved his finger south and pointed at the fort. "This is where the defenders, who accompanied me, fought the last battle of Fort Defiant.

After fighting a pitched battle all night, an earthquake destroyed the fort and the city was lost. I suspect drathva involvement."

"Hmm … yes. A drathva would eliminate it to prevent any organized defense. As you say, the campus is on the edge of the city and would be a defensible position. Did the enemy come from the west?"

"The Elven survivors reported devastation coming from the northwest. The daemia army crossed the Misty River, which at that time was much smaller and spanned by three bridges. Once across the river, they attacked the city, devastating it, and then pushed south, killing all in their path."

"Yes, I see. Lacking organized resistance, it was a simple matter of slaughtering the survivors." The colonel spread out the maps and pondered them in silence. "This gives me what we need. We will study it and form a battle plan."

Chapter 37

Jake collapsed onto a cot and stretched out. Although weary, sleep fled from him, and miserable consciousness robbed him of rest. His mind wandered through time to where their journey began. He wished he could step back into his former life, return to yesterday, and choose a different path. Such dreams, however, dissolve when the present returns and our shoulders bear the burden of the future.

The tent flap flew open and Reggie strode into the tent. She sat with her arms crossed and scowled. Jake turned over and refused to give up his quest for sleep. His thoughts returned to Juliana like a melody that he could not forget. She haunted his thoughts, and he was sure it would ever be thus.

"I can't get this thing off," Reggie said.

"Uh huh," Jake grunted. "You mentioned that."

"What's the matter with you?" Reggie touched the choker that circled her neck, and her fingers glided over it. "Are you still brooding about Juliana?"

"No. Yes. Leave me alone," he said.

Charlie entered the tent, and when she saw Jake, she cocked her head and said, "What's the matter with him?"

"He's pouting because he misses Juliana," Reggie said.

"No. I am not pouting. Okay, So what if I am? I'm glad she survived, but I lost her just the same," he said.

Before Charlie could comment, Linda entered the tent with his father close behind her. "Quit moping. We will be moving out soon. You need to get ready."

Jake turned over and sat on the end of the bed. His searched the faces of his friends and family for the meaning of their intrusion into his personal misery, and an epiphany came to him: elves are telepathic. They live as a community both in body and mind. "Our whole world is gone. Everyone I ever knew is dead. No more Main Street, no trips to get a burger, no drives in the country, I never thought it would end. It was supposed to last forever."

His mom rushed to him and gave him a hug. "I know. We all feel it, but the pain will fade. Just give it some time."

He pushed away and combed his fingers through his blonde locks. "I don't want it to fade. I want my life back. I want Juliana back." He pressed his hands to his face and groaned, "I hate this. Our whole world, the United States and everyone we ever knew, is gone. What are we supposed to do — forget them?"

"We are doing what we can," Gunner said, "instead of what we can't."

"Yeah, I know," he sighed.

Thor stuck his head into the tent. "We are going to move out with the troops in the morning. We will act as liaison to the human community."

Linda cringed, put her arm around Jake, and asked, "They can't want us to fight. This is ridiculous. We're not trained warriors." She thought about Gunner and Thor's military service, and then said, "Some of us aren't warriors."

"We are not fighting. They only want us to meet and coordinate with the local officials. Grab your gear. We have —" Thor started to say.

"Let me guess," Jake said. "We have to get going. It's an emergency, and we have to move out right away. We haven't had a chance to catch our breath or rest since this whole nightmare began. Now comes the running and the screaming."

"Something like that," Thor said. "Now get your stuff, and let's go." He tossed a bundle down with a clank. "Put on your Elven battle gear."

"Wonderful," Jake mumbled. He picked through the armor and gear. "These metal cups are cold." Then he noticed Reggie's perturbed expression. "Oh yeah, I guess you've got it worse."

Some time later, Jake pushed aside the tent flap and exited the tent. His right hand glided over the cool metal clasped around his lean frame. Both adornment and function, both beautiful and ugly, and both restrictive and mobile, the armor declared, "Be aware, an Elven warrior walks among you." When the Sons of Thunder, Gunner and Thor, exited their tents, men took notice. The sight of such powerful Elven warriors inspired both awe and fear, but the sight of Charlie not so much. She pranced along behind them, a cheerleader following the team.

"Much better," Brother Henry said. "Now you look like Elven warriors of old and renown." Linda and Reggie led over the horses. The sight of Reggie — clad in a glossy black slip-suit that contrasted her silver armor — inspired awe within Jake. Her scale, chainmail tunic appeared like a tight silver mini-dress, but it stopped mid hip; and when she moved just so, he caught a glimpse of her silver maiden's belt. Reggie had always been a great friend, a companion on life's journey, but in that instant, she became something more. He saw her for what she became, not for who she had been.

Never more than just a friend of her youth, Reggie saw Jake with new eyes. His flaxen hair, pointed ears poking through his locks, vibrant blue eyes, and warm smile captivated her, yet there something more about him — a non-human presence that whispered of mystery and lore. She understood why the men paused to watch them pass. Elves shunned human contact and secluded themselves from the sons of men.

She sensed the gulf between herself and humanity. When she approached women, the conversation ceased, and they moved away when decorum allowed. She was eternal, forever young. When she ran, she did not grow weary. She ran faster, jumped higher, heard the scamper of a mouse, and saw with the eyes of a hawk — yes, the gap was real: men were wisps of smoke, appearing for a moment and passing from sight.

Men tested their shields; women strung their bows; horses skittered about and neighed; troops assembled in formation; pennants flapped atop poles, and the clarion of trumpets called all to battle. Jake mounted his steed and surveyed the clamor: warriors glinted in the morning light and a long column began to march. He and the others joined the cavalry unit at the rear. When they tapped their spurs, the horses moved. They passed in front of the foot soldiers and galloped through the gate.

The road weaved through an apple orchard, little green apples upon each twig. The sun emerged from behind the Black Mountains and reflected on the Misty River, burned away the morning fog, and warmed the land. Armor, a backpack, and battle gear made Jake wish that he wore shorts and a T-shirt, but he was glad for the protection. His thoughts raced ahead to tomorrow. Like all those before him, he wondered who would survive the day and where the end would find him: victorious or dead, face down in some bloody field.

Charlie chewed her lower lip and stared at the horse's mane. The chatty girl languished in silence, her thoughts brooding and full of despair. Jake rode up next to her and said, "I love your outfit. It's the best that I've ever seen on you." She touched her Elven armor and then primped her red curls. A smile brightened her face. He said, "Don't worry. We'll be with you."

"Okay," she said in a soft voice.

Reggie drew in a deep breath through her nose. "Horses stink. They look so beautiful. You wouldn't think it, but they do. Maybe mine needs a bath. Nah, it just stinks. What do you suppose Brian and Bain are doing?"

Chapter 38

Bain repelled down the sheer rock face through the all-consuming gloom. Acidic water dripped for hidden heights and stung his eyes. Even with gloves, the rough rope left his hands raw, and weary legs kept searching for the bottom. Everything ached — yet it was the best day of his life: for the first time, he walked among his people, and he belonged.

At long last, his headlamp reached the bottom, and he saw Brian gazing up at him. He was the last dwarf down the cliff, and the second he reached the bottom, they resumed their trek. They scampered over jagged rocks that lined an underground river, and an unexpected wind gusted from the opposite direction. They drew near the exit. However, there would be no rest. When they emerged, it was their duty to hike up the mountain and join the battle.

Master Kairn raised his fist, and they stopped. He sniffed the air. "There's a foul stench on the wind. Daemia and haugr are near. Each dwarf readied their weapon and moved in silence. When they rounded a bend, daylight blinded them. The faint smell turned into a festering stench, and all were nauseous. They followed the river to the mouth of the cave. The waters leaped off the sheer cliff and plunged over the waterfall. It emptied into a lake set in the foothills. Black tents spread across green fields, and countless axes chopped at pine trees. One after another, twigs snapping, branches breaking, a deep thud from the earth, trees crashed to the ground. Daemia appeared more numerous than ants upon the ground. They constructed siege ramps to reach the air vents and invade the dwarven city.

Kairn sat upon a broad, flat stone and gulped a swig of whiskey. He handed it to Og, and in turn, it passed to each dwarf. "Well brothers, there you see it: the end of Marek. Those accursed daemia will haul those ramps all the way up the mountain on the Broad Road. It's long, but it has a tapered grade. The city defenders will be in the tunnels, repelling the haugr diversion. They will invade from above and take the city unaware."

"We must do something," said Gladgrac.

The master dwarf scanned the cliffs above them. Sentries stood upon the cliff's edge and guarded the high camp. "Going down is certain death, and so is going up, and we cannot go back." He gripped his war hammers and eyed the stairs to the top. "We will rush the camp above us.

One of us might make it through. If so, he will warn our people of their pending doom."

"As fond as I am of a suicidal charge," Bain said, "we have another option. We could travel up the river and search for another way out. The water has to enter somewhere."

"Aye, that's true enough," Kairn said and stroked his beard. "If we fail, we can always return and use the cover of darkness. It's a good plan. Let's go."

They retreated from the harsh light of day, and once again, the welcoming arms of the earth received them: the cool air, the firm stone, and the sacred darkness. After retracing their way up the river and beyond, they arrived at a fork in the river. While the others searched for a way to forge the swift moving waters, Kairn saw a natural bridge above them. "This way," he said and scaled the wall. The others scampered up after him. When they reached the top, they found a long forgotten bridge carved from solid stone, a long forgotten road of the dwarven people.

Kairn returned to the cave's mouth where the road emerged. Layers of grime and muck covered a flat rectangle. He wiped away the filth with his hand and studied the chart. "This is the old trade trail. Legend has it that our ancestors used it before the mountain shifted to Earth. Hundreds of miles of these roads passed through the Wolf's Maw Mountains on our homeworld of Eden. One could go all the way to Midway City." He found a spot on the map that excited him. "Look here. He traced backward on the map. It passed close by where we found that abandoned human restaurant, and then it travels right up to the city."

"We can use it to return home," Og said.

"Nay, the bulkheads are closed. We would never find a way through them. No, we must exit and climb the mountain. Let us hurry." Kairn sprinted away from them, and they chased after him.

Chapter 39

Hope kindled upon their arrival at the dead city. Colonel Briggs sat atop his mount at the top of a foothill. He searched the surrounding countryside, but his hungry eyes found only ruins: a bit of weathered concrete, the tattered remnant of a red brick wall, a sunken hole filled with vegetation, rectangular structures covered with vegetation, and cool blue water.

Gunner rode up to the colonel's side and pulled the Dragon's Eye Amulet out from beneath his clothing. The colonel looked at it, and the Dragon's Eye looked back at him and blinked. "We wish to travel back to a time before the city fell." The eye closed, and when it opened, a golden dot hovered in the air before them. It spread out in a great, golden curtain, one that reached to the heavens, into the earth, and spread out before them. It shimmered and waved as if caught in a breeze; sweet smelling spices and the scent of flowers hung in the air; and its glow renewed their flesh, restoring their vigor and refreshing their soul.

Gunner tucked the medal away. "Now we ride through it. It's harmless, like passing through a waterfall." The horse, if it noticed the curtain at all, paid it little heed. He rode through it and disappeared. The colonel took a deep breath and forged his courage. He signaled his captains and led the way.

When the colonel emerged on the other side, it took a few seconds for his eyes to adjust. The sun shifted back to sunrise in the eastern sky, and despite the sun of a later summer, an indefinable chill nipped at his nose. Red and golden leaves still clung to the trees, and buildings, dozens of them, rose up like ghosts.

White tents, carnival music, a meandering crowd, and the aroma of food stunned the colonel. He knew Fort Defiant as a ruin, bereft of life, yet the students that passed between buildings and eyed him with curiosity. He rode up to a young man clad in a bulky sweater, faded blue jeans, and canvas athletic shoes. "Excuse me, boy, where are we?"

The young man cocked his head and gave the colonel a sideways glance. "This is Fort Defiant State College. Are you some sort of renaissance re-enactor here for the festival?"

"No. I'm with the King's Army. Run and tell the school officials that I have arrived." The young man gave the colonel a curious examination and then walked toward the administrative building, looked back several times, and scratched his head. When the colonel turned his horse around, his face went ashen. He covered his mouth and stared at landscape. He turned toward Gunner and asked, "Where are the Black Mountains?"

"They haven't arrived yet. I would say they won't be here for another three hours, perhaps less." Gunner took a swig from his canteen. "It's flat as a pancake right now. I never thought that would change in the blink of an eye."

"It's astonishing." The colonel became weak and struggled to stay in the saddle. "The myths are true. I-I can't believe it. It's impossible but true. Will angels wing down from heaven? What is impossible?" When the troops broke formation and looked about in dismay, the sergeants barked orders, but no one listened. They were too astonished, and it took them precious time to regain control.

"With me," the colonel shouted. He strode toward the administrative building, and the others followed him. They charged up the stairs with a clatter of armor and slammed open the doors to the main building. No matter what century, military installations had similar style architecture: a plain face, square, simple, functional, a defensible building that suited the military mind. It reassured him that these were his ancestors, and it provoked a kinship that transcended time.

Standing in the hallway, Selwyn Rogers paused from speaking with his secretary Rose. He cocked his head and squinted at them. Clad in silver armor, swords on their left hip, and smelling of horse, they appeared unreal, phantoms from some ancient battle. "Excuse me, can I help you?"

The officers marched past him without answering. A series of maps — the town, the old fort, and the surrounding counties — hung on the ecru walls. "These are ideal for our needs." He pulled the county map off the wall, and his men gathered around him. "It is as we hoped. Three main bridges cross the Misty River. If we control them, we control access to the town."

"You're going to use a Thermopylae Defense?" asked Gunner.

The colonel pondered the question for a few seconds and nodded. "We can hold two of the bridges with 500 troops at each, but the third bridge is too far, and we don't have enough personnel."

Jake pushed through and pointed to the third bridge. "That bridge is going to be destroyed. A fuel truck explodes on it. Both spans fall into the water. Only the center pier remains intact."

"But we crossed it after it had been rebuilt," Gunner said, "but that was later."

"Can I help you?" asked Selwyn.

"You are in charge of this facility?" asked the colonel.

"Um … yes," Selwyn said, spread his feet, and crossed his arms.

"We have need of it as a field hospital. We will evacuate the wounded and the civilian population here. If you have any defensive measures in place, you should activate them. The town is about to be overrun," Colonel Briggs said.

Selwyn took a step back, turned his head sideways, and eyed them. "What? Is this some sort of drama or reenactment?" Then he saw Jake. "What is going on with you? You charged into my office and ran out. A few seconds later, you rush back into the building dressed … well … dressed like that."

Jake looked through the open office door and through the window. He saw himself running across campus toward the student union. "We don't have time to explain. Some people … um … creatures are going to attack the town. These people are here to stop them. They need your cooperation."

"This is insane." When Jake started to go, Selwyn grabbed Jake's left arm. "I need to know what's happening."

"Search your heart. You know that queasy feeling: that sense of dread, that certainty something terrible is about to happen?" When Selwyn nodded, Jake said, "It's real. All we are asking is that you make provisions for the wounded and help those who evacuate from town. It's like those civil defense drill you made us do last year. Will you help us?"

"I guess," Selwyn said.

"Fantastic, all we need from you is to activate the civil defense measures. The sudden drop out of all the phones and other technology would justify it. Just get the plan and put it into action." When Selwyn nodded, Jake said, "I have to go." He rushed out of the building and sprinted after himself.

Jake circled around the building and slowed to a stop. Amidst the crowd, he saw the back of his car as it cruised away from the student union, and then his hawk-like eyes focused on Juliana. The innocence in her eyes, her love for him made his soul ache, and he yearned to chase after her; but there was no time — lives depended on him. He noticed the other students staring at him and at the soldiers that assembled on the parade ground.

"This is one screwed up day," Doug said. "My car's wiring is burnt; the battery is melted, and you look like a 'renaissance fair' reject."

"Huh," grunted Jake. "Oh, yeah, well, your day is about to get a whole lot weirder." He pointed east. "You see that empty space on the horizon. Well, don't get used to it. The biggest damn mountain range you've ever seen is about to appear. It's going to cause earthquakes so bad it will reshape the earth."

As if on cue, the thick sod pushed up to their left, and Brian's head appeared. He pushed aside the thick clumps of green grass and brown earth, and then he climbed out of a hole. Bain came next, followed by the rest of the dwarves. Brother Henry lumbered past them and rubbed his ponderous belly. "You're the last person I expected to see, Kairn."

Kairn brushed off the dirt and said, "Shaft 37 was overrun by Haugr, and Marek is under attack. We followed the emergency escape shaft to the Echo Waterfall, but there had to be at least 10,000 daemia in the plains below us and even more above us. They built siege ramps to access Marek's air intake shafts. We reversed our course and happened upon the ancient trade trail. We were almost to the end when we encountered a curtain of golden light." He looked up at the empty sky where his mountain home should have been. "What happened? The mountains have vanished."

"No," Brother Henry said and patted Kairn on the shoulder. "They haven't arrived from Eden yet. We have to act. The daemia are about to attack Fort Defiant. Saving the ancient city is the only way to safeguard the future …."

"And what of Marek? Who will save my people?" asked Kairn. "We must warn them what happened."

"Your people will have no dealings with an unknown dwarf of dubious lineage and no clan. They will brush aside your words and disregard your warnings." Brother Henry's hand rubbed his belly and screwed up his face. "I am a member of the Wizard's Council and a holder of the Sacred Flame. Although I never met with these dwarves up to this point, the royal assembly in Drendain accepted my counsel, and the dwarves of Marek will have no choice but to accept my words. I must be the one to go."

"Aye," Kairn said stroked his beard. "We will stay."

"I must leave once the Black Mountains arrive," Henry said. "However, I will return as soon as possible."

"I do not understand all of this. What of our battle to save our home?" Og said. "We cannot abandon our people. We must go with Brother Henry and fight."

"Do you see mountains? For I do not. Perhaps Tsuur, in his infinite wisdom, has brought us here for this very moment. And I tell you this, that army we saw in the planes is beyond our reckoning. The battle to save Marek is here and now. Take hold of your weapons and join the battle to save our people."

Chapter 40

The statue of Magus Vakhal — founder of Fort Defiant and an American Civil War hero — watched the army in quiet repose. He died in battle, a glorious death by all accounts, but the living wished to avoid such glory. Do the dead even know that their death was glorious? Even if they do, what good does it do them? They are dead.

Doom consumed their thoughts, because in all the stories — the fall of the ancient world, the destruction of Fort Defiant, and the end of the Golden Age of humanity — death was a foregone conclusion. Despite the cool air, the sun baked the pavement and dust stung their eyes. Shoppers and merchants alike exited the Main Street Shopping Mall to watch the strange procession. Bob's Barbershop emptied one man with an apron around his neck. Patrons dining alfresco spoke in whispers and speculated about a renaissance convention. Children on bicycles rode along and joined the excitement. Milton Barnhouse, sheriff deputy, radioed the station. "Was a parade scheduled?"

Three bridges — the Holiday Bridge, the McCormick Ferry Bridge (the Mac), and the Coronado Bridge — spanned the Misty River. The next closest bridges were 73 miles north and 56 miles south. Colonel Briggs climbed down the riverbank and inspected the bridge. "Our ancestors were … are skilled engineers," he said to Captain Rowan. "It would take us a week to demolish it, and we have only hours."

"We can block the bridge with debris," the captain said.

"Our enemy is ruthless but efficient. They would soon remove any fixed obstacle. Jake reported that the Coronado Bridge will be destroyed by an explosion. They used petroleum to fuel their machines. He called it gasoline."

"Gasoline?" asked Rowan.

"Yes. Suicidal in our time, rhunite would detonate any such fuel." They climbed back to the top of the embankment. He opened his mouth to speak when an earthquake threw them to the ground. The sun smeared across the sky. "IT'S HAPPENING," he shouted and held up his right arm to guard his face. The Earth screamed as if giving birth, and brilliant yellow light washed across the sky, and clouds like giant waves rolled over the land. The heavens rent and a jagged rip revealed stars set in the midnight sky.

When the Black Mountains appeared, the ground heaved, twisted, and broke. Ripples, like waves on the ocean, flowed across the land, and the river ran in the wrong direction. A tremendous explosion occurred in the south and hurtled concrete debris hundreds of meters into the air. They rained down upon the city with catastrophic effect. The troops raised their shields and deflected this lethal debris.

When they rose to their feet, the summits of the Black Mountains now appeared in the east. Foothills solidified and bedrock jutted from the earth like broken bones. Alarms whirred through the city, and black pillars rose from a multitude of fires. Vehicles stopped and lay scattered on the streets. The occupants staggered from their stricken cars and scrambled over the bridge toward the wounded city.

"Use those vehicles as a barrier. Push them into place," shouted the colonel. It took the troops a minute to gather their wits. Groups pushed cars and trucks into place and then tipped them on their sides. The dwarves retrieved great blocks of stone, pushed up from the ground, and formed crude barriers. "I want a patrol to tell me our enemy's location and strength."

"What can I do?" Jake asked the colonel.

"Spread the word throughout the town. Have them evacuate to the campus, and have them mount patrols to safeguard it. Our duty lies here," the colonel said.

Jake turned and ran to his horse. In true elve fashion, he leaped onto the horse's back and galloped away. The others of his group rode with him. They charged up Main Street and made a left on Center Street. The city complex lay at the top of the hill. They rode across the lawn, dismounted their horses, and surged up the stairs. They threw open the double doors and entered town hall. Mayor Waylon staggered about as if drunk, blood flowing from a wound on his balding head.

"Are you all right?" Jake held the mayor and inspected the gash. "Get a first aid kit." Charlie ran toward the restrooms and found one mounted to the wall. She snatched it and returned. After opening the box, Reggie cleaned the wound and applied a gauze pad with some tape.

"I'm fine," he gasped. "What happened?"

It was an all too familiar question, one without a believable answer. "You have to come outside." They helped him out of the building, and when he saw the Black Mountains, he turned ashen and began to faint. They helped him over to the courthouse steps and Reggie fetched him a glass of water.

He took a sip and said, "Sweetheart, I need something way stronger than water. Get me a shot of scotch from the Clock Restaurant." After she went back inside the building, he struggled to his feet. "This is impossible. Mountains just don't appear. I can't understand this." He bent over and vomited. When Reggie emerged with the glass of whiskey, he swallowed it in one gulp.

"How doesn't matter," Jake said. "They are here, and the world is changed. Enemies are going to attack Fort Defiant from the west. We've blocked off the bridges, but it may not be enough. We need you to follow the civil defense plan and evacuate everyone to the campus."

Another explosion rocked the building and a ball of fire rose up from behind the courthouse. "The propane tanks exploded," Jake said. "Come on. We need to get busy." They ushered Mayor Waylon into the courthouse, and Sheriff John Stone exited his office.

"The whole city is in crisis and now my radios are failing. All I get is static." When he saw Jake and the others, he asked, "What's their story?"

"Step outside, look east, and then come back in," said the mayor. When the sheriff crossed his arms and glared at him, he said, "Just do it, John." The sheriff snorted and marched out of the building. When he returned a minute later, he covered his mouth with his right hand and was ashen.

"Are you okay?" asked Jake.

"Where the hell did those mountains come from? It's not possible." He wandered into a restaurant and grabbed a hidden bottle of whiskey. He poured two drinks, one for himself and one for the mayor. After tossing back the drink, he said, "What do we need to do?"

"These … young people want us to evacuate to the college campus," the mayor said. "They say someone is about to attack us from the west."

"Of course, they are," the sheriff replied and poured another drink. He gulped it and poured another. "Do we have any idea who is attacking us?"

"It's more like what," Charlie said. "They're called daemia."

"Daemia? What in the hell is a daemia?" asked the mayor.

"Monsters," Reggie said and sat on a barstool, "and I have seen way too many of them. We don't have much time before they attack."

"Right." The sheriff took a swig from the bottle and walked toward his office. When Gwen, his secretary, was about to ask him a question, he held up his left hand for her to stop. He flipped open a panel marked "Civil Defense Siren". After he pressed a large red button, a siren wailed and its twins echoed all over town.

―――

The earsplitting siren caused Colonel Briggs to turn toward the town. Whether the call of a horn, the ring of a bell, or the wail of a siren, it was the same message: mortal peril has overtaken the city. It was some small progress.

Captain Rowan led his recon patrol up to the colonel. "With your permission, Thor and Gunner have agreed to join our patrol." The colonel nodded, and they rode toward the barrier. The soldiers paused from their work, and grim faces watched them pass in silence. The colonel walked toward the barrier and leaned upon the cool metal. Too often, he sent men to their death, and he always hoped that they would return, but the Great Spirit seldom answered his prayers. He saw fear in the eyes of his troops, and he wished for a thousand more cavalry and ten thousand more infantry, but such wishes are futile.

―――

Gunner drew back on his horse's reins and then took a swig from his canteen. Yet another abandoned vehicle lay on the side of the dirt road. When the Black Mountains arrived, an electromagnetic pulse from rhunite destroyed most electronics, such as the computer in most vehicles. Scores of people marched in a slow dirge, their bodies softened from years of industrialized living; they dropped on the side of the road, never to rise. The winding road traveled through a few oak trees and then a pasture.

Smoke formed a black column and rose above the treetops, a mark of destruction. He dug in his spurs and galloped toward it. The patrol chased after him. When his horse rounded the trees, he saw a field of blood. It covered every blade of grass, and pools soaked into the earth. As far as the eye could see, bits of skin, flesh, and bone littered the ground. They marked what had once been a dairy farm.

Off in the distance, a solitary white farmhouse and a red barn lay in the center of the bloody field, a classic American pastoral scene turned into a nightmare. Flames leaped out of the house's windows and curled around the roof. He dug in his spurs and charged across the field, the powerful animal eating up the ground, throwing up clods of earth. As he neared the burning structures, the stench of burnt plastic and synthetic chemicals stung him.

Two bodies lay upon the ground between the farmhouse and barn. Armless and legless, a bloody mess of guts and tattered clothes, had this once been a man and a woman? He dismounted and approached them, but the horror made him turn away. Gunner dropped to his knees and vomited.

Thor strode up to the macabre scene and snarled. His army training included that of a field medic, so he witnessed many bloody corpses. He squatted next to the bodies and drew his knife. After he had examined the corpses, he returned to Gunner and placed a hand on his shoulder.

"I'm sorry." Gunner wanted to be strong, a man of action, like those he admired in his youth. However, time, children, and love changed him. He now valued family above all else, and the humanity of these dead strangers overwhelmed him.

"No need to apologize old friend. It's as bad as I've ever seen."

"Daemia," Captain Rowan said. He removed a pair of binocular from his saddlebags and searched the horizon. A clear path of blood stained the grass and marked the daemia's direction. "Daemia are carnivores, so they require a constant supply of fresh meat. They often sent out hunting parties to gather supplies. It is an easy matter to find the main body. What is in that direction?"

"Fairplains is a stone's throw from here," said Thor. He pointed toward a water tower, once white, now tinted with rust. "It's about 15 miles that way."

"Mount up," shouted the captain. "Leave the dead."

Gunner understood — no more harm could come to the dead — but he hated it just the same. He focused on saving the living and mounted his horse. His entire body tensed as he rode away from the carnage, and he never looked back. However, he wondered about the farmer and his wife. What kind of people were they? Rising at dawn, work until exhausted, saved every penny, reused what others threw away, loved to see things grow, he knew the type.

The blood trail followed County Line Road, and at a T-intersection, it made a right on Beeline Highway. Several cars burned ahead of them. The windows shattered and the tires exploded as flames licked out from underneath it. The rhunite contained in the daemia armor provided enough ionizing energy to spark the gasoline. The oily chemical smoke clung to them and made them gag. Likewise, the power lines melted off the telephone poles, and the transformers burned. A blind man could follow the trail of destruction.

A small bridge spanned a meandering creek, and thickets choked the ground on either side. As they crossed the bridge, a man ran from the woods, waving his arms and shouting. Gunner's right hand moved to his sword, but he paused. "Help me!" the man shouted. "They took my family."

"How long ago," asked Captain Rowan.

"An hour ago," the man said. "Please, you have to help them. I was in the woods taking a piss when they attacked. There was nothing I could do." He sank to his knees and sobbed. "Please don't let them die."

The captain wanted to promise the man he would rescue the man's family. However, cruel experience taught him to refrain from empty promises. The man's family would live until they reached their destination, and then the daemia would butcher them, a drama seen too many times. Hurrying might lead to mistakes, and mistakes get warriors killed. "We will do what we can."

The column rode past the sobbing man still on his knees. As much as their hearts might want to, they had no comfort to give. They rode in silence, each person consumed with thoughts of home and loved ones. When they reached the crest of a small hill, they saw Fairplains. The town lay in a small valley, and it was little more than Main Street with a single traffic light. Daemia moved about the town. Two red brick buildings and the sheriff's office burned. In a far field, the daemia gorged on the bloody flesh.

Due to their elvish eyes, Gunner and Thor spotted the captive town's folk. The survivors languished in a cattle pen with two guards nearby. Ignorance kept the people compliant. If they knew what the daemia had in mind, they would have fought to the last person.

Captain Rowan made a note on a road map. "This looks to be the advance group for the main attack force." He made a few mental calculations and said, "They will feast into the night, and when they are joined by the main force, they will attack Fort Defiant. It should be sometime in the morning. We return to the town to warn the colonel."

"What about the captives?" asked Gunner.

"We have no means to rescue them. There are ten thousand daemia in that town and surrounding area. Our only hope of returning to warn our people is stealth. " The colonel turned his horse to leave.

"We could ride in, kill the guards, and carry off the survivors," Thor said.

"You see those six limbed creatures." The captain pointed at a far hill. Gray insects, the size of horses, scrambled around the fields of wheat and stripped it. "Those are Spine Bugs. They have crushing mandibles, stingers with formic acid, six limbs that can scramble up vertical walls, and a top speed of 97 kph (60 mph). However, they do have weaknesses. They can only sprint short distances, a hundred meters or so; then they move at a crawl, and they spend a deal of time-consuming vegetation. They are like locust in that regard; they will strip an area of foliage. And they are very susceptible to insecticide grenades."

"If I remember my entomology, bugs don't have lungs. I'm surprised they can get enough oxygen to survive," he said.

"They are genetically engineered to have lungs."

Gunner turned his face to the wind. "What if we started a fire? Prairie fires can run faster than a horse. It would chase them away, and we might be able to rescue those people. They wouldn't know we were here until it was too late," Gunner said.

The captain deliberated and rubbed his chin. "It would drive them away from Fort Defiant and destroy their food. Very well," he said. "It's worth the risk." Each warrior carried two glass vials in separate saddlebags. These vials contained a binary accelerant, once mixed produced "Greek Fire". They spread out along the rolling hills and poured the first vial in a horizontal line relative to the town. At the captain's signal, they poured the second vial. Blue flames, hot enough to burn metal, erupted. The dry prairie grass caught fire, and the wind picked carried it.

A daemia guard strolled out from an alley, chewing upon a steer femur. When he saw the fire, the bone dropped from his hand. A wall of flame rushed at them with the swiftness of the wind. It screeched an alarm and sprinted toward its mount. The perplexed daemia walked around the buildings, and when they saw the fire, they too fled in reckless abandon.

The cavalry chased after the flame, sabers drawn for battle. The mounted daemia charged away from the flame and crested the opposite hill. Those on foot were soon overtaken and burned. The guards around the human prisoners turned and ran.

Covered in manure, blood, and mud, Holly Temple rose to her feet and climbed over the horse fence. "COME ON," she shouted. The other survivors followed after and scrambled over the fence. She ran toward Thor.

"We're here to rescue you." Thor said and grabbed Holly's wrist. He hoisted her onto the back his horse with one pull. The giant elve warrior waited until the others warriors arrived and then shouted, "Hurry, climb on with them." Together, Thor and Holly sped back through the town. Meanwhile, the wall of flame chased the terrified daemia over the prairie.

———

Fort Defiant Citizens filled every seat, stood in the aisles, and flowed out the back door, disappearing into the starless night. Mayor Waylon waved his hands and tried to hush the din. "Please, speak one at a time, and remember, we don't have a microphone so speak loudly. Now Vern Hendercot, I believe you were next to speak.

"What the hell are you talking about?" Vern chewed a wad of tobacco and tipped back his ball cap. "That is the most asinine thing I've ever heard. Mountains just don't appear. It has to be some sort of trick, maybe a hologram or some such thing. I say we send out a team to investigate and find out what's going on."

"We know what's going on," Jake said. "Earth and Eden are reunited. The mountains came from Eden, and things — monsters came with them. They are going to attack and wipe out the town. We need to evacuate.

"You look like a reject from a renaissance fair. Mayor, tell me you're not taking what he says seriously. It's the most unbelievable —"

"LISTEN TO HIM!" shouted Holly. All heads turned toward the back. Gunner and Thor escorted her into the hall. She pulled free from them, and everyone watched her in silence. Both mud and manure stained her white bathrobe and caked on her bare feet; cuts and scrapes covered her legs; twigs tangled her hair into knots, and a large bruise covered half her face. She limped down the aisle, and a fat lip and two missing teeth made speaking painful.

When she reached the front, she turned toward them. "Some of you know me. I've lived in Fairplains my entire life. I went to school and college here in Fort Defiant. My husband …" she choked back tears, "his family was one of the founding families." She mumbled and sobbed.

"What did she say?" asked Ashley Roland.

"I said, "Kevin, my husband, is dead." She fought back the tears, clenched her fists, and used her rage to continue. "The things, monsters, came after the earthquake. There were thousands of them. We didn't know what we were looking at …."

―――――

"Kevin, what is that?" asked Holly. Their 127-year-old building had a commanding view of Main Street and the rolling plains behind it. She brushed aside the white gauze curtains and looked out the second-floor bedroom window. Her head cocked, she tried to understand what her eyes showed her. Black specs, thousands of them moved across the plains. Most were on foot, but a few were mounted. "Is there some sort of weird roundup?"

Kevin exited the bathroom and buttoned his shirt over his beer belly. He combed his fingers through his thinning hair and then rubbed an itch from his face. "I've got to get to Fort Defiant. We need more cattle feed."

"Baby, come on over here." When he joined her at the window, she pointed at the small humanoid figures in the pasture behind the town. "Who is that? What are they … oh my gosh," she gasped. Blood sprayed the severed artery in a steer's neck. It ran ten paces and then collapsed. Five of the figures drew crude, machete-like cleavers and hacked bits of flesh from the animal.

A cow collapsed, and then three more hit the ground. Archers launched volleys at the docile animals, slaughtering them. When the herd panicked, the mounted rider sped around the cows with unbelievable speed. They launched arrows and hurled javelins. Glistening red blood sprayed from them and covered the field in red.

"Son of a bitch," Kevin said and clenched his fists. "What the hell do they think they're doing? They're slaughtering our entire herd." He ran through the house and into his den. He grumbled about useless government rules as he dialed the combination for the gun safe. He yanked open the door and grabbed a 30-30 rifle and a box of cartridges. He loaded his gun and then filled his pockets. After he had strapped on his revolver, he hurried from the room.

Holly waited for him by the lamp stand. "I tried to call the police, but my phone is dead. The screen is all black and charred." When she saw him heading for the stairs, she rushed after him. "You need to get help. There are too many of them for you."

He charged down the stairs, his footfalls thumping the wooden stairs. When he burst out the door, he saw several other men gathered by their trucks and jeeps. "Did you see those rustlers?" asked Pete.

"Yeah, I saw them," Kevin replied, "and I'm going to shoot their asses. Are you boys coming?"

"Hell, yeah," Pete said. "Let me get my gun."

"Now Kevin, you be careful." Holly clutched her terrycloth robe closed and shivered in the early morning chill. "I'm going to drive up to the sheriff's office." Kevin said something about staying home, but she ignored him. Keys in hand, she sat down on the icy driver's seat of her 1979 Jeep Cherokee, manufactured before computers. After the engine started, she threw it in reverse, and then sped away, leaving rubber on the pavement.

The new sheriff's office for Cheyenne County was a few miles outside town. She raced through town and sped through the single traffic light. When she turned on the radio, wisps of smoke came from it. She pressed on the accelerator and shot through the sparse trees. Her jeep almost seemed to float as she raced for the office.

When she arrived, she slid to a stop right in front of the glass doors. She leaped out and ran into the building. "Your phones are out. Someone is slaughtering all the cattle. Kevin and the boys are going to see who they are?"

"Shh," hushed Sadie. She and a deputy, Ben, stood close to an old, analog radio. "We know all about it. The sheriff is going to investigate." Holly joined them at the radio.

"I've reached Glenview Road. I see a whole bunch of them," radioed the sheriff. When they looked out the glass corner windows, they saw his jeep speeding toward the rustlers, red light spinning, and siren wailing.

Sadie watched through a pair of binoculars. "He's stopping near them and getting out of the jeep. He's got his gun raised. Oh my god, an arrow nearly hit him. He fired at one of them; it went down. Two more are rushing at him. NO," she screamed and lowered the binoculars in shock.

"What?" asked Holly. "What happened?"

"The handgun on his hip and the gun in his hands exploded," Sadie said and stared with empty eyes. Holly took the binoculars from Sadie and raised them to her eyes. She saw two halves of a mangled corpse on the pavement. Raw, bloody flesh covered the front of the jeep. The jeep's gas tank exploded, and it did a summersault in the air. It landed on the roof and burned.

"Kevin," Sadie whispered. She ran through the office, dodging desk and leaped over the counter. The front doors slammed open as she ran to her jeep. Three more explosions rocked the ground and the building disintegrated behind her.

When she rose up from the ground, she saw her husband's white pickup truck in flames. Kevin fled the monsters and threw away his handgun. It exploded and stunned the daemia, but they recovered a moment later. "KEVIN," she screamed as an arrow hit him in the back. He staggered and two more arrows struck him. When he collapsed, she sprinted toward the field. Then she saw the mounted figures coming toward her, and she ran back to the jeep.

When she slid to a stop in town, shoppers and merchants viewed her with curiosity. "You have to run," she shouted at them. "They're coming." However, the people ignored her and moved away from this crazy woman. "Listen to me; they're killing everyone."

It was too late. The daemia riders raced through the center of town. When an arrow struck Tom, the grocer, he staggered and fell into the street. A woman near the produce stand screamed, and an arrow hit her in the neck. She dropped her bags and collapsed onto Tom.

Holly threw open her front door, two arrows struck it. She bounded up the stairs to her second floor condominium with something chasing after her. "HELP ME!" she screamed. A terrifying roar caused a surge of adrenaline within her and propelled her through the house. She ran into the kitchen and grabbed a butcher knife. When she spun around, her knees became weak, and her urine hit the floor. The creature was too hideous to be real. Crowned with horns, the face of spider, rows of jagged teeth, the daemia raised its sword. "You killed him," she screamed and rushed at the beast with her knife. It blocked her feeble thrust and bashed her face with its fist. She spun around once and crumbled to the floor.

Holly awoke with her left cheek in the cool mud. When she pushed herself upright, manure and mud squished through her fingers. The left side of her face throbbed, and her blurred vision made out the form of women and children huddled near the side of a barn. The primal screams inside the barn made her heart race and hands tremble. She crawled through the mud to the others and huddled in the cold.

After the screams ceased, she smelled smoke and struggled to her feet. Fire swept through town, setting buildings and fields ablaze. Cut and bloody, she climbed over the split rail fence and saw flashes of silver armor. As if in a dream, a man in armor charged up to her and hoisted her onto his horse. A moment later, they galloped away from the carnage.

———

Holly trembled and then sank to her knees. Several women and men rushed over to help her. They helped her to exit the room. When she reached the door, she yelled through her tears. "Tens of thousands of them are coming. You have to do something."

Chapter 41

The sunrise found the defenders looking west, searching the fields and forest for the approach of their enemy. They stood upon a crude barricade composed of granite blocks scavenged from the riverbank, overturned automobiles, and pikes set at acute angles. A trench filled with scavenged motor oil lay before the barrier. They tried to take solace in it, but it was a feeble structure, the product of a desperate night's work.

Brian rubbed an itch from his nose and adjusted his grasp on the pike's staff. The other dwarves lay on the ground like casualties and slept. Every so often, he looked north and saw Bain on the other barricade. The brothers locked eyes and shared a moment. They wondered if they would ever see each other again.

What happened to their family? The question refused to leave his thoughts. The Black Mountains replaced Gleason Kansas and several other towns. Were their graves beneath a mountain of stone? He refused to believe it. In his heart, he knew that they were alive. He pondered the Dragon's Eye Pendant. Perhaps he could use it to go back in time and save them, perhaps warn his father of a pending heart attack. However, all the other dwarves, and their human allies, had the same thought. Each of them pondered a moment in time, a moment if changed, would alter the course of their lives. However, Brian knew the problems of life lacked simple answers, and it would be an abuse of the pendant.

Most dwarves are nearsighted. After all, how far does one need to see in dark caverns and twisted tunnels? However, he saw something: a black spec, then another, and then the distant beat like drums. It might be the enemy, or it might be the wind blowing debris again.

Reggie used her backpack as a pillow and slept on the ground near the barricade. Her silver scale-mail tunic slid up her bottom, and it afforded Brian a view of her glossy black ass cheeks with the silver cable of her maiden's belt buried between them. The view both amused and aroused him. Using the blunt end of his pike, he poked Reggie in the bottom. "Cut it out," she moaned and batted at the pole. He poked again. "Stop it," she said and glared at him.

"I see something. I need your elvish eyes to check it out," Brian said.

Jake and Reggie scrambled onto the fortification and searched the distance. "THEY'RE COMING," she shouted. The others sprang to their feet and crowded onto the barricade. A black mass soon differentiated into an army. Drums thundered; silver-tipped spears flashed, and swords smacked shields. Berserkers sprinted ahead of the comrades and charged at the barricade.

When a hand touched Reggie's shoulder, she yelped and spun around. Colonel Briggs forced a smile and said, "I need you for a mission. You are to ride through town and sound the warning. I was hoping there would be only a thousand, but I estimate a minimum of ten thousand daemia and … they have battle trolls among them. This position will last an hour at the most. The only hope for the citizens of Fort Defiant is to flee. They might find shelter with the elves or the dwarves. Have them climb the Merchant Road and don't stop for anything. The sick, the weak, or the handicapped will have to be evacuated first."

Reggie stared at him in silence, and then she surveyed the warriors. Brian, Bain, and the others were about to die. She longed for some reprieve, some shred of hope, but she found none in the Colonel's eyes.

"Go now," he said and guided her to a horse.

Kairn asked, "Should we begin work on the bridges? If we collapsed them, it might buy them more time."

"Too late," Colonel Briggs said. "We ran out of time." He nodded toward the enemy. "And they've brought pontoon bridges." Kairn saw wooden rafts atop crushed automobiles, and great beasts pulled them. "They intend to the permanent bridges and surround us on both sides, negating our defensive positions. The Misty River is too narrow and shallow. In the future, it would have been wide enough to thwart them, but not now. Have the archers slow the enemy as they deploy those pontoon bridges."

They waited in silence as the enemy drew near. Each warrior's thoughts returned toward their home, unfulfilled dreams, and the face of a lover or a child. The drums drew near and drove the courage from their hearts. Many eyed the bridge and contemplated retreat.

"We are honor-bound to serve the King by oath and love for kin and home. I feel the fear that would make me a coward, to run, to save my life, but I would rather die on my feet than live on my knees. I will stand and fight. Will you join me?" said Colonel Briggs. The troops shouted and raised their weapons. "Blow your trumpets. Tell these beasts we are guardians of life and that they may go no farther."

The sharp, clarion call of the trumpeters cut through the din of the enemy. The troops began chanting, "Death,

death, death." The trumpets blasted the "King's Battle Cry" and gave the enemy pause.

The daemia formed into battle lines. Their angry cries rolled like thunder. The enemy commander, Grack, raised his sword and roared. When he brought down his sword, the archers loosed their arrows, and a thousand black arrows sailed through the sky. "Shields," the colonel shouted. The warriors raised their shields and formed a protective shell. The arrows rained down upon them and bounced off the protective metal barrier.

A few, however, passed through the seams, and an arrow sank into the thigh of a man next to Brian. The man cried out in pain and sank to the ground, blood flowing from the wound. The blood, the wound, and the cries of agony made the moment real. Brian wanted to shout, "Everyone, stop! Someone has been hurt." But this was no game: those creatures wanted to hurt and then kill them. It was a difficult moment for a peaceful mind to absorb. He awoke from the dream of peace to the reality of war, and sleep would never be so sweet and the world so safe because of it.

Grack shouted, and the berserkers broke through their lines. They rushed at the barriers in a wild frenzy of screams and roars. "Pikes," ordered the colonel, and a hundred bristling shafts protruded from their position.

The berserkers ran at the fortification and leaped over the trench. A few made it over, but many fell into the oil. Their rhunite infused armor set the used motor oil ablaze, and agonized screeches ripped from them. They scrambled out of the trench and spun in a wild dance, engulfed in flames. A few ran back toward their lines, only to be cut down by their archers.

With a nod from Grack, the drums beat out new orders. The line moved as one, and a continuous flight of arrows rained down on the defenders. The aggressors formed a wedge with the pontoons near the peak. When they approached the river, more oil ignited and formed a wall of flame between the bridges. The archers loosed their arrows and cut down the daemia. The enemy answered with more arrows. As arrows flew back and forth across the sky, men, women, and daemia were injured or killed.

Medics carried the wounded away from the battle and tended to them, but their efforts would be short lived. When the daemia crossed the river, they would kill and eat them. However, the medics struggled for every life and rushed into the battle to save the fallen.

Some of the trolls pushed the pontoons toward the river, and others pushed siege ramps toward the barricades. "KILL THE TROLLS," shouted the colonel. The archers aimed at the trolls, but their armor plate and stone bodies were too dense. They heaved and pushed the siege ramps into place. A stream of daemia rushed up the wooden ramps and leaped over the barricade. The warriors swung their axes and swords in a crazed frenzy. Black and red blood covered the ground as humans and monsters collapsed from mortal wounds.

A troll rushed at Colonel Briggs and brought down his great hammer. The commander brought up his shield at the last moment, but the power of the blow sent him sailing backward. He rolled over the concrete bridge, arms and legs flailing. The troops rushed at the troll with their pikes and pushed it backward. The creature stumbled over the curb and fell backward. It broke through the railing and hit the river with a great splash. The weight of its armor and body dragged it to the muddy bottom, never to rise.

The medics grabbed the colonel's unconscious body and dragged him to safety. Captain Rowan took command and ordered his reserve troops into battle. The daemia did likewise, and they rushed over the burning ramps, leaping at the defenders. The captain lowered his shield and surveyed the enemy. Only a fraction of the enemy's troops fought them. Nine thousand remained in reserve, ready to join the fray at any moment. He was about to shout an order when a heavy bolt from a ballista punched through his chest and protruded out his back. He spun in a half circle and collapsed to the ground.

Although the daemia had no chemical explosives, they had a precious supply of rhunite bombs, difficult to make and even more difficult to transport. However, Grack wanted the bridges taken intact and launched the pontoons to outflank the humans. Catapults flung blue, rhunite bombs in the air. For a moment, they hung at their apex, fingers of brilliant white light shooting from them. "Take cover," Kairn shouted. They leaped from the barricade just as the bombs hit. A tremendous explosion hurled metal, stone, and concrete into the air. Dust formed a thick cloud, and when it cleared, the both barricades were demolished.

The pavement shook beneath the colonel, rousing him. He struggled to his feet as the dust cleared. Both barricades were down, the battle was lost. He prayed that the town's people made it into the mountains. Then he saw bolts fly through the air. Ballistas — constructed from automobile leaf springs, wood, cable, and ratchet crank — positioned on rooftops launched heavy bolts hundreds of meters. They cut down the daemia trying to carry the pontoons to the river.

The sharp tap of drums echoed through the city. Terror flashed through the medics and wounded. Had the daemia outflanked them? The colonel limped to the corner of a building. Thor rode before a procession from the heart of town. Four rows across and thousands deep, men and teens marched down Main Street, and another column, three blocks south, marched down Center Street. They wore football, hockey, and cycling helmets; and sports gear, a patchwork of metal plate, and layers of leather. Baseball bats, machetes, swords, spears, and javelins filled their hands.

The drummers hammered out an angry beat. "The hell with running," shouted Vern. "It's our home and we're pissed. If they want the town, let them try and take it."

Columns of armed men and women marched past the astonished colonel. As they crossed the bridge, the daemia abandoned the pontoons and fled back to their lines. Thor rode over to the colonel and helped him onto the back of his horse. Gunner led the column that crossed the center bridge. Thousands of armed citizens crossed the bridge and formed up ranks.

Ten thousand armed citizens of Fort Defiant formed ranks on the opposite side of the Misty River. The town's people raised primitive shields made out of wooden doors cut in half and covered automobile sheet metal, secured to their arms with rope. Thor raised his sword and shouted, "Attack." A great shout rose up from the Fort Defiant defenders that shook the trees, and they rushed at the daemia troops.

Grack roared, and his troops rushed at the humans. A great crash of metal and a groan came from the collision. Weapons met in furious combat. The remaining archers formed ranks behind the battle line and let their arrows fly at will. The town's people fought for their right to survive.

A warlock — ugly and gnarled by dark magic — climbed atop an abandoned minivan and raised his cooked staff. The tip of his staff glowed red and a power surge leaped from it. It struck one of the ballistas, hurtling the crew through the air. The remaining ballistas answered in rage and launched bolts at the sorcerer, but he raised a shield, and the bolts bounced off them.

Colonel Briggs heard the clatter of hooves. Brother Henry led an Elven cavalry charge, his staff raised in anger, and trumpets called for war. An energy blast of brilliant white light leaped from the tip of his staff, it sliced through the air and punched through the warlock's red shield. It blasted the warlock and flung his broken body through the air. They galloped across the bridge and circled around behind the Fort Defiant troops. They caught the daemia cavalry trying to outflank them. They crashed into one another with the clang of metal. They kept moving in sweeping turned, neutralizing the greater speed of the daemia insect mounts.

Unknown to all, the dwarven army arrived by night. The only part of the most southern bridge that remained was the central pier, but it was enough. Using scavenged materials of wood and stone, they built a new bridge atop the central pier and crossed the river. They charged north on their mountain goats, attacked the enemies defenseless left flank and then strafed them with bolts from their crossbows. Too late, Grack realized his mistake: sending all of his cavalry to one side of his lines and leaving the opposite side vulnerable. The dwarves threw the enemy lines into chaos and cut down their enemies.

The remainder of his troops pressed into the human lines, but the defenders rode behind the daemia lines and attacked them from the rear. Chaos broke out in the daemia lines, and the daemia dead piled up on the ground; black blood soaked into the earth. The classic "hammer and anvil strategy" shredded the daemia, as if fed into some great machine.

The enemy commander climbed on his mount and fled the battle. He retrieved his Dragon's Eye Amulet and a curtain of darkness spread out before him. Upon seeing their commander flee, half the daemia troops fled after him, but the other half went south. A victorious shout erupted from the people of Fort Defiant.

———

Over 3,000 years in the future, General Leland McCloud waited for inevitable destruction. Using binoculars, he surveyed the enemy forces. More numerous than locusts, he estimated their number at 180,000, higher than what the command predicted. They lounged in their camp, eating and reveling with mugs of grog. They cast the ultimate insult upon him: they ignored him.

Of the squads that he sent out to harass the enemy, only a fraction returned. The remainder died in battle, suffered an injury, or deserted. He bore little malice toward those who deserted. The stand he took was little more than suicide in the name of duty, yet he wanted to die as he lived — with honor.

He donned his best uniform: dark blue with gold buttons and polished boots. Of course, his silver, ceremonial cuirass, gauntlets, greaves, and helmet accompanied it. His troops copied him, and they too donned their dress uniforms. As a last act of devotion, they mounted their steeds and waited for his orders to charge the enemy.

The daemia watched this activity with amusement and jeers. A few artillery units employed their catapults to fling excrement at the humans. They laughed with roars and drank their grog. If the humans wanted to die and fill their bellies, they would accommodate them.

"Mount horses," the general commanded. A cool morning breeze turned his cheeks ruddy and ruffled his helmet's red mane. "Draw swords," he said and the scrape of metal withdrawn arose from the warriors. "I am proud to serve with you, and even prouder to die with you. We shall meet in the undying lands and have a mug of ale."

He raised his sword and was about to order the charge when a great wind arose. The horses skittered about as the ground shuddered. A black curtain rose up from the earth and soared into the heavens. It spread out to the right and left, as far as the eye could see.

A daemia commander, atop an insect mount, surged out from the curtain. Several hundred daemia chased after him. At first, the general thought it some new dark weapon, but the black curtain disappeared. When the enemy saw the general and his troops, they skidded to a stop and fled in chaos to their lines.

The general heard the faint call of clarion trumpets. He turned his mount about and gaped in astonishment. As if a mirage, translucent walls, and skyscrapers shimmered against a pale blue sky. A roar arose in the heavens and trumpets blasted. Phantom riders charged up behind them. A city emerged from the translucent to the solid. At first, he thought it some deception of the enemy. The walls were higher, the buildings taller, and foundation broader than all the kingdoms of the realm. The silver spires reached up to the sky, of a type not seen since the Golden Age of Man. They were more numerous than silver tipped war pikes.

A vast army emerged from the mist. Covered in silver and gold plate armor, they spread across the hills. The general could scarcely believe his eyes. At least 300,000 troops spread out to his right and left. Colonel Nathan Briggs and his command staff thundered up the road. When they reached the general, he came to a swift stop. "Reporting as ordered," the colonel said. He retrieved an ancient envelope, yellowed and brittle with time, and handed it to the General. "My ancestor, Colonel Conrad Briggs, charged his son with care of this letter. It has been handed down, father to son, ever since that time."

The general took the envelope from the phantom colonel. Using his knife, he sliced through the aged envelope and removed a letter written upon parchment. It read as follows:

To General Briggs,

Alexander, I am sure you have many questions. It is my hope, my belief that my ancestors, my sons will join you in battle, and that they will explain the events that overtook us. I, we, traveled to the distant past and made our stand. Since you are reading this, we are victorious upon the field of battle, and the city of Fort Defiant is safe. I decided to stay here in the past and make it my home. They need me. I pray that I am up to the task for much depends upon it.

Your friend and companion,

Colonel Conrad Briggs

The general cleared his throat and took a few seconds to collect his thoughts. "This is unbelievable, yet the proof is right before my eyes." It made no sense, but one does not question a miracle. He cleared his throat and said, "We have a battle to fight."

Colonel Nathan Briggs surveyed the enemy and sniffed. "One would think the enemy would bring more troops to take Fort Defiant. It's a bit of a disappointment. The other half of our army, our strategic reserves, was eager to see some action. We will just have to make due."

"Trumpeters, sound the battle charge." Silver trumpets called out through the morning air. The enemy camp erupted into confused chaos. "Attack!" the general shouted and brought down his sword. The warrior's footsteps shook the earth and thundered. So many arrows sailed through the sky as to block out the sun. Three hundred thousand swords and shields stood at the ready.

When the armies clashed, the daemia ranks crumbled and black blood covered the ground. Cavalry units emerged from the flanks and attacked behind daemia from the rear. The daemia ranks crumbled and Fort Defiant army charged the fleeing enemy. "Kill them all; let none survive," General McCloud commanded, and they slew the daemia army, littering the ground with their dead bodies before the great city.

Chapter 42

In the past Fort Defiant, Colonel Conrad Briggs sat upon a square granite block and rubbed his right knee. His muscles ached, and his knee swelled. He retrieved a silver flask, a gift from his late wife, from his jacket pocket and removed the cap. After taking a swig, he savored the flavor and the heat as it burned his throat. When a shadow fell upon him, he saw Gunner and Thor blocking out the sun. If there were ever bigger elves, he had not seen them. They appeared like giants as if a myth came to life. Black daemia blood coated their silver armor and their unsheathed weapons. He held up his flask. "Care for a drink?"

"Hell yeah," Gunner said and took a swig. He then handed it to Thor. "We heard reports that part of the daemia force circled around the dwarves and headed south. By now they've crossed the rebuilt Coronado Bridge, but most of the city in the south is empty."

"Not all of it," Thor said. When Gunner furrowed his brow and cocked his head, Thor said, "Jake, Charlie, the others, and I are at his house." When the colonel raised an eyebrow, he said, "We are here a second time. I mean we previously existed here ... in this time-period. Help me out."

"This is our second presence in this time," Gunner said, "our normal lives and then this."

"I understand," the colonel said.

Thor looked toward the setting sun in the west, and his face lost all expression. "It was about this time of day we were first attacked. They came at us like a stampede. We had to fight all night to survive."

"Time travel is strange." The colonel took a swig from his flask and returned the cap. "I won't be born for another 3,000 years." He struggled to his feet and limped over to the concrete railing. The waters of the Misty River flowed as they had his entire life. "I was born up river from here. My family owned a farm. I loved sitting by the river and fishing, but I suppose that timeline is gone forever."

"And yet you're here," Thor chuckled.

"So I am. Time like quantum mechanics is confounding." He sniffed and asked, "Where is Brother Henry?"

"He is helping with the wounded," Charlie said as she scampered to them. She handed the colonel a plain brown bottle, about the size a sample shampoo container. "Brother Henry said, 'This will cure what ails him.'" The colonel opened it, sniffed, and scowled – it smelled like piss. He snarled and drank the foul liquid.

Brother Henry waddled up and asked, "Did you have the colonel rub that medicine on his knee?"

"Rub?" gasped the Colonel.

"Oh well, it won't hurt you to drink it, I suppose," Henry said. Thor and Gunner roared with laughter. Soon the Colonel joined them and threw back his head. "I'll fetch another bottle, but apply this batch to your knee."

Jake rode up and leaped off his horse. "The daemia are burning the south side of the city. Should we assemble the troops and go after them?"

"We need to be methodical. We can't afford to let the daemia flank us. I know lives are at risk, but many more are at risk in the northern half of the city. Have the troops to go on a house-by-house search. We will force them south, toward the old fort. Is it empty or is it defended?"

"Oh, it will be defended — by us," Thor said. "The attacks forced us south. We fought to defend the old fort, and we won," Gunner said. "But it cost us many lives."

"An aftershock is coming in two days. It toppled the fort, and we went south." Thor used a rag to wipe the black daemia blood off his armor. "This stuff is like glue."

"And smells like manure," Gunner added.

"Yes, hazards of war," Colonel Briggs said. He limped to a horse and mounted it. When Henry handed him another vial, he said, "I'll rub on this one."

"It would be wise," Henry said and rubbed his belly. "They're serving us something called 'cold cuts' on submarine sandwiches. It sounds perplexing but good."

———

Two days later, Reggie sprinted across the street and dodged behind the corner of a house. He slotted an arrow and readied it. He stepped around the corner and saw Jake locked in mortal combat with a daemia. Their swords clanged and armor flashed. They circled around each other so Reggie could not get a clear shot. When the daemia knocked Jake into a wall, her arrow flew. It sped from the bow, closed the gap, and struck the daemia in the throat. Black blood spurted from the severed artery. Jake scrambled back to the battle and stabbed the daemia in the joints between its armor. The mortally wounded creature staggered backward and tried to flee. After three steps, it collapsed to the ground and a raspy growl escaped its lips as it died.

He grabbed a rag from the ground and wiped the sweat and grime from his face. Reggie took a drink from her flask and handed the canteen to him. Lukewarm water never tasted so good. "We're almost to the fort. We need to go this way."

They scrambled over a divider fence and dropped into another backyard. A German Shepherd, trapped in a chain link enclosure, snarled and snapped at them. Its dead owner lay across the yard, face down in the grass with bloody wounds on his back. Jake approached the enclosure and whispered to the dog. The animal sensed his intent and calmed. When Jake opened the kennel door, the dog shot out of the cage and over to his owner. It whimpered and lay next to the corpse, its head resting on the dead man's shoulder.

When Jake began to leave, Reggie said, "Should we just leave him?"

"He's still grieving," he said.

"I meant the body," she said.

"No time to bury the dead yet," he said.

Charlie scrambled into the backyard, and shouted, "Daemia." In a blink, Reggie and Jake slotted arrows and drew their bows. When three daemia barged through the gate, they let them fly. The dog dashed across the yard, leaped into the air, and grabbed the third daemia's throat. It whipped around and ripped away a chunk of flesh.

Blood spurted through the daemia's fingers. More arrows hit the daemia, but the other two still stood. Gunner entered the backyard and chopped them down with a bearded war ax.

"Stop fooling around. Don't play with them; kill them," he said. "We're almost to the fort." Charlie crossed her arms and sashayed by him, nose in the air, feeling a bit insulted. They followed her, and when they rounded the house, they saw scores of dead daemia. They littered the front yard, street, and surrounding yards. Several fires burned and smoke rose from the broken windows. The breeze carried the stench of urine, feces, and rotting flesh.

A daemia shattered a bay window and hit the ground. Brian leaped out and sank his war hammer in the creature's skull with the sharp crack of bone. Bain exited with an egg sandwich in one hand and a juice box in the other. "There's plenty of food in the pantry," he mumbled, his mouth full. Brian gave the daemia another whack just to make sure it was dead.

"I'm hungry," Jake said and rushed into the house.

"We need to get to the fort," Gunner said. "You can eat later." Even Thor ignored him and sought out a quick meal. Gunner stomped into the house. The bodies of three daemia lay among the ruins of the living room. The clank of dishes and a hushed conversation came from the kitchen. When he entered, he saw Charlie cooking eggs and bacon in iron skillet on a propane stove; Reggie set the table. The others sat around the table, mugs ready for the coffee to brew. Gunner sat at the head of the table. "I guess we could have a quick bite to eat."

A short while later, slurps and smacking lips replaced conversation. They heard a knock at the front door and turned to see if the owner returned. "Excuse me," Toni said. "Wait. How did all of you get here, and where did you get those costumes?" Laughter erupted around the table. "What's going on? I just left you back at the fort. I came searching for food." They laughed so hard that they cried.

"We have a story to tell you," Jake said, wiping the tears from his eyes. "Have a seat." After joining them, the youth group entered behind her. They told their unlikely story of elves, dwarves, and daemia.

"Where's Linda?" Toni asked.

"Back in the city with Brother Henry," he said. "They are treating the wounded." An aftershock shook the house. The light fixtures danced and the house groaned. However, it withstood the tremor. "The old fort just collapsed."

Toni asked, "What are we going to do now?"

Epilogue

Juliana had many questions and few answers. One minute she stood in Fort Defiant as the earthquake hit, and the next she woke up in her home in Golden, Colorado. Her entire family had Elven bodies complete with pointed ears. Her first thought was to contact Jake, but all technology — including phones and computers — stopped working. Without a car and with martial law imposed, she had no choice but to remain at home.

Her back ached, but she continued to work. She pulled up weeds and watered their crops. Like so many others, her family transformed their front-yard and backyard into a garden. Gray clouds and a frigid wind from the Rockies declared that winter was upon them. The ground would soon freeze, but rhunite caused plants to grow with astonishing vigor and speed, so they would soon have a harvest to sustain through the winter.

When her little brother threw down his spade in disgust, she decided it was time for a break. She leaned her spade against a shrub and tried to rub away the pain from her lower back. After dipping a ladle into a cooking pot, she drew the icy water to her lips. Her mother, Marjory, exited the house with her dad, Thomas, behind her. "We have to go into town," Marjory said. That was much easier when they still had gasoline for the car. Even if it did have gas, most of the working cars that encountered buried rhunite burst into flames or exploded. No, travel by foot, bicycle, or horse was the only means of safe travel.

"There's nothing left in town," Juliana said. "All of the emergency supplies are gone or stolen. We could go out to the fields again and try to harvest some more wheat."

Her father descended the stairs and walked past Juliana. They turned to see what he looked at. Oak Lane climbed a hill and curved before their house. They saw a group of teens on horseback riding up the road. They laughed and talked as if on some great adventure. Juliana took three steps, and her elva eyes grew wide with joy. "Jake," she shouted. She sprinted toward them. Jake dismounted and she leaped into his arms. They kissed, and he held as if he would never let her go.

Brother Henry rubbed his belly and waited until his patience grew thin. "We don't have time for this. We are on a mission of utmost urgency." But Jake and Juliana kept kissing.

The End

www.ingramcontent.com/pod-product-compliance
Lightning Source LLC
Chambersburg PA
CBHW031424240626
47154CB00001B/196